over. Although Ladisias faced away from him, preventing any observation of his face, Zeeran knew his brother. He had worn a stoic expression on their journey thus far, but Ladisias was concerned. It showed in the way his shoulders slumped every night when they were forced into their tents and in the heaviness of his eyes and the dark circles beneath them.

Papa wore the same mask of emotion, but Zeeran would offer him no sympathy. Their predicament was, by Zeeran's estimation, their father's fault. Papa could point fingers at their uncle all he wanted, but the blame was not one man's to bear.

"This is foolish," said Zeeran, knowing Ladisias was likely listening to his restless movements. "We never should have left Verascene, and we never should have left Feya."

A muffled groan escaped from beneath Ladisias's blanket. "We've been through this. Papa was only trying to make things right, make things better for all of us. You continue to hold him responsible when—"

"Uncle Morzaun is not to blame!"

"Hey!" Rook's gruff voice settled over them from the other side of the cloth. "Keep it down in there, or I'll tell the general you're stirrin' trouble. Curfew means you're to go to sleep, not conspire."

"And if I don't want—"

Ladisias's hand shot over Zeeran's mouth. "Our apologies. We'll quiet ourselves."

Rook gave a harrumph, and his shadow rolled over the cloth tent and disappeared. Zeeran ripped his brother's hand from his face and scowled.

"Don't give me that look," whispered Ladisias. "Learn to hold your tongue. Our situation is precarious at best, yet you insist on antagonizing the soldiers."

"And you"—Zeeran shoved a finger into his brother's chest—"insist on cowering before them. We have magic, Ladisias. *They* should be taking orders from *us*. You're too much like Father."

Ladisias shook his head. Darkness surrounded them, but the firelight that percolated through the tent cloth allowed Zeeran to witness his brother's shaggy blond hair sweep against his forehead. The two of them were different in nearly every way, from their appearances to their dispositions. Zeeran looked least like his parents with his dark hair and eyes, and his quick temper was certainly nothing like Papa, who had spent years hiding his family from the world.

How he resented the solitary life his father had forced them to live. He resented a great many choices the man had made.

"I do not cower," said Ladisias, his voice an almost growl. "I obey their commands because I value my sister's life. I value *our* lives."

His brother's words sucked the anger from his body. The last thing Zeeran wanted was for his actions to put Feya in danger. The king could not be trusted to keep his promises, and one false move on their part would land his sister a meeting with the guillotine.

Zeeran heaved a sigh. "You're right. I'm sorry."

"Of course I'm right. I'm older." Ladisias patted Zeeran's shoulder and then flattened onto his back. "Go to sleep. We'll need plenty of rest for tomorrow."

"Another day of endless walking. What does Ivrin think? That Uncle Morzaun is going to step out from behind a tree and say 'you found me!' The general is ridiculous and a complete fool."

"Perhaps, but Ivrin said he had a lead on our uncle's whereabouts. I trust he would not move camp so hastily if that were not true."

Zeeran crossed his arms. "And what if we do find him? What does the general expect of us? I will not harm someone I believe to be innocent."

Ladisias said nothing in response. He didn't have to for Zeeran to understand. Of all the members of his family, Zeeran was the only one who believed in his uncle's innocence. The man had done wrong, of course; he could not deny that. But he also would not blame him—not when the previous king of Izarden had pushed the man to act. Uncle Morzaun would not have used his magic to harm others had he not felt threatened. Had he not experienced so much loss.

As predicted, Zeeran slept little that night. His mind wandered to the palace of Izarden where Feya was being held captive. In exchange for the pardon Zeeran's father desired, King Delran had demanded that Zeeran's family assist in the finding and capture of Morzaun. Zeeran's uncle was responsible for the death of Delran's father, and the king sought revenge.

But Delran did not trust magic nor anyone who could wield it. To ensure he was not betrayed, the king had kept Feya at the palace, swearing that no harm would come upon her so long as Zeeran's family cooperated. Once Morzaun was delivered into Izarden's hands, Feya would be allowed to go free and the pardon granted.

Zeeran scoffed, the soft sound alone in the darkness of the quiet hours before dawn. Trusting King Delran to keep his word was yet another mistake to add to his father's list of failures. How many more would Papa make before one of them got hurt—or worse?

For now, Zeeran could do nothing but play along like a pawn in a chess game, continually led by more powerful players. But Uncle Morzaun had taught him the intricacies of the game, and even a pawn could take down a king.

* * *

Morning light trickled through the small gap in the tent cloth, announcing the end of another night. The chatter of Izarden's army mixed with the clatter of men striking camp created a cacophony not even the deepest sleeper could ignore.

Including Ladisias, and that was saying something.

"Did you sleep well?" asked Ladisias as he rolled up his sleeping sack.

"I'd have to sleep at all to have a chance at doing it well." Zeeran tied a knot in the rope around his own roll of blankets with a hard pull. "A hard feat for *some* of us."

"Already in a mood, I see." Ladisias crawled to the tent opening and pushed open the cloth. "Hurry, or Rook will be down our throats before the sun has fully risen."

"Hurry or not, he will do so. He takes pleasure in our misery." Zeeran crawled out of the tent after his brother and tossed his bedroll onto the ground.

"Then do me a favor and hold your tongue. I would prefer not to have my breakfast withheld due to you insulting the soldiers."

Ladisias's lips twitched. "Or to you toying with them with your magic."

Zeeran restrained a grin. "I haven't any idea what you're referring to."

"No? You mean to tell me Rook suddenly sneezed suds of his own accord? Perhaps he should see a medicine man, though his symptoms did seem to disappear before curfew last night."

A laugh escaped Zeeran, the first he'd experienced in days. "Very well, I confess, but you can't deny the man deserved it. No one will speak to our mother with such a foul mouth if I have any say in the matter."

"Yes," said Ladisias with a chuckle, "he deserved it, but that doesn't mean we should use our power that way. Irritate them too much, and it's our sister who pays the price."

Zeeran folded his arms, whatever cheerfulness he'd experienced fading. "Mama has seen nothing to suggest Feya will be harmed, but how do we know her visions can't be wrong? We should go back for Feya."

Ladisias shrugged and began removing the cloth from their tent's frame. "Our lack of success in ever getting away with mischief these last twenty odd years seems proof enough to me that her visions can be trusted."

Their mother was a Seer, and in his twenty-four years of life, Zeeran had never known any of her visions to fail. But that didn't mean it wasn't a possibility nor did a lack of a vision mean Feya was safe. Visions came as they pleased, sometimes offering glimpses of the future years in advance, but more often, only a few minutes. If Delran were to decide Feya no longer held value, minutes would not be enough time for them to intervene.

Ladisias gripped his shoulder, his expression solemn. "The best thing we can do is find Morzaun. He needs to be held accountable for his crimes. Innocent people died due to his actions. Their families deserve justice."

Zeeran could not disagree with his brother's words, and his heart ached for those who had lost family members, but the last thing Morzaun would receive was a just trial. Delran wanted revenge, and that would not end well for Zeeran's uncle.

The two of them packed their tent and loaded the supplies onto their horses. Zeeran rubbed a hand along his black mare, once again contemplating how easy it would be for them to escape. But with Feya in the king's clutches, it wasn't an option.

A hand appeared next to his own, and Zeeran turned to face his father, an older version of Ladisias in appearance. The man's gentle gaze settled on him, studiously surveying Zeeran's face. "Still haven't slept, have you?"

"I don't expect to sleep any time soon."

"Zeeran, I know you don't agree with—"

"Betraying my own family?"

"That isn't fair. None of us forced Morzaun to do the things he did. He made a choice. I could argue that *he* betrayed us. We're all being judged because of his decisions."

"Judged but not killed." Zeeran shook his head and ran his hand along the mare's back. "His capture may as well be a death sentence."

His father sighed and opened his mouth to respond, but shouts from behind them cut him off.

"Aldeth!"

A man with sandy brown hair marched toward them. General Ivrin may have been equal in stature to Zeeran, but the man held a commanding presence. And while Zeeran admitted to carrying a sour mood as of late, Ivrin's expression displayed a constant look of someone chewing on a lemon.

The general stopped in front of them and withdrew a folded piece of parchment from beneath his black armor. "Here, Aldeth." He thrust the paper into Papa's hand, and Ivrin fixed him with a hard stare, his blue eyes dark like the sea during a storm. "Send this to my brother, Lieutenant Strauth, immediately."

The general crossed his arms over his chest and narrowed his expectant eyes. The scrutiny made Zeeran shift on his feet despite the fact that he was not the one under the man's intense glare. Ivrin didn't trust magic wielders, which was just as well. Zeeran didn't trust him, either. But the general donned a murderous look on the regular. His treatment of them the last few days had been despicable at best, but Zeeran sensed something far more sinister lurked beneath the surface. The general was hiding something.

Papa summoned his magic. Sparks of green glittered in the morning light in a dazzling display. The color matched the deep hues of the grass and forest, unlike Zeeran's blue aura that mirrored the sky.

The magic dissipated when a brown-feathered bird landed on Aldeth's shoulder. He handed the letter to the creature, and it took the piece with its talons. Without a word from Papa, the animal lifted into the cloudless sky and disappeared.

"I expect to make some headway in our quest today," said Ivrin. "I also expect complete cooperation from you"—his hard gaze flicked to Zeeran—"and your family. If I give you an order, you had best follow it. Is that understood?"

Papa bowed his head. "Of course, General."

Zeeran bit his tongue, the only way to keep it from saying things it shouldn't. His parents' compliance in all of this added fuel to his already burning anger.

A smug smile erupted over Ivrin's lips. "Good. Be sure your wife and other son are aware. We wouldn't want to give the king any reason to harm his guest."

"Prisoner," Zeeran corrected. "Feya had no desire to stay. A guest wouldn't be concerned about their own safety."

"Zeeran." His father's voice came as a low warning. The man rarely lost his temper, and it seemed whenever he did, Zeeran was often the cause. The two of them struggled to see eye to eye on most topics, but his father's lack of willingness to fight the injustice against them was the greatest sore spot of them all.

Ivrin's expression twisted into a sneer. "Then you should keep yourself in line or your sister will pay the price. Her *safety* means nothing to me."

Zeeran clenched his fists and weighed his options. He wanted nothing more than to punch the smug expression off the general's face, but before he could decide whether to follow through with the desire, shouts sounded through the camp. A young soldier raced toward them, his breathing heavy.

"General." He bent into a bow and took a moment to catch his breath. "Our men have captured the sorcerer."

Zeeran's blood ran cold. "Captured?"

"That's excellent news," said Ivrin. "Bring him to me. The man needs to be incapacitated."

"We have him bound with—"

"That's not enough! I will not allow him to slip through my grasp. Bring him."

The young soldier nodded and made a hasty retreat. Morzaun had been captured; their search was at an end. King Delran would release Feya and grant their pardon.

Zeeran's stomach curled. He should be happy about the possibilities on the horizon.

But happy was the last thing he felt. Morzaun would be put to trial, and the punishment would undoubtedly be death. They were trading his uncle's life for redemption—for freedom—and he wasn't certain this was a price he could willingly pay.

CHAPTER TWO

Choosing Sides

Zeeran sprinted after his father and General Ivrin to the center of the camp. Sunlight poured into the clearing through the dense trees surrounding the meadow, and tiny blooms of red and orange dotted the unoccupied spaces between half-packed tents, men, and horses. Shouts and taunts filled the area and settled over Zeeran like an ominous cloud.

His uncle had been captured. A mixture of emotion swarmed through him, but none stood as bold as the dread swelling in his stomach.

A soldier with a thick, scruffy beard yanked a familiar figure forward, his hand gripping the man's arm. Morzaun's black hair hung to his shoulders, but the two red strands, one on either side of his face, were new. It had been years since Zeeran had seen his uncle, and the addition of wrinkles on the man's forehead and near the corners of his eyes reflected the passage of time.

A rope was wrapped around Morzaun's wrists, binding them together in front of him. His dark clothing matched his solemn features, and the leather armor covering his chest bore symbols Zeeran had never seen before. In the first light of dawn, he could make out the shape of a triangle, though the symbols within it were less clear.

General Ivrin brandished his sword. "Morzaun, sorcerer of dark magic and traitor to Izarden, you are hereby remanded for crimes against our kingdom. You will be escorted to the palace and detained until the court has allocated your punishment through fair trial."

Zeeran bit his tongue. There would be nothing fair about Morzaun's trial. The people of Izarden hated magic, and even though his uncle had long since lost his ability to wield it, they still wanted blood.

"What have you to say to the accusations brought against you?" demanded Ivrin. "Do you deny your involvement in treason? Have you any refutes?"

Morzaun lifted his chin. "If by treason you mean bringing to pass the death of a tyrant, the death of a man who had betrayed his own people, then I do not deny your claims. I wholly admit to them and rejoice in the outcome of my efforts."

Ivrin clenched his fists. "You rejoice in the death of others? I believe that tells me—and everyone in this kingdom—all we need to determine what you deserve."

"Everyone?" Morzaun's lips lifted in a slight grin. "Are you certain? I know people who would disagree with your assessment, including your father."

Ivrin stormed forward and placed his blade against Morzaun's throat. "Do not mention my father." He lowered his voice, and

Zeeran could no longer hear the exchange. Morzaun's expression betrayed nothing, not even a hint at fear or concern.

"Ah, General. You would like to end me yourself, wouldn't you? Accuse me all you wish, but you are no more innocent than I am. Dark deeds do not change their marks, no matter the intention fueling them."

"You murdered–"

"I did, and I would do so again." Morzaun's gaze shifted to Zeeran's father. "Hundreds of lives would not have needed to be lost if Sytal had died the first time, but some of us value the life of a devil more than the innocent. Isn't that right, Aldeth?"

"Our magic does not give us the right to issue judgment," said Aldeth. "You abused your power. You didn't deserve it."

"And yet you passed judgment and saved a man undeserving of your sympathy. How many people died at the hands of the former king and would have lived had you not healed him?"

Papa turned away, the muscles in his jaw constricting. Zeeran knew his father held regrets, but Morzaun was right. King Sytal had done more damage by being permitted to live. Had Morzaun not taken it upon himself to enact justice, Sytal would have never paid for his crimes. How was that fair to those who had suffered?

"Why bother hauling me back to Izarden?" asked Morzaun. "Kill me now, and save yourself the trouble."

Ivrin growled. "You will stand trial."

"So I may be issued a death sentence? I'd rather face my fate now."

Zeeran held his breath. His uncle was mad to tempt the man. The general walked the line of obsession and insanity, and Zeeran had no doubt he would seize the opportunity to end Morzaun. King Delran would never punish him for it, either.

"Last chance, General." Morzaun grinned, not an ounce of fear in his dark eyes. He met Zeeran's gaze and winked.

Ivrin lowered his weapon. "As I said, you will be taken to Izarden—"

His words cut off with a sharp inhale as Morzaun thrust his bound fists into the general's stomach. Ivrin bent with a groan, and Morzaun slid his hands against the general's blade, slicing his skin in addition to the thick rope binding him. He moved so quickly, the soldiers surrounding them had no time to react. Morzaun ripped the sword from Ivrin's hand and pulled him into a headlock. He settled the edge of the blade against the general's neck, pinning the man to the leather armor adorning his chest.

Soldiers brandished their weapons. Blood rolled down Morzaun's arm and dripped from his elbow onto the dark green grass. Ivrin fought his hold, but each attempt to move dug the blade into his skin.

"You forget yourself, General," said Morzaun. "You may have experience, but so do I. Once second in command under your father, I've received the same training as you and have had far more years to perfect my skill."

The soldiers inched closer, shouting orders for Morzaun to release their leader.

"You'll never get out of this alive," grunted Ivrin. "You're as good as dead."

"Morzaun!" shouted Aldeth. "Let him go. We can do this without bringing harm to anyone else. You cannot fight off so many, especially when magic stands against you."

"Perhaps not, but I'm not entirely convinced I don't have magic on my side." Morzaun's attention shifted to Zeeran. "Does everyone agree with your decisions, Aldeth? You have allowed these people to force your family into hiding. You have allowed them to treat you no better than the dirt beneath their boots. And for what? Hope that they will see the err in their ways? You're a fool."

Morzaun was right; he and Zeeran's parents had fought for Izarden—defended the people from foreign invaders when they first acquired their ability to wield magic. Izarden had thanked them with prejudice and disdain. His family had been outcast and hunted. They didn't owe King Delran anything, and his father had requested a pardon when they'd done nothing wrong.

Zeeran clenched his fists. He would not spend the rest of his life fighting to convince people that magic wasn't evil, not when their minds were already made on the matter.

Green light erupted around Aldeth's hands. "Release him, Morzaun. Do not force me to use my power against you."

"You took no issue in doing so before. Tell me, have you felt any remorse for stealing my magic? Or do you reserve such emotions for those who don't deserve them?"

"Stop this!" A petite figure in a lavender gown ran toward them, her long blonde hair catching the breeze. Zeeran's mother grabbed her husband's arm, her blue eyes pleading. "Aldeth, please don't hurt him."

"He hasn't changed, love." Aldeth's fierce gaze flicked to Morzaun. "And I don't think he ever will. Your brother must pay for the crimes he's committed, but more importantly, we must keep him from continuing this chaos. It ends here."

She tightened her grip on his shirt sleeve. "I know. I just..." Her voice broke. Zeeran wanted to scoop her into his arms. This entire situation was difficult for all of them, but it affected his mother the most. Morzaun had taken care of her since the day the two of them lost their parents, and the siblings' connection ran deep. Zeeran's father may not regret relieving Morzaun of his power, but his mother did, and Zeeran sympathized with her wholeheartedly.

"I won't hurt him," Aldeth whispered, wrapping his arm around her waist and pulling her close. He placed a soft kiss on the top of her head. "I'll put him to sleep."

Zeeran swallowed against the lump that had lodged in his throat as his father whirled his hands. Green light followed their movement, the specks of glittering magic catching the morning sunlight like the droplets of dew on the grass.

This was unfair. Taking Uncle Morzaun to Izarden would sentence him to death. How could his parents accept that fate for a member of their family?

Zeeran had always looked up to his uncle. The man had taught him to fight and helped him gain control of the magical energy passed down to him through his parents. But that training had been cut short when the previous king of Izarden murdered his uncle's wife. After that, Morzaun had disappeared. Zeeran had lost the one person who'd always understood him.

And he was about to lose him again, this time, for good.

Aldeth concentrated his aura into an orb. Throwing his palms forward, the spell shot straight for Morzaun in a beam of glittering energy. Sparks of purple ignited from his mother's hands, and a faint glow illuminated protectively around Ivrin's body.

Zeeran sucked in a breath. His body moved, his mind only half certain of the course he would take. Ladisias's shouts rang in Zeeran's ears, and his brother's fingers fumbled for purchase on his shirt. Zeeran ripped free of Ladisias's grasp and darted forward. Lifting his hands, shimmering blue light erupted into a dome-shaped shield in front of him. Aldeth's spell collided with it, and the magical energy split in two, flowing to either side and dissipating into the air.

The area went silent. Zeeran allowed his shield to fade, giving him a clear view of the shock on his parents' faces. A thud behind Zeeran drew his attention. Ivrin lay on the ground, his hand pressed against his throat and blood seeping between his fingers, while Morzaun hovered over him with a satisfied grin.

"Traitor!" a soldier shouted. "He's defended the sorcerer!"

Defense had certainly been Zeeran's intention. He stared down at the general, his mouth agape. He hadn't meant for Ivrin, despicable as he was, to be killed. Crimson painted the man's skin and soaked the visible parts of his tunic. Zeeran imagined what was hidden beneath the man's armor was just as drenched.

Ivrin gagged, and blood spewed over his cheeks as he struggled for air. Zeeran's stomach twisted. This was his fault.

Morzaun backed away when Aldeth shoved past Zeeran and kneeled next to the general. Aldeth began muttering the words to an incantation, ones Zeeran recognized as a healing spell. His father's magic sealed the gash in Ivrin's throat, and after a few eternal moments, the man sucked in a sharp breath.

Papa looked up at Zeeran, his brows furrowed. "What have you done?"

"Detain...him." Ivrin ground out the words with a great deal of effort.

No. Zeeran was as good as dead if he allowed himself to be taken. Fear coursed through him, and he stumbled backwards as soldiers advanced, shrinking the surrounding circle with each step, their swords raised.

A hand fell on Zeeran's shoulder, and he jumped.

"You must get us out of here or we'll both face the guillotine," said Morzaun.

"I...how?"

"With your *magic*." Annoyance laced his uncle's response. Morzaun tilted his head and gave Zeeran an incredulous look. "You have power; use it."

"I don't want to hurt them."

Like Morzaun had hurt Ivrin. A shiver ran down Zeeran's spine.

"So don't. Knock them over. We only need time to escape." Morzaun's gaze flicked to the thick grove of trees beyond the camp and then to the soldiers slowly moving toward them. "Now would be an excellent time to begin."

Zeeran whirled his hands, summoning his aura. Shouts and orders muffled the sound of his mother's scream. Zeeran sent a wave of magic away from him in every direction. The spell toppled the Izarden soldiers like a harsh wind blew over trees.

Morzaun gripped his arm. "Run!"

Zeeran's legs obeyed, carrying him farther and farther from his father's demands and his mother's pleas. Images of Ivrin clutching his bloody throat forced their way into Zeeran's mind, but he shook them away, focusing on the white trunks of the birch trees they passed and keeping his feet from entangling on the vines and underbrush.

Morzaun grabbed Zeeran's tunic and yanked him behind a large, boxwood bush, panting heavily. "You must transport us out of here."

"Transport? What are you talking about? We need to keep running."

His uncle shook his head. "I will teach you the incantation. We can't outrun them all. Besides, I have more important things to do."

"More important things than hurting someone?" Zeeran glared at him. He didn't regret saving Morzaun, but he also didn't approve of his uncle's actions. Ivrin deserved it, to be sure, but Zeeran had no desire to be responsible for the general's death. Fortunately, his father had stepped in.

"Would you have preferred General Ivrin kill the both of us?" One of Morzaun's dark brows lifted. "We may turn ourselves in now if that is your preference."

"No...of course not." Zeeran heaved a sigh. "What is this incantation, and what exactly does it do?"

Shouts resounded in the distance followed by the swish of leaves as soldiers pushed their way into the forest. Morzaun leaned against the oak tree shielding himself from view. "Can you picture the city of Rowenport? Or, preferably, the road beyond the city walls?"

Zeeran and his family had left Verascene, their island home, and arrived in the port city of Rowenport only a few days ago. It had been Zeeran's first time setting foot in Izarden since he was a young boy, and the sights and sounds of the city were ones he'd committed to memory. "I can picture it fairly well. Why?"

"Because that's where we're going." A grin pulled at his uncle's lips. "It's my destiny to help you, Zeeran, for one can never arrive at their destination without a bit of direction."

CHAPTER THREE

A Traitorous Plan

Zeeran repeated the strange words in his mind. He'd performed a number of spells since his magical abilities manifested a few days after his tenth birthday, but none had ever tongue-tied him as much as this. Even his mind stumbled over the foreign language, one that seemed different from the words his mother had spent years teaching him.

Shouts encroached upon their hiding place among the trees, and Morzaun shifted closer to him. "We must go. Are you ready?"

Hardly, but what choice did they have? Zeeran could manage a handful of soldiers, but if his parents and brother decided to subdue him, there would be little his lone magic could do. "Ready as I can be. What happens if I don't get this right?"

Morzaun tugged at his armor. "My advice is don't get it wrong."

Comforting.

"Alright," muttered Zeeran. "I picture the place in my mind, say the words, and...how do I take you with me?"

"Simple. Hold onto my tunic." Morzaun narrowed his eyes. "Be sure not to let go even when the nausea sets in."

"Nausea?" His stomach was already a ball of knots. He didn't need to add more discomfort to it.

The undergrowth rattled. An armed young man with honey brown hair pushed through the branches and came to a dead halt. His eyes rounded, and indecision played over his features.

"Do it now, Zeeran!" Morzaun shouted.

Zeeran pictured the colorful rooftops of Rowenport and the sparkling sea. He imagined the dirt roads extending from the city into the rolling hills that stretched toward Izarden. The incantation stumbled from his lips as his hands cut through the air. A trail of blue magic followed the movements, and its appearance seemed to pull the young soldier from his dazed condition. The man drew his sword and called for reinforcements, then took a hesitant step forward.

An odd sensation swept through Zeeran's stomach. He reached out for his uncle, finishing the spell with a quick flourish of his wrist, and gripped the man's shirt at the shoulder. The world around them blurred the way dye bled on wet fabric, the colors mixing together until everything was no longer clear and defined. He could make no distinction between the green of the trees and the lush boxwood bushes. The sky smudged and spun until up became down...or at least, he thought it did. Perhaps it was him who was no longer upright.

Bile rose in his throat, but he swallowed it down and made certain to tighten his hold on Morzaun. The world rearranged, and for several long moments, looked more like the starry night sky than the shadowed forest where they'd hidden from the army of Izarden.

Color swirled into view. Trees, a dirt road, and in the distance, a glittering sea. Zeeran landed on solid ground with a thud, his lungs burning. Had he taken a breath that whole time? The way his lungs demanded he gasp for air suggested he hadn't.

He pushed himself onto all fours. Nausea hit him with more force than he could withstand. His stomach clenched, and he lost everything he'd eaten for breakfast. The morning meal hadn't tasted so great the first time let alone a second.

Black leather boots appeared in his view. Zeeran glanced up to find his uncle staring down at him with sympathy. The man heaved a sigh. "You'll get used to it. The first journey is always the worst."

"I don't intend to do that again," muttered Zeeran, accepting his uncle's outstretched hand.

"It will grow on you. The amount of time saved alone makes the spell useful, but imagine how much less your muscles will ache."

"Perhaps, but next time I'll be certain to refrain from eating beforehand."

Morzaun chuckled and turned his attention to the city resting beyond the meadow. "You did well for your first attempt. At least we made it in one piece."

If one didn't count the pieces Zeeran had left over the ground.

Zeeran ran his hand through his hair, ignoring the way his stomach still churned. "What now?"

"That depends on you." Morzaun turned his steely gaze on Zeeran. "On where your loyalties lie. You committed an act of treason, but if you have any thoughts of returning—"

"No. I won't go back there. They all want to see you tried for your actions, and we both know it's a mere formality. Delran will ensure you're put to death."

"Indeed. And you don't believe me deserving of death?"

Zeeran shifted on his feet. The way his uncle analyzed his responses made him nervous, but he spoke the truth. Morzaun didn't deserve to die. "I believe your actions were justified."

For several moments, his uncle said nothing. The distant sounds of the city filled the awkward silence, but the longer Morzaun withheld his response, the more anxious Zeeran became. What would he do if his uncle abandoned him? He *had* committed treason, and the thought of striking out on his own with such a heavy mark on his head was daunting.

"You may come with me," said Morzaun finally. "But know that I have no intention of turning myself in, nor will I sit idly by while Delran hunts me down."

"You have a plan, then?"

Morzaun smirked, but for some reason, the expression didn't comfort Zeeran as much as he would have liked. His uncle started down the road toward Rowenport and waved for Zeeran to follow. "I have a plan, but I won't give you the details yet. You will forgive me, I hope. I am slow to trust even my family."

Zeeran couldn't blame him for that. After all, much of this mess with the Izarden king had been created because Zeeran's mother and father had objected to Morzaun's actions. Delran's father had held Morzaun's wife captive for years, and Papa had encouraged him to do nothing to retaliate. Papa believed their powers were a gift, that they needed to be used responsibly and for good. But who got to decide which causes were worthy of their talents?

Who decided what was right and wrong?

Zeeran padded after Morzaun. He would show the man he could be trusted, that he didn't believe as Papa and Mama did. "What can I do to prove myself? I'm on your side. Sytal got what he deserved, and Delran is no different than his father. I want to see true justice served."

"In time it shall be, but we've a long way to go before then. If you wish to prove your loyalty to me, then let us start with this: what do you know of the gems your father and I brought back from Kantinar?"

The gems? Zeeran had been told the stories of the magical stones of Kantinar since he could remember, and while the colorful rocks were the source of their magical abilities, Zeeran failed to understand why his uncle would want access to *his* knowledge. Surely Morzaun knew more about them than Zeeran did.

"I know what my father has told me," said Zeeran. "When you, Mama, and Papa traveled to Kantinar in search of a weapon to defeat the invaders who murdered your families, you found a scepter embedded with gems. Upon touching it, the magical energy it contained transferred to you."

"Yes...or at least some of it. The Virgám retains more magical energy than any human could tolerate. That amount of power would likely rip the soul apart. It would take a special person, indeed, to wield it. But regardless, we were infused with some of its energy, and our magical gifts were passed to our children."

A flicker of pain spread over his face. Uncle Morzaun had lost his wife when the previous king murdered her, but he had also lost his son. Before Zeeran's aunt died, she had convinced one of her handmaiden's to take their young son and flee, fearing what King Sytal might force the boy to do with his magic.

Morzaun had learned of this when Mama had a vision. Zeeran's uncle and father had traveled to Izarden straight away, but they were too late. The vision had come to pass. Aunt Senniva was dead and Eramus gone. It was then that Uncle Morzaun committed his first act of treason against the kingdom, nearly killing King Sytal.

"The chamber where the Virgám lies is covered in symbols," continued Morzaun. "Your father and I eventually returned to study them, and between our notations and the voice guiding your mother, we learned a great many spells. But that was not the only thing we brought back with us to Verascene."

"You found more gems."

Morzaun nodded. "We did, and they contained the same magical energy as the Virgám, though far less powerful. Your father and I studied them for a long time, but for the most part, they remain a mystery. I have made some progress in coming to understand them since I began my life of solitude."

Intrigue pricked at Zeeran. "And what have you discovered?"

"I merely have theories, and we can discuss them later. For now, I believe we should keep our talk of magic to a minimum."

He pointed forward, and Zeeran's gaze followed. They were close enough to Rowenport now that he could see the bustling merchants and shoppers crowding the streets. Talk of magic made the people of Izarden uncomfortable, and their glares and murmurs made Zeeran uncomfortable in turn.

He buried his mound of questions. There would be time to discuss the gems later. For now, he would concentrate on where they would go next, and hope it was his legs that would carry him there rather than magic.

* * *

Zeeran followed Morzaun through the crowded streets. His uncle made several purchases as they moved down the long corridor of merchants, adding the items to the satchel that hung on his right shoulder. Zeeran hardly noticed what the purchases included, distracted as he was by the bustle around him. Verascene had only one village, and there were more people on this one street in Rowenport than lived on his entire island home. He quite enjoyed the energy the large city exuded.

"I believe that's everything." Morzaun stuffed a pouch of fragrant, powdered spices into his satchel. The lingering aroma left Zeeran's nose tingling the way sniffing a flower might, which he had experience with given the number of times Feya had shoved her wildflower bouquets into his personal space. The scent wasn't unpleasant, but it made his face tighten all the same.

"Now what?" asked Zeeran.

"I could use a bite to eat. What about you?"

The thought of food made Zeeran's stomach rumble. Everything he'd eaten this morning had been regurgitated after using the transportation spell, and he was quite aware of his stomach's emptiness. "Food sounds good."

"Come. I know a place where we can get a decent meal."

Zeeran followed Morzaun around the corner of a brick building and through a shadowed alley. They exited on the opposite end to a street that was far less crowded, but the amount of people going about their daily business still baffled Zeeran. He could stand in the streets all day watching the array of colorful characters roaming between buildings and never grow bored.

The street inclined, and his already tired muscles burned with the extra effort. They climbed the hill, and at the top, Zeeran looked over his shoulder. In the distance, sunlight glinted off the sea, and a multitude of ships moved into the harbor. For a brief moment, a pang of homesickness stirred in his stomach.

Morzaun approached a wide, wooden building painted a soft shade of yellow. Or at least it had been at one time. The paint chipped away from the planks, cracked and weathered, and the glass in the window panes were covered in a mixture of fingerprints and grime.

They were eating *here*?

Zeeran tried not to wince as they entered and the pungent smell of alcohol wafted up his nose. The room rattled with boisterous chatter. Men and women alike chugged the contents of their mugs and engaged in an open display of familiarity that would make genteel society balk.

A woman with braided dark hair waved and offered a coy grin when she caught Zeeran's eye. He quickly turned away, shifting his attention to the back corner of the room where his uncle was leading him.

They sat down at a small table with less proximity to the other occupants of the pub, but Zeeran could feel the gazes set upon him. The people were watching *them*, perhaps, but Morzaun didn't appear bothered by it the same way Zeeran was. His expression remained as stoic as ever, and not a hint of anxious energy radiated from the man.

The pub owner made his way to them and took their requests. A plate of cooked lamb, boiled vegetables, and bread rolls arrived a few minutes later. Zeeran and his uncle ate in silence, which gave Zeeran's mind permission to wander. To think. To reconsider.

Had he made the right decision in protecting his uncle? He believed in the man's innocence, of course, but choosing to side with someone deemed a traitor would have ramifications for more than just him. What if Delran punished his parents? What if he punished Feya?

Zeeran pushed his plate away, his twisting stomach too unrelenting to allow him to finish. Morzaun leaned back in his chair and crossed his arms. "I've come to a decision."

"About what?"

"I know how you can prove your loyalty to me." Morzaun tapped his finger against his arm, pursing his lips. He glanced around as if to make sure no one were near enough to hear and lowered his voice. "As I told you, I've been studying the gems. I have one in my possession at present, but if I were to have more, perhaps better progress could be made. The gems may be the key to removing Delran from the throne."

Zeeran's brows lifted high on his forehead. "You plan to dethrone the king?"

"I would like to, yes. Delran is a replica of his father. He leads this kingdom to war as often as his father, and while those endeavors have found success, they will not always prove fruitful."

"And who would reign in his stead?"

Morzaun lifted his cup and drank deeply. When he returned the empty vessel to the tabletop, he lifted a shoulder. "I was once told to take the position should Sytal prove lustful for power. Delran's heir is young, and with the princess deceased, the role naturally falls to me."

"To you?" Zeeran scoffed. "I mean no disrespect, Uncle. You would make a fine king, but I can't imagine the people of Izarden will feel the same way."

"Likely not, which is why I have yet to make a move in that regard. The gems, however, could assist if we understood their power more fully. Your father is in possession of the others, and they will do no one any good sitting idle in his house."

Zeeran leaned forward and clasped his hands on the table. "What is it you want me to do?"

"Take us to Verascene. I imagine you know where a few of the gems are. Help me obtain them. Your family is not on the island at present, therefore no one will be in our way."

Zeeran nodded slowly. "Working out the gems' abilities would be beneficial to us all. My father is too stubborn to see reason. We will never be accepted because of our power. We need to be prepared—always keep a watchful eye over our shoulder. The more we understand our connection to magic, the better."

Morzaun's chair slid across the wooden floor with a wail. He stood, a wide grin stretching over his face. "Well said, Zeeran. Tomorrow, we leave for Verascene."

CHAPTER FOUR

Spells and Gemstones

Though sleeping on a worn straw mattress at a less than respectable inn was only a small step above a tent and bedroll, Zeeran felt well rested. A morning meal of biscuits and hearty gravy had also given his spirits quite the boost. Neither, however, had kept at bay the nausea that came with practicing the transportation spell.

The world contorted and spun, the dark green colors of the trees mixing with the sky and ground until nothing was recognizable. Then, they separated, each part of the landscape taking on its natural form and hue.

Zeeran clutched his stomach, demanding what little remained of his breakfast to stay there, but it was no use. He cast up his accounts for the seventh time that morning. Or perhaps eighth? He wasn't sure anymore.

Morzaun clapped from where he sat at the base of a tree, his eyes dancing with mirth. "You've developed good control over it now, I think. A few more successes, and the nausea should fade."

Zeeran spat out the bile lingering on his tongue. He had transported himself yards down the dirt road outside of Rowenport. According to his uncle, moving one's body to a location closer to the starting point was more difficult than miles across the continent. Zeeran hadn't believed this until his first attempt to move himself from one side of the road to the other. The notion still seemed strange, but Uncle Morzaun insisted it was difficult for the mind to discern between where one was and where they wanted to go when both locations were so near each other.

His uncle pushed himself up from the ground and dusted off his trousers. "It's time." He stepped to Zeeran's side and placed a hand on his shoulder. "Imagine Verascene, perhaps outside your home."

Zeeran nodded. He had no desire to attempt transporting them inside a building. Too many things could go wrong, really. What if they ended up inside the hearth, jabbed through by the fire poker, or knocked over his mother's favorite clay pot? Both would have similar ramifications and were far too risky for his tastes.

Gripping Morzaun's shoulder, Zeeran allowed the incantation to spill from his lips. The world bled into a mixture of color like the way ripples disturbed a reflected image on a watery surface. He pictured his home—the thatched red roof, the boxes of purple flowers beneath the window, and the mountains stretching into the clouds that backdropped it all. The world twisted, and his stomach did the same.

Zeeran clenched his jaw and balled his fists. The air in his lungs grew stale. Slowly, the world shifted into something familiar. The cottage he'd grown up in came into view. Wispy clouds splayed across the sky, and trees—a mixture of flowering maples and palms—dotted the dirt path leading into the village.

Vomit rose in his throat, but he pushed it down. Not that he had anything left to shower the ground with.

"Well done," said Morzaun. "Now the real work begins."

His uncle marched to the cottage door and let himself inside. Zeeran drew a steadying breath before following. The inside of the cottage was dim with the clouds hiding much of the sun's light, but Zeeran could maneuver this place with his eyes closed. Everything was as they had left it. The knitted blankets his mother had created—all featuring her favorite deep purple color—draped the chairs. A vase full of wildflowers sat in the center of their dinner table, its contents withered and dry but still pretty in their own way. Ladisias had even left a pair of his smelly socks on the stone hearth.

Another pesky wave of homesickness gnawed at Zeeran's insides, but he ignored the sensation. He could not call this home any longer, could he? Leaving his family the way he had...they would not want him back. He believed in his decision, but no one else would support his actions. It was a sacrifice he had to make to fully embrace and acknowledge his stance, but only now did the full extent of the costs become apparent.

Morzaun rummaged through a few trunks in the corner. He knew Papa's hiding places as well as Zeeran, and after a few minutes of searching, pulled out a small trinket with a grin. "Ah. I've found one."

He held the object into the shallow stream of light coming in from the window, revealing the metallic luster of a silver ring, and the blue gem it contained caught the beams with a shimmer. Zeeran had never paid the gems any heed given that none of them understood much about them. He could sense the magic pulsing from each stone, but beyond that, they were useless. What good did such relics do if the power could not be tapped?

But perhaps he was wrong to assume it couldn't. They need only discover how to draw out the magical energy.

"Ladisias forged that for Mama," said Zeeran. "But she refused to wear it. She didn't like the idea of having the gem so close to her all the time."

"Caution." Morzaun dropped his hand and placed the ring into a pocket on the inside of his cloak. "Your mother is wise to abide by it. We know not what the gems are capable of, and I would certainly prefer to be the one studying them than to put her at risk."

Zeeran preferred the same.

"Can you sense the others?" asked Morzaun. "The last time I was here, I struggled to access my connection to all of the gems we brought back from Kantinar. I suspect your father may have hidden some of them."

"Why would he do that?"

Morzaun rubbed a hand over his mouth, a hint of irritation flickering in his dark eyes. "To keep them from me, I presume. He has lost all trust in me, and as I have lost all connection to the Virgám and can no longer feel the presence of magic, I place *my* trust in you. Can you sense any of the other gems here or not?"

Zeeran closed his eyes and concentrated on the gentle pulse he sensed emanating from the gem in Morzaun's pocket. He pushed his focus past it, searching for the others, but found nothing.

"The other gems aren't here," said Zeeran. "My father must have moved them. There's a chance some of them are still at the forge."

A good chance, Zeeran believed. Ladisias had shown a natural aptitude for forging at a young age, and the local blacksmith had taken him on as an apprentice not long after they arrived on Verascene. Once his skills grew beyond that of an amateur, Papa had given Ladisias permission to turn the gems into more...to create shells for them.

"Excellent suggestion," said Morzaun. Why don't we pay Fernden a visit. I presume the forgemaster is still alive?"

"Yes, he is, but we may have to wait until he's gone home. Papa will have instructed—"

"Come, Zeeran." Morzaun pushed past him and pulled open the door. "We don't have time to waste."

Zeeran followed him outside. The sun had slipped through the clouds, basking the world with light and warmth. The dirt path leading to the village twisted between trees until it came to a clearing where the few island inhabitants bustled about with their chores. Many of them offered looks of curiosity and confusion, and a few glared at Morzaun.

News from the mainland rarely reached their isolated home, but his uncle had not been on good terms with a few of those residing here, either. His emotions made him explosive at times, and that in congruent with his ability to use magic—or past ability, rather—made him dangerous. It was that precise combination that had taken an innocent man's life several years ago, a man who also happened to be the father of General Ivrin.

But none of that mattered. Morzaun couldn't lose control of something he no longer possessed. They could focus on saving Izarden from suffering under the hands of another tyrant.

Morzaun stopped outside of the large forge and tilted his head. The sound of metal smacking metal hit Zeeran's ears, and each clank made him blink uncontrollably in rhythm with the sound. Beams of thick wood held up the thatched roof, and the back side of the forge had a wall where shelves were lined with various tools. On the left, a giant stone hearth contained a blazing fire, its flicker reflected in the cooling trough next to it.

In the center of it all, Fernden's arms moved with power and force, each swing warping the piece of hot metal he held with long tongs. Sweat beaded above his thick, auburn brows, and his concentration on the work kept him from noticing the watchful eyes set upon him.

Morzaun entered the forge and waved his hand to catch Fernden's attention. The burly man didn't cease his work, but gave Morzaun a nod. "I'll be with ye in a minute. I'm nearly done."

As they waited, Zeeran closed his eyes and focused his mind on sensing the presence of magic. He found a faint glow on the opposite side of the room, the blue aura illuminating in his mind like a candle. Another gem.

But where were the others? Zeeran wasn't certain how many his uncle and father had brought back from Kantinar, but he knew very well it was more than two. Uncle Morzaun was in possession of one already—a dagger embedded with a blue stone, forged by Ladisias some time ago—and they had found a ring in the cottage. Ladisias carried a sword he had made for himself, one that possessed a green gemstone not unlike the aura that came from his magic, but there were more stones than that.

Zeeran opened his eyes and bit his lip. Why had he not paid more attention?

Fernden placed his hammer on his work table and with a quick shuffle submerged the glowing orange metal into the water trough. An angry hiss rent the air, accompanied by a giant waft of steam that crashed into the ceiling and radiated outwards until it dissipated.

For several minutes, Fernden kept still, whistling as he waited for the hot metal to cool. Once it had, he placed it on a rack and made his way over to them. "Morzaun, havna' seen ye in a spell."

Fernden's expression remained stoic, but Zeeran could see the suspicion in the man's blue eyes.

"Indeed," said Morzaun. "It's good to see you're still at it, Fern. I would expect nothing less. I imagine my nephew has been hard at work creating masterpieces as well?"

The blacksmith's eyes narrowed slightly. "Aye, Ladisias puts his talents to work. The lad will likely take over for me soon. Havna' seen him in several days, though. Aldeth gave me the impression they were leaving the island for a time." His gaze shifted to Zeeran. "Thought ye'd be accompanying them."

Zeeran swallowed. Fernden knew of his family's ability to use magic—everyone on the island knew—but a spell that allowed a person to transport from one place to another in the blink of an eye was new for Zeeran. It would be new for the islanders as well, and knowledge of such spells would undoubtedly pique their interests. Verascene was not a place those stranded here could escape without magic, what with its sharp cliff faces and rough waters. The very thing that kept people from leaving also kept Zeeran and his family safe from Delran. The idea that someone could leap to the mainland with a few words and wave of the hand would become a commodity many would not turn down should they find out.

"I decided to stay behind," said Zeeran. "Keep an eye on things."

The way Fernden stared at him with that calculating look made Zeeran's insides squirm. Why was he lying, anyway? It wasn't as though he had no right to come home. There was nothing suspicious about that.

Zeeran glanced at his uncle. Perhaps it was not Zeeran's presence that Fernden found dubious, but Morzaun's. The man did have a way about him—intimidating and unreadable.

"I see." Fernden's analytical eyes finally moved away, and Zeeran exhaled like he'd forgotten how to breathe. Nothing about this conversation should make him feel so tense, but it did, and that was more unsettling than anything. Tendrils of guilt gnawed at his stomach, but he brushed them aside. He had no reason to feel that way.

"What can I do for ye?" asked Fernden. He wiped a trickle of sweat from his temple with the back of his hand. "I'm right busy, but I'll do what I can."

"We were hoping you had a few of the gems Aldeth and I retrieved," said Morzaun. "I want to study them for a time while my brother is away."

That hard look returned to Fernden's eyes, and Zeeran's heart picked up speed. "We could discover how they work. Surprise Papa when he returns. Besides, it's important we understand them so their power can be controlled." The words had tumbled out in a way that would certainly not appease Fernden's distrust, but Zeeran couldn't recall them now. He smiled, and hoped the expression appeared genuine.

Apparently, he failed.

Fernden's forehead wrinkled. "Aldeth instructed me to keep the gem hidden until he returned. If that's what ye've come for, then I have to disappoint ye. I gave 'im my word."

"Surely you can make an exception for us?" Morzaun's tone deepened, and he spoke through gritted teeth. "We're his family."

The blacksmith considered him for a moment, his gaze flicking to Morzaun's balled fists. "Nae. No exceptions. I dinna trust ye, Morzaun, and I think ye right well know it."

The muscles in Morzaun's jaw clenched. Fernden turned and shuffled back to his work desk, whistling his tune.

"Can you sense the gems," Morzaun whispered, his gaze locked on the blacksmith.

"Only one, but—"

"Get rid of him."

Zeeran's heart skittered. "What?"

"We need that gem if we're to take down Delran. It's for the good of everyone in Virgamor that we study those stones. I will not allow this *blacksmith* to stand in the way of that." Morzaun turned his dark gaze on Zeeran. The coldness there sent a shiver down Zeeran's spine. Morzaun had always been different—strong, reserved, and slightly frightening with his natural commanding presence. But this wasn't the same. A darkness lingered there.

"If you want to prove your loyalty to me," said Morzaun. "Then take care of this fool."

CHAPTER FIVE
A New Home

Take care of Fernden? That phrase could have any number of meanings, but the way Morzaun was staring at him crossed a few off the list of possibilities. Of course, his uncle didn't intend for him to *kill* the man.

Did he?

Another wave of ice slithered up Zeeran's back and into his shoulders. Fernden may be acting a fool, but he didn't deserve to die. Zeeran was overthinking this; his uncle certainly didn't mean his order that way.

Zeeran stretched his palms out before him and muttered an incantation. He would deal with this easily enough—and in a way that didn't involve murder. Blue light swirled around his hands, and an inconspicuous beam of light crept toward the blacksmith, who paid no heed to his visitors. The spell hit Fernden as he raised his mallet to strike a piece of metal. The tool wavered with the droop of the man's eyes, and for a moment, Zeeran worried Fernden would drop the heavy mallet on his foot. It fell to the ground with a thud that made Zeeran wince, but upon inspection, appeared to have missed any appendages, leaving an impressive dent in the earthy floor instead.

Fernden swaggered for a few seconds before his body toppled to the ground. Zeeran raced to his side and crouched. The blacksmith's face had smoothed over, and his chest rose and fell in deep, steady heaves.

"A sleeping spell," said Morzaun. "I suppose that will do. Now, the gem. Where is it?"

Zeeran pointed across the room to where the aura had illuminated in his mind. The clank of metal filled the open forge as Morzaun fumbled through tools and bins for the stone. Zeeran stood, keeping his gaze on Fernden. The man would awaken in an hour or so, well-rested and likely annoyed that the gem was gone. He would tell Papa...eventually.

Zeeran hadn't the faintest idea when his family would return. How long would they search for Morzaun? For him? Perhaps Delran would send them home.

He *hoped* the king would send them home, for the alternative was far less appealing. But what could the soldiers or king do to them, really? Zeeran's family had magic, and the thing that deemed them the enemy also made them risky to attack.

Zeeran's mind wandered to his sister, Feya. She possessed magic the same as Zeeran and Ladisias but had struggled as of late. Her power was unreliable, to say the least, due to her fear of losing control, and Zeeran worried after her. The rest of his family may be safe from Delran's assaults, but Feya remained vulnerable, perhaps unwilling to fight back should the need arise. And she was all alone.

"I've got it."

Zeeran couldn't see Morzaun's face, but he could hear the smile in the man's voice. His uncle turned, holding an object up in front of him. He gestured Zeeran forward with his free hand, his eyes fixed on a round amulet, hungry as though he hadn't eaten in several days.

Zeeran obeyed the command, coming to a stop right in front of Morzaun. The piece of steel wasn't much to look at, a few intricate vines and flowers etched into its surface—Ladisias might have skill with forging, but his artist aesthetics needed work—but the gem in the center oozed with power. With magic.

"You're certain you don't sense any others?" asked Morzaun.

Zeeran channeled his focus, expanding his search as far as his mind would allow, past the glowing blue aura of the gem in Morzaun's hand and pocket and to the edges of the village. "No. You're likely right about Papa hiding them. They could be anywhere on the island."

"Perhaps. Or not on the island at all."

Zeeran bit his lip. Why would Papa go to such lengths to hide the gems? Sure, they possessed magic, but it wasn't as though they were sentient beings capable of using the power inside them against mankind. His family didn't even know how to access it.

At least not yet.

Zeeran's gaze flicked to Morzaun, who was studying the amulet with an intense look in his dark eyes. Had Papa feared someone *would* learn how to access the power of the gems? But that didn't make any sense. Morzaun had lost his power, or it had been taken from him, rather. After his uncle devastated the army of Izarden and killed the previous king, Zeeran's parents had feared the power Morzaun wielded. Together, they'd faced him and used a spell to absolve the man of his ability to wield magic.

Without that ability, Morzaun couldn't even sense the gems' presence, let alone access the energy stored within them.

Or so Zeeran believed. Admittedly, none of them knew enough about the stones or the origin of magic to make assumptions. The realization flooded Zeeran's stomach with anxious energy, like dozens of dragonflies swarming the edges of a pond. He'd wanted to pledge his loyalty to his uncle—been so certain the man's cause was just. Yet something niggled at him, a sense of dread he couldn't quite comprehend.

Morzaun slipped the amulet into his pocket with the ring. "Let's be on our way. We can study these properly once we're home."

"Home?"

A wry grin pulled over Morzaun's lips. "You *do* still wish to join me, don't you?"

Zeeran nodded. "Where is home, precisely?"

Morzaun patted Zeeran's shoulder and made his way out of the forge. Zeeran followed close on his heels, suspecting they would use his newly acquired means of transportation to go *home*. His stomach already felt the effects, churning with anticipation and angst.

"We'll return to Rowenport first," said Morzaun. "Catch a ship to Croseline overnight." Morzaun paused and turned to face him. His eyes wandered over Zeeran, analyzing. "But before we do that, I think it best you give yourself time to rest. Transporting via magic has surely left you exhausted after so much practice this morning, no?"

He did feel tired, and given what could go wrong should he perform the spell incorrectly, Zeeran wasn't saddened by the idea of resting. "A nap should put me to straights."

"Good. We'll return to Rowenport once you've rested. We'll have plenty of time to find passage."

"And after that?"

"We go where your parents won't find us. And *then*, we begin."

* * *

Even after an hour of walking, the smell of the sea tickled Zeeran's nose. Soon they would be far enough inland that the air would lose the familiar scent, replaced instead with those of the surrounding pines and flowering plants.

The road from Croseline lacked for company, not another soul passing them once they had journeyed beyond the rolling hills overlooking the coastal town. Croseline was comparable to Rowenport in size, but unlike the kingdom of Izarden, Selvenor was yet in its infancy. There were few towns beyond the port city and the kingdom's capital.

After spending another evening on Rowenport's bustling streets, the quiet of the ship Morzaun had bartered passage on was deafening. Eating breakfast in Croseline had livened the morning, but now they walked in eerie silence.

Zeeran increased his pace until he matched his uncle's gait. "How long until–"

"Patience, Zeeran. We'll be there by this afternoon. And once you've seen the place, you won't have to make the journey on foot ever again."

Admittedly, after smelling the inside of the cramped cabin onboard the ship, Zeeran would prefer a faster means of getting about. It would save him coin as well, not that he had paid for anything since joining his uncle. Zeeran *had* saved the man's life, and from what his parents had said of Morzaun, the man knew how to make a living with or without magic and had quite the savings from his time as second in command of Izarden's army.

The lack of hesitation to pay for Zeeran's food and passage certainly proved Morzaun's coffers were full enough, at least for a man who seemingly lived in the forest.

Zeeran glanced around. The woodland stretched endlessly before them, and the road weaved between the trees, following the path of the river that ran alongside it. The area was quiet and peaceful, but anticipation kept Zeeran from enjoying it. His uncle had spent years evading Delran, and being shown his new home felt like being let in on some enormous secret.

"We'll cross here," said Morzaun. "The river is wide but shallow. Perhaps a few feet deep."

His uncle splashed into the ripples diverging around a rough stone, and Zeeran followed. There was no road on the other side, leaving them to fight through thick brambles and undergrowth. Leaves clung to his wet clothes, and dirt found its way into his boots, turning to mud beneath his soppy socks.

When the sun hovered above the treetops overhead, the forest thinned, and Zeeran welcomed the reprieve. He was exhausted and filthy. Hopefully wherever *home* was, he'd find a river or stream nearby for a bath.

Morzaun halted and turned to face Zeeran. "We've arrived. Make yourself familiar with the area. You may stay with me for a time, but I expect you to construct your own place over the next few weeks. I prefer my privacy."

"Construct?"

A lopsided smirk lifted Morzaun's lips. "You have magic, Zeeran. You're plenty capable of building yourself a house."

Zeeran bit his lip. Uncle Morzaun had a point, but just because Zeeran possessed magic didn't mean he knew *how* to build a house.

Morzaun started forward, leaving no time for argument. Zeeran would figure it out. How difficult could it possibly be?

They entered a clearing dotted with yellow and white wildflowers. To his left, Zeeran took in the worked ground of a small garden, several plants putting on a display of colorful vegetables. Next to the garden stood a shed, its outer walls covered with tools hanging from hooks and long nails. Split firewood was stacked against one side, and Zeeran wondered how cool the nights were this far north. Verascene remained warm year round, but the weather here was different. He would need shelter for when the air turned foul.

Zeeran shifted his attention to the other side of the clearing. Two cottages rested at the edge of the surrounding tree line. They were much smaller than his parents' cottage on the island, likely a single room each, but the size seemed suitable. Zeeran would study his uncle's home and replicate the structure's designs.

Morzaun stopped in front of the first cottage and outstretched his hands. "Welcome. I know it's far humbler than what you're used to even on the island, but we make do. Of course, having you around to transport us to Croseline will be useful when we run out of things, as we often do."

Zeeran blinked. We?

"I'll teach you to hunt," continued Morzaun. "I'm certain your father has never taught you that particular skill as it would involve actually using a weapon. Trapping is important, too. If you are to stay, I'll expect you to pull your share of the work, and in return, I'll teach you everything I know."

A thrill shot through Zeeran. "Even sword wielding?"

Morzaun chuckled. "Ah. You wish to finish your training. Yes, we can do that as well. But for now, we should rest. It's been a long journey, and you have an exhausting few days ahead of you."

Right. He had to build a house. "I hope you intend to offer me a few pointers; otherwise, I may severely injure myself. House-building is not something I have experience with."

"Everyone needs some guidance, but I also believe there is value in letting you figure things out on your own. Balance is key."

"I suppose that's fair." Zeeran turned his attention to the second cottage. The other half of his uncle's *we* must live there, but who were they? Zeeran had assumed Morzaun lived alone. Someone in hiding would want as few people to know of their whereabouts as possible, which meant that whoever lived there must be someone his uncle trusted.

Morzaun chuckled again, drawing Zeeran's attention back to him. His uncle folded his arms and grinned. "You're wondering who lives there. I can't blame you for being curious." He started toward the second cottage, waving for Zeeran to follow. "Come. Now is as good a time as any for you to meet her."

Her? More questions swarmed through Zeeran's thoughts, but he held his tongue. After all, he would soon find out who had earned his uncle's trust when Zeeran, a member of the man's own family, had yet to do so.

CHAPTER SIX

Hidden Scars

Morzaun knocked on the cottage door, and an illogical amount of anxiety swept through Zeeran's stomach. He imagined a middle-aged woman on the other side, perhaps with as many years of life experience as his uncle, complete with wrinkles and a brow that could chide him without words.

The door swung open. A woman no older than Zeeran with hair as black as midnight stared back at him. Her hair was braided tight against her head above her ears and then the long strands draped over her shoulders, the color transitioning to a deep red as though they were being consumed by flames—flames that matched her piercing green eyes, calculating and untrusting—ready to burn unsuspecting victims.

But the woman's most distinguishing features were the scars that crossed her cheeks. One found its way over her nose and between her brows, a trail of red, healed and aged with enough time to allow it to fade. Zeeran wondered at the extent of the marks, which must serve as an unrelenting reminder of some truly horrendous event. Somehow, the deformation only deepened her beauty, like living irony that drew a person in out of curiosity and made them beg to know her secrets.

"Have you finished gawking at me?" The woman folded her arms, her gaze roaming over Zeeran. "Who's the dolt?"

Zeeran scoffed. "Pleasure to meet you as well."

Morzaun chuckled. "Play nice, Sicarii. My nephew will be staying with us indefinitely. I expect you to keep your daggers away from his heart."

Was he serious? Zeeran glanced over the woman, taking note of the leather belt and straps serving as sheathes for a multitude of weapons. Just who was this lady?

Sicarii harrumphed and topped her disdain off with a dramatic eye roll. "And why have you gone and adopted a pet? I thought being discreet and unnoticed was your aim?" One of her dark brows lifted. "Your puppy looks as though he'll bark loud for all to hear at the first sign of trouble."

"I've no need to bark," spat Zeeran, "but you are correct about one thing—I will hardly go unnoticed should trouble arise. I'm plenty capable of defending myself."

"Zeeran can wield magic," explained Morzaun. "He will be an asset to our cause, more so once I've had the opportunity to train him."

Sicarii shrugged, playing off a façade of disinterest. She failed to fool Zeeran, however. He could see the intrigue flickering in her eyes. Given her age, she'd likely never seen Morzaun use magic—likely hadn't seen anyone use it. That sort of curiosity was difficult to hide.

"So, the puppy can do tricks. How fascinating." Sicarii examined her nails with a level of nonchalance that irked Zeeran. Maybe he wasn't the best fighter or even the best at wielding his power—Ladisias had always outshone him on those fronts—but his abilities *were* an asset. Perhaps this woman required a demonstration to fully grasp his gift.

Light erupted around both of Zeeran's hands. Sicarii's gasp only fueled him more. He concentrated on the weapons dangling around the woman's waist. Blue light encircled them, lifting the daggers until they slipped from the leather sheaths and hovered in the air in front of her. Sicarii stepped backwards, her mouth agape.

Zeeran smirked and gave his wrist a flick. The daggers rotated so that the blades faced the woman. Sicarii's eyes rounded, a reaction Zeeran took great satisfaction in before ending his spell and allowing the daggers to drop to the ground with a series of thuds.

Sicarii glared at him. "Am I supposed to be impressed?"

"You looked rather impressed."

"Well, I'm not, so you can calm your ego and temper that ridiculous expression. There's no reason to be so pleased with yourself."

She bent over and snatched up her weapons, her scowl creating a deep line in her forehead. Zeeran's grin grew. The woman was stubborn, and whether she wanted to admit it or not, she was impressed...or, at minimum, fascinated.

Sicarii straightened and swept her hair over her shoulder. "I take it we are to have a discussion? Things did not go according to–"

"Not here." Morzaun nodded to his cottage. "You and I will discuss that in private."

Private? Clearly Uncle Morzaun still didn't trust him. Zeeran had done everything the man asked, even saved him from Ivrin and the soldiers. But trust required time, and given what his parents had done to the man, Zeeran would be patient.

"Fine," said Sicarii, irritation lacing her tone. "But don't you dare blame me for what happened."

She stomped past them and headed for Morzaun's cottage without so much as looking back over her shoulder before throwing open the door and disappearing inside.

Morzaun sighed and ran a hand over his face. "I don't recommend pestering her...or taunting her if you wish your heart to keep beating."

"What happened to her?" asked Zeeran. "How did she get those scars?"

His uncle shrugged. "I don't know because I'm not foolish enough to ask her about something likely to get me stabbed. I suggest you take that into consideration."

"Noted. Am I to wait outside while the two of you discuss things?"

Zeeran attempted to hide the annoyance from his tone, but he'd probably failed. He'd be lying if he said the secrets didn't bother him. But he would earn his uncle's trust. He would give Morzaun every reason to take him into his confidence.

"Perhaps you might take a few minutes to think about your cottage," said Morzaun. "Best to have a vision of what you want before you begin."

Zeeran nodded. "Very well."

Morzaun patted Zeeran's shoulder. "I'll tell you more in time. We've much work to do, and I believe you will play a key role in my plans."

His uncle returned to his cottage, and Zeeran plopped down on the grassy ground, staring at the empty space before him. Building a house would be difficult work, but designing one's own abode had its perks. He could do whatever he liked, shape and mold his ideal home into what he wanted.

He smiled. He would do the same for his future and, with any luck, find the contentment that had thus far eluded him.

* * *

Zeeran shrugged off his coat and tossed it into the grass. His shirtsleeves stuck to his skin, making them more difficult to roll up to his elbows. He retrieved his sword from the ground and held it at the ready.

Morzaun chuckled and shook his head. "Loosen your grip. I know you're excited for lessons, but holding your blade so tightly will not give you more control. Relax, Zeeran. Give the weapon some room to breathe."

Zeeran obeyed, relaxing his hold. His brother had trained with Morzaun for months when they were younger, and Zeeran had watched from the sidelines. Ladisias had taken to the sword quickly, and his skill had rivaled their uncle's in time. But when Zeeran's turn arrived, he hadn't been given the opportunity to fully test his natural aptitude. A few weeks were hardly enough to develop much skill before his uncle left Verascene for good.

"Today we will focus on your footwork, but remember to keep your grip light," said Morzaun. "Now, I would like you to mimic my motions."

His uncle stepped to the right, and Zeeran mirrored the movement. For several minutes, Zeeran copied each shift in Morzaun's feet, his gaze pinned on the man's boots. It seemed an almost silly game, but Zeeran trusted his uncle's techniques. The man had been second in command of Izarden's army once. He knew what he was doing.

"Good," said Morzaun. "But watching my feet is a bad habit. Keep your eyes on my face, and mimic without looking down. Your attention should never waver. It only takes a moment for me to strike, and if your focus is elsewhere, you'll be less prepared to counter."

Zeeran and Morzaun rotated in a complete circle. Keeping his attention from shifting to the ground proved more difficult than Zeeran thought, and he chided his eyes each time his gaze flicked to Morzaun's black boots.

Morzaun changed directions so quickly that Zeeran tripped over his own feet trying to follow. He recovered his steps, but Morzaun changed direction again, increasing his pace and making his movements more unpredictable. Mirroring the man's actions grew impossible, and the effort soon had Zeeran heaving for breath and flailing his limbs like a fool.

"Are we dancing or training?" came a feminine voice from the tree line.

Zeeran straightened and lowered his sword as Sicarii left the shadow of a giant oak to saunter into the clearing beyond the cottages. Her lips were tipped up in a smirk, and the red in her hair caught the sunlight, making it almost glow like fire.

"Honestly, both choices are insulting," she said, stopping next to Morzaun. "That is the worst form I've ever seen for both activities."

"And you were an expert the moment you picked up a blade, I presume?" asked Zeeran. "How incredibly convenient for you. Or, perhaps, you mock me to make yourself feel better about your inadequacies."

Zeeran knew that to be untrue. He'd watched Sicarii last night as she practiced throwing her daggers. Her precision was nigh on perfect, and part of him felt sorry for the tree she'd mutilated. But then he'd stared as she practiced lunging, evading, and blocking. The way her body moved, training and dancing were not so dissimilar. Her movements were smooth as a calm lake. Each flowed into the next effortlessly, and the entire performance had mesmerized him.

Still, he had no intention of revealing such observations. The woman didn't need a boost to her ego.

"My inadequacies?" Her brow lifted, amplifying her smirk in a way that oddly twisted Zeeran's gut. "Would you like me to demonstrate how *inadequate* I am?"

The wise part of him encouraged him to say *no,* but the foolish part talked rather loudly, drowning out logic. "Yes, I would."

Morzaun sighed, but laughter danced in his eyes. "Very well, Sicarii. I leave the rest of today's training to you." He walked to Zeeran's side and patted his shoulder. "Try not to get yourself killed, will you?"

"No promises," Zeeran muttered.

His uncle chuckled and left Zeeran alone in the clearing with Sicarii. She removed a dagger from one of her sheaths and tossed it into the air. The weapon did several flips before she caught it by the hilt.

Show off.

Zeeran reigned in the desire to do some fancy twirl with his sword. He was more likely to slice his finger off than to impress her.

Not that he needed to impress the woman.

"Do you not wish to use a sword instead?" asked Zeeran, nodding toward the short blade in her hand. "Seems a bit unfair."

"You're right. I should dispose of my weapons entirely to even out the odds."

Zeeran scoffed. "Fine. But don't say I didn't offer."

He lunged, sweeping his blade toward her abdomen. Sicarii swiveled out of range, rotating until she stood directly behind him with such speed Zeeran had no time to blink before she thrust her elbow down on his shoulder.

He bit back a groan and turned. He jabbed his blade at her chest, but Sicarii evaded with a side step. She swung her dagger, and Zeeran jumped backwards. The steel missed his skin but snagged on his tunic, leaving a long slit from the center to the hem.

Zeeran strode forward, and the determination in his step seemed to take Sicarii by surprise. She matched his gait with a retreat, but Zeeran increased his pace and swung his sword. Sicarii twisted to avoid the blade, but it sliced through her hair as she twirled out of reach. A fistful of red hair fell to the ground.

Sicarii scowled. "You cut my hair!"

"You cut my shirt."

The woman lunged, the energy she exuded rivaling that of an angry bear. Zeeran blocked the first plunge of her dagger, but Sicarii procured a second blade from her belt and slashed it across his forearm. He screamed, and Sicarii backed away, her expression a mixture of anger and guilt.

Blood trickled over Zeeran's skin, the pain pulsing up his arm and into his shoulder. He dropped his sword and placed his hand over the wound. Blue light appeared with his muttered words, and his skin stitched itself back together.

"How convenient," grumbled Sicarii. "I think we're done here."

She spun around and headed for the trees.

So, she intended to nearly cut off his arm and simply walk away? Not happening.

Zeeran chased after her, the shadows consuming both of their bodies when they entered the thick of the forest. Zeeran grabbed Sicarii by the arm and pulled her to a stop. "Are you jealous of my magic?"

"Jealous?" She ripped her arm from his hold. "Why would I be jealous of a spoiled brat who can heal himself?"

"I didn't always have magic. My power didn't manifest until I was ten years old."

"Oh, and is that small differences supposed to make me like you? How many scars do you have? I'd wager very few, because you can fix your injuries with nothing to remind you they ever occurred. How nice it must be to save yourself from marks that would define you."

Zeeran studied her face—the way her green eyes threatened to burn a hole in him and the way the shadows danced over the faded red lines on her cheek. Of course she would resent him for the ability to heal when her past had left an inescapable reminder.

Zeeran lifted his arm and turned it so that the little light percolating through the treetops fell over the faint line on his skin. "Magic doesn't prevent scarring, though it can lessen their appearance sometimes."

"Good for you."

He sighed and took a step closer. Sicarii tensed, distrust settling in her features. He tilted his head, bringing him close enough to smell the flowery scent of her soap, and lowered his voice. "We all have scars, some visible and others buried where only we can see. Those at the surface make us feel vulnerable, but it is the ones that hide within our memories that do the most damage. Those are the scars that truly define us if we allow them."

Her expression softened, and her green eyes searched his face as if looking for the very marks he tried to hide. "And how do we keep them from molding us into something we don't wish to be?"

"By accepting our past is unchangeable and refusing to let it determine our future. It's the most difficult battle we face, and the most important victory we can claim."

She remained quiet for several moments before a small smile

lifted her lips. "You are not what I expected, you know."

"Is that good or bad?"

Sicarii shrugged. "I haven't decided yet."

"I have time to influence the decision, then. Do let me know when you've figured it out."

She narrowed her eyes, but her smile grew. "I believe we both have work to do. Your house isn't going to build itself, though magic likely makes it come close." Sicarii slipped past him, and her arm brushed against his, sending a rush of chills down his spine.

Zeeran turned to watch her fight through the overgrowth. "Admit it. I'm growing on you."

"Like warts grow on toes, perhaps," she tossed over her shoulder. "That doesn't mean I want you around."

Her words should have been offensive; instead, Zeeran found himself grinning. Like a fool. A complete and utter dolt.

He tempered the expression and marched after her. "I'm the most lovable wart you'll ever have, though."

Sicarii laughed, *genuinely* laughed, and Zeeran began to doubt his own wisdom. Perhaps the most important battle he could win had nothing to do with himself, for every smile he made appear on Sicarii's face felt like the grandest of victories, and he was determined to win the war.

CHAPTER SEVEN

To Live Forever

Zeeran wiped the sweat beading on his forehead with the back of his hand, the other tightening its grip on the hilt of his sword. The sun was merciless today, and despite training in the shadows of the trees, his clothes had become drenched. Of course, he owed much of it to spending the morning removing bark from the trees he'd downed the day before. Magic proved a useful companion for preparing the wood for construction, but Zeeran found he liked to do some of the work by hand as well. Keeping himself busy gave his mind time to think, analyze, and study.

Turns out a man could learn much from studying his own thoughts.

Zeeran found he had no regrets about his decision to leave his family and join Morzaun, and though there were things—secrets that his uncle had yet to divulge—that irked him about the situation, he was ultimately satisfied with the choice.

Still, he worried about his family. Missed them, even. Delran was not a man to be trifled with, and Papa had agreed to leave Feya behind as *insurance* to set the king at ease.

Zeeran lunged, jabbing the tip of his sword in the air with far more force than the empty space required for conquering. Papa had made a mistake in leaving Feya on her own. She had no way to defend herself given her struggles with magic, and Zeeran had made certain Papa knew how much he opposed the decision. If something happened to her, it would be Papa's fault.

The shuffle of Zeeran's feet stirred dust into the air. He sliced the particles and whirled around to stab at the nonexistent opponent approaching on the other side. He backed against the tree, holding his sword at the ready. What would he do if he were surrounded by foes and had no way to escape?

His uncle was a brilliant strategist, and if Zeeran wanted to be half as good as him, he needed to start *thinking* like a strategist. As a boy, imagining such scenarios was nothing more than a game, but now the practiced notions held merit. He was an enemy to the throne of Izarden, a traitor, and he needed to be prepared.

Though no danger actually existed in the quiet shadows of the forest near his new home, Zeeran's pulse quickened at the imaginary challenge. Power surged through his veins, prodding just beneath his skin, waiting to be released.

But he would not use his magic. He shouldn't rely on that ability alone. He wanted more than anything to be strong without it. Once he'd mastered sword fighting, his gift of magic would serve as an even greater asset.

Zeeran lifted his weapon and reared back to strike. Something whizzed through the air, barely missing his cheek, and struck the bark of the tree next to him. He stilled, his gaze searching the shadows, but nothing moved in the silence.

Another flash of metal swept past his face and lodged into the tree. Zeeran tightened his grip on the hilt of his sword. "Who's there? Come out and face me."

The chuckle that followed eased his constricting stomach. He recognized that laugh, having heard its taunting sound a great deal over the last few days. Sicarii stepped out from behind a tree, a wide grin smeared over her face.

"Your form is terrible," she said. "A child could do better."

"Forgive me. Not all of us have had years of training." Zeeran gripped the hilt of the dagger protruding from the tree behind him and yanked it free of the bark. "I confess your aim deserves praise."

One of her dark brows lifted. "I missed."

Zeeran grabbed the second dagger, shaking his head. "Once, and I might have believed you, but I know better. I've watched you practice. You don't miss, and certainly not twice."

"Would you have preferred I aimed for your head?"

Her grin disappeared as he crossed the grass to stand in front of her. Sicarii had not given him the opportunity to learn much about her over the last few days, but Zeeran had noticed that his proximity ate away at her confident façade . Anytime he drew near, something beyond aloofness flickered in her eyes. He thought it might be fear, but that made little sense. Someone capable of defending themselves so proficiently had no reason to be afraid of him.

Then again, Zeeran did possess magic, and his uncle had proven how unpredictable magic could be.

Zeeran offered her the weapons. Her green eyes darted between his face and the daggers, uncertainty still lingering within them. Sicarii slipped them from his hands, gently, with perhaps the most hesitation he'd yet seen from her.

"Thank you," she whispered, her attention fixed on the ground. Or perhaps his boots. Zeeran wasn't entirely certain, nor did he understand why he couldn't bring himself to step away. Having such a small gap between them clearly made her uncomfortable, but then, she hadn't backed away from him, either.

He cleared his throat and forced his feet to move, placing a larger space between them. "If my form is as horrendous as you say, then perhaps you should teach me."

"I said terrible, not horrendous. And I'm no teacher."

"Ah. Only a critic? How am I to improve if no one shows me the proper way?"

Sicarii sheathed her daggers. "Perhaps try asking your uncle. His barrel of patience is far fuller than mine, especially for men who—" She turned away and stared off into the shadows.

"Men who what?" asked Zeeran.

She met his gaze. Uncertainty filled her green eyes again. "Never mind. I'm in no mood to teach you, nor do I have the time. Morzaun has a mission for me to complete."

Sicarii spun on her heels and headed toward the clearing where their cottages—well, Zeeran's could not truly be considered a *cottage* yet, but he'd made progress this morning—rested in the surrounding grove of pine and birch.

"Wait." Zeeran jogged to reach Sicarii's side and then kept pace with her. "What mission is he sending you on?"

"If you want the details, you'll need to speak with Morzaun."

Zeeran bit his lip. His uncle hadn't been the most forthcoming about his plans, especially not in regards to Sicarii's involvement. The secrets both irked and intrigued him, the latter more than Zeeran cared to admit.

"He hasn't confided anything to me," said Zeeran. "I doubt that will change anytime soon."

"That's hardly my problem. He's your family. Perhaps he doesn't believe you worthy of his trust."

Zeeran's foot caught on a stone, and he nearly stumbled to the ground. Sicarii's march seemed intent on escaping him, but he wasn't finished. There was more on the line than earning Morzaun's trust. For some inexplicable reason, he needed her trust as well, and something told him it would be far harder to win.

"My family betrayed my uncle," said Zeeran. "I can't blame him for being leery of me."

Sicarii halted, her expression as cold as stone. "And you've done the same thing. You betrayed them, and that doesn't exactly prove you capable of loyalty, does it? It seems to me this runs in your family—a constant stream of disloyalty."

An icy sensation ran down his back. She wasn't wrong.

He ran a hand through his hair. "You're right, and proving myself is what I want more than anything. But how can I do that when neither of you will give me a chance? Am I to be forever judged for the actions of others? My choices have done nothing but lead me here."

Sicarii studied him, her gaze searching for answers to questions he wished he could hear. What did she think of him? There was disdain, certainly, but also something more. Zeeran sometimes saw through her hard exterior—caught moments when she dropped her guard long enough for him to glimpse the person she kept hidden.

Sicarii's shoulders slumped, and she crossed her arms. "Fine. I'll show you some things when I return, but don't ask me to divulge anything in regards to Morzaun's plans. He warned me that if I told anyone—"

"I won't ask. You have my word."

She gave him a firm nod and continued along the worn dirt path toward the clearing. "Very well. We'll begin in a few days. Until then, perhaps your uncle can teach you proper stance."

"I'll be certain to make the suggestion and look forward to your return."

They had reached her cottage now, and Zeeran stopped a few feet from the door, not wishing to intrude on her more than he already had. To do so would only destroy the progress he'd made.

Sicarii paused with her hand on the doorknob. "You should know, I won't go easy on you."

"I had rather hoped not."

Her lips twitched, and with the turn of the handle, she disappeared inside.

* * *

Zeeran followed Morzaun through the forest, keeping to the worn game trail to avoid being completely shredded by branches and thorny plants. His chest burned from the practice session they'd had. An hour of training with Morzaun every day would certainly whip him into shape sooner rather than later.

As Sicarii had suggested, Zeeran had requested Morzaun teach him proper stance yesterday. Having mastered that, they'd moved on to maneuvers today. A smile crept over Zeeran's lips. Perhaps the woman would be impressed with his improvement when she returned.

"When should we expect Sicarii?" asked Zeeran, hoping his tone sounded less interested than he actually was.

"Not for several days. It takes time to reach Izarden from here, especially on foot."

Zeeran halted. "Izarden? You've sent her to the city? Why?"

Morzaun chuckled, seemingly unphased by either the questions or Zeeran's unmoving feet as he pushed through some low branches. "Are you concerned for her well being already? You've known her not more than a week."

True, but Zeeran shared a connection with Sicarii. She loathed him, and he loathed her.

Or at least, he pretended to. So much emotion rested beneath her steely outer shell, and the desire to discover her secrets fueled him. Why, he couldn't say. Sicarii was a mystery he simply needed to unravel.

"She intrigues me," admitted Zeeran. "I've never met a woman like her."

"Seeing that your father has kept you prisoner on an island for most of your life, I can't imagine that should be surprising."

It wasn't. Few people lived on Verascene, and the majority of them were not his age. One of the locals had taken an interest in Feya, but she seemed disinclined to accept the attention. Neither Zeeran nor Ladisias had any prospects that lacked wrinkles and gray hair...or still drooled and spoke nonsense.

"What can you tell me about her?" asked Zeeran. "You know nothing of her scars, but surely you know her somewhat well. You've given her a great deal of your trust."

"I know she hasn't had an easy life, but all the specifics were irrelevant. She wasn't always as strong willed and skilled as she is now. When we first met, she showed faint promise. So, I made a deal with her. In exchange for my training, she would assist me in my plans."

Zeeran wanted to know exactly what those *plans* comprised, but knowing his uncle was not ready to divulge the information, he settled on a different question. "You trained her to wield the daggers? What purpose did she have in learning such a skill? A woman of her beauty—"

"Would be highly sought after?" Morzaun scoffed. "Indeed. I suspect therein lies the scourge of her past. I don't know all the details, as I have told you before, but I'm not a fool. I know what it is to seek revenge. It's a fire—a passion—that one cannot easily douse."

Revenge. Morzaun wanted it, and apparently Sicarii had sought it as well. Had she found justice or satisfaction? If she had, the success certainly hadn't made her happy. Sicarii had buried her true self beneath so many layers, Zeeran wondered if anyone was capable of reaching her. Perhaps if he knew what trauma lay in her past, he could help her find the surface again.

But that was a problem to solve at a later date. He could do nothing to understand Sicarii when she was presently absent.

"Where are we going?" asked Zeeran.

"Just a little farther. I thought you might wish to wash off all that sweat in the stream."

That certainly sounded appealing, but Zeeran refused to believe that was the only reason for their trek through the forest. Morzaun was not a man to lounge about, always busying himself with something constructive. Everything he did had purpose.

They pushed past the swaying branches of a young tree and the river came into view. The water trickled over the rocks, creating a soothing harmony that matched the quiet of the surrounding forest.

Morzaun removed his coat and rolled up his shirtsleeves. He crouched next to the shallow bank and splashed water on his arms and face. He hadn't appeared as sweaty and exhausted as Zeeran, but perhaps he only hid it better.

Zeeran joined him and rubbed the cool water over his skin. The process was certainly refreshing but did little to ease the ache in his muscles. He plopped down onto a fallen tree and sighed, picking at the peeling bark. "I wish the distance between amateur and master was not so great."

His uncle chuckled and turned to face him. "These things require time. The achievement would mean less for you if it were easy. Besides, if such skills were so easily obtained, everyone would master them, thus defeating the point of being highly trained."

Zeeran kicked at the ground. "I suppose. Ladisias seemed to take to this much faster."

"Perhaps the sword. He has a natural aptitude for it; however, the same cannot be said of his magic. You learn spells far faster than he does."

"Because I'm a Protesta...like you. Magic comes naturally to me. That gift isn't something I perfected on my own. It was merely handed to me at birth."

"And because of that, it shouldn't be counted? Skill is skill, Zeeran, no matter how long we've spent perfecting them. A wise man knows his strengths, but an even wiser man accepts his weaknesses and works hard to turn them into strengths despite the difficulty. You may never be as talented at the sword as Ladisias, but knowing how to wield one will only add to your defense and reduce vulnerability."

Zeeran shook his head. "How did you become so wise?"

Morzaun sat down beside him. "Experience, much of it tragic and painful, but I am better for it. Stronger. And knowledgeable enough to pass on some wisdom to you." He held up a finger and arched one of his dark brows. "But that is not why I brought you to the river. I need your help."

Something rose within Zeeran at the opportunity to prove himself. "Anything. Just tell me what I can do."

His uncle smiled. "I knew you could be counted upon. I'm glad you made the decision to come with me."

Pride swelled in Zeeran's chest. He had earned his uncle's trust, or at least enough to be granted some praise. A small step, perhaps, but one he would gladly accept.

"When your parent's stripped me of my power, I lost all enchantments I had performed on myself," said Morzaun. "There is one in particular I'd hoped you would restore for me."

"What sort of enchantment?"

"One that stops the effects of time."

Zeeran's mouth fell open. "You mean there is a spell that will make you immortal?"

"There is. It is recorded in the spellbook your mother created, but I'm guessing she hasn't mentioned this to you. Not surprising, of course. Neither of them approved of my using it the first time."

Zeeran tapped his fingers against the bark. "Living forever...that appeals to you?" He wasn't sure how he felt about it himself. Like anyone, he had no desire to die, but to live continually? To never age? He'd never given thought to such a thing, but now that he knew it was possible and the choice lay before him...

Well, he had time to make a decision. He wasn't performing the spell on himself today.

"You would like me to make you immortal again," said Zeeran.

"Yes. I have much to accomplish, and one lifetime simply will not be enough. As I have lost the ability to wield magic, I hoped you would be willing to perform the spell on my behalf."

Zeeran shrugged. "I see no reason not to if that's what you want."

"The spell is called the *amortias.* It's surprisingly simple considering its effect."

"Then teach me the incantation."

Morzaun grinned, and within the hour Zeeran had both learned the words to perform the spell and successfully restored his uncle's immortality. The incantation had been simple, one he could easily conjure for himself if he decided a single lifetime wasn't enough, though the more he thought on it the less he believed he would ever feel that way.

Morzaun stood and grabbed his discarded coat from the ground. "I need to leave for a day or so. I expect that cottage to have a roof by the time I return."

"I may not meet your expectations, but I will certainly try." Zeeran scratched the back of his neck. "Where are you going?"

"Not far. I have some things to see to, but I will return soon. I wish to discuss what I've discovered about the gems with you then."

Zeeran straightened. "You've discovered more?"

"I have, but I can't discuss it with you now. I need to leave before the sun has fully set." Morzaun slipped his arms into his coat and tugged on the front to straighten the fabric. "Thank you, Zeeran. I appreciate your willingness to help me today."

"Of course." He would do whatever he needed to earn the man's trust. It seemed his diligence would soon be rewarded. Morzaun had learned more about the gems' capabilities, and that knowledge would help them rid Virgamor of Delran. They needed only to gain the peoples' trust first. Perhaps Morzaun would allow Zeeran in on his plans, and their plot to overthrow Izarden's ruthless dictator could truly begin.

CHAPTER EIGHT

Hidden Abilities

From his position on the cottage roof, the sun was merciless. Without the shadows of the trees, Zeeran quickly became drenched in sweat. He rubbed the back of his hand over his slick forehead and then gave his wrist a flick. Blue light encompassed his hand and the worked lumber on the ground below. The plank lifted into the air, and Zeeran guided it toward him.

After securing the board in place, he repeated the process. Time passed quickly, he found, when he kept himself busy. Using more of his magic would have made finishing the work faster, but what would he do with himself the remainder of the day? Both Morzaun and Sicarii had yet to return, leaving him alone in the quiet of the forest.

So, he worked on his cottage. Another few days, and his new home would be complete enough for him to move in. Sleeping on the hard floor next to the hearth in Morzaun's cottage had left his muscles aching nearly as much as working on his own home had.

Zeeran leaned back on his heels and drew in a deep breath of warm air. Only two boards remained. Then he could take a break.

Movement in the trees drew his attention. A figure cloaked in black weaved through the shadows. Sunlight illuminated Morzaun's face as he entered the clearing, revealing his tight features. The man stormed across the grassy plain with a fury that made Zeeran's pulse race.

Zeeran slid to the edge of the roof to where his makeshift ladder leaned against the side of his cottage and climbed down the rungs. Morzaun had reached him by the time his feet touched the ground.

"You're back," said Zeeran.

"Obviously," Morzaun snapped. "I see you've at least made use of my time away."

Zeeran pinched his lips. His uncle was in a foul mood, but did he dare ask the reason? He'd finally gained some ground with the man, and the last thing he wanted was to lose it. Zeeran wiped his sweaty hands on his breeches. "Can I get you something to eat? I'm sure you're exhaust—"

"No. But you can come with me. We have much to discuss."

Morzaun marched away, and Zeeran followed to his uncle's cottage. Once inside, Morzaun gestured for him to sit at the table while he took up an aggressive pace from one side of the room to the other. For several minutes, Zeeran watched him, silence reigning over the small space.

Morzaun halted and rubbed a hand over his stubbled chin. "I need to ask you some questions, and I need you to think them over carefully."

Zeeran nodded, his gut twisting. He'd never seen his uncle this agitated, and the presence his rage established was unnerving.

Morzaun took a few steps toward the table and placed his hands palm down on the surface. "If your parents were to hide something of extreme importance, where might they do it?"

"I...are you speaking of the gems? I haven't any idea where they might have hidden them."

"No, not the gems, though I would like to find those as well. Once again, your parents have taken something from me, and it's essential I recover it."

Taken something? Zeeran's mother and father had used their magic to extinguish Morzaun's powers. None of them had seen him since then—not until his uncle had been captured by General Ivrin's men, an event Zeeran now wondered whether was on purpose. But what else did Morzaun have that his parents would feel the need to take? They were likely yet unaware that he and Zeeran had stolen the two gems from Verascene.

"Did you see them?" asked Zeeran. "My parents?"

Morzaun scoffed. "Unfortunately, I did. Somehow they managed to locate my hiding place." Morzaun waved his hand dismissively when Zeeran's brows knitted. "Not here. I have a place not far from our camp, a cave where I spent much of my time after Senniva's death. It is there that I recorded many of the spells I've learned over the years—spells your parents were unaware were possible to perform."

"Recorded?"

"On the cave walls, but also in a spellbook of my own making, much like the one your mother has." He threaded his fingers through his black hair and scowled. "But your parents have completely destroyed the markings on the cave wall. My most important knowledge obliterated."

"What about the book? Is that what they've taken?"

"Yes. It is of the utmost importance that I retrieve it. I can remember many of the spells within, but there are a few in particular, ones far more complicated, that are essential to my plan. I must have that book."

Zeeran swallowed. This was the most his uncle had ever shared with him, and he longed to know more. "What good is a spellbook to you if you cannot wield magic?"

Morzaun looked him over, his stony expression calculating...analyzing. Zeeran held his breath. Had he done enough to earn the man's trust?

His uncle moved to the table and sat down across from him, his face still stoic. He leaned forward, his dark brows drawing together. "You will tell no one, understand?"

"Not a soul."

Morzaun's eyes narrowed, but he nodded. "After your aunt was murdered, I left Verascene to set out on my own. I was determined to have my revenge—to bring the man responsible for my wife's death to justice. I came here, to this very forest, but I was not alone. Just as your mother hears a voice that has taught us many of the spells we've learned over the years, I also began to hear one."

"And it taught you new spells?"

"Yes. Many, and I recorded them first on the cave walls and then within the bindings of my book, *The Irrilám*."

Zeeran's mother had named her book of spells as well. *The Tahctya* had been a resource to his family for years, a guide for learning to control their powers. Zeeran had spent hours as a child memorizing the odd symbols and mastering the incantations it contained.

"Several of the spells are exceptionally complex," Morzaun continued, "but there is one that I've been studying for quite some time. Only recently did I discover a way to complete it, but your parents have destroyed all traces of its instruction in the cave and taken *The Irrilám*."

"And what did this spell do?"

Morzaun's lips curled into a wicked grin. "It restores one's magic."

"You could get your power back?"

The surprise in Zeeran's voice only made his uncle's grin grow. "Precisely. But I need the book. The spell is more ritual than a simple incantation, hence why it was not one I memorized, though now I see the error in that decision."

"Do you believe my parents knew about that particular spell?"

Morzaun shrugged. "I cannot say, but I suspect the voice that guides your mother may have informed her of it. They were there when I arrived at the cave and, of course, refused to tell me what they had done with the spellbook. I presume they sent Ladisias away with it before I arrived. So, I ask you again; do you have any idea where they would hide something they deemed of great importance?"

Zeeran searched his mind. He'd grown up on an island with only a small village to its name. They were surrounded by a thick forest and a mountain that reached into the clouds. His mother and father could have any number of hiding places, and that number only grew when one considered his father's elemental abilities allowed him to leave the island.

"Papa could have hidden it anywhere. He's made trips to the mainland over the years, and I wonder if this was his purpose. Perhaps he hid the gems. It's likely the book is wherever they are."

Morzaun sighed and slumped back in his chair. "Just when I believed I had everything I needed to proceed...well, begin, at least."

"What do you mean?"

His uncle tapped a finger against the table and then stood. "I could use a spot of tea. It's been a trying day. Would you care for some?"

"Sure," Zeeran replied as his uncle stood and crossed the room. "What else did you need besides the book?"

Morzaun chuckled as he lit a fire in the hearth and hooked a kettle on the rod hovering over it. "I've won your curiosity, have I? The spell requires more than words, as I've told you. The details are vague to me, and while I remember the important requirements, I don't dare attempt it without exact instructions. You needn't worry about the rest. Until we have retrieved *The Irrilám*, we can do nothing more."

Zeeran shoved down his irritation. His uncle would tell him no more about the spell today, it seemed. But there were other things they still needed to discuss, and Zeeran hoped the man would oblige his questions.

"Before you left, you mentioned discovering more about the gems' abilities."

Morzaun removed the kettle from the hearth with a cloth, and with his back to Zeeran, prepared their tea. "Ah, yes. I had intended to speak with you about that as well. I've discovered something quite extraordinary on that front."

Zeeran's leg bounced up and down. If Morzaun had recently discovered something, then Zeeran was likely the first person to know. Being in the man's confidence sparked pride in him. He wanted to be a part of Morzaun's plan, and earning enough trust to be included felt like a great accomplishment.

All through his childhood, Zeeran had often felt second to his brother. Ladisias had stolen his uncle's time and focus with his natural aptitude with the sword. Morzaun had trained Ladisias from a young age, leaving Zeeran to receive very little of his uncle's attention.

And Zeeran desperately wanted to learn, to be considered good enough for training. Papa was not a fighter, and Morzaun was the only person on the island who had any sort of combat skill. But despite the many hours Ladisias had spent with Uncle Morzaun, it was Zeeran who sat in his cottage now. It was Zeeran who had defended the man against Ivrin and his parents' designs.

Morzaun rejoined him at the table, a cup in each hand. He offered one to Zeeran before taking his seat, and the steam wafted over Zeeran's nose. With a deep inhale, Zeeran allowed the herby scent to fill him.

"The gems each carry different abilities," said Morzaun. "In a way, they represent different spells."

Zeeran took a sip of his tea, careful not to drink the hot liquid too quickly and burn his throat. "So, no two are alike?"

Morzaun tilted his head from side to side. "Not the ones in my possession, at least." He sat his cup down on the table and held up his hand to where the sunlight beamed in through the window, catching on the blue gem embedded in the ring on his finger. "This ring is capable of creating a glamor. Essentially, a disguise. There is a spell that allows for the same, though it requires more than a simple incantation. The ring bypasses the need for any of that."

His uncle closed his eyes, and the gem illuminated. The blue aura surrounded Morzaun's head, the swirl of glistening magic creating a veil that obscured Zeeran's view. The magic faded, and Morzaun stared back at him with a face that belonged to someone else. His black hair had faded to gray, his chin had taken on a square-like shape, and his eyes had shifted to a lighter hue of brown. Had the transformation not happened before his eyes, Zeeran would have never guessed it was his uncle who sat across from him.

"How?" Zeeran sputtered. "You lost your ability to wield magic. How is it possible for you to activate the gems?"

"How is irrelevant, and not a question I have an answer for. My best guess is that although my magic was stolen from me, I still hold a connection to it. That connection allows me access." He shrugged.

"Or perhaps one doesn't require a connection to access the power they contain. Once Sicarii has returned, we will know for certain."

Sicarii? What did she have to do with the gems?

The ring illuminated again, and in another swirl of magic, Morzaun's façade faded. He looked down at the piece of jewelry with a wide smile. "Rather useful, isn't it?"

Zeeran drank more of his tea, and Morzaun's dark eyes watched him carefully. It was a hot day, but something about the way the liquid warmed his insides was comforting. Soothing, even. "Yes. I imagine it will be useful. Having a thorough disguise makes any mission easier."

Morzaun reached into his cloak and pulled the amulet from within. "This allows one to transport like the spell I taught you."

"And does it come with nausea as well?"

His uncle chuckled. "As I'm quite used to traveling that way, I don't know. I imagine it still has the same effect on those unaccustomed."

"And what of your dagger?" asked Zeeran. "Have you discovered its ability also?"

Morzaun returned the amulet to his cloak, his brows furrowed. "I have not, I'm afraid."

Zeeran clenched his jaw. He knew the man well enough to recognize the lie, but he wouldn't push Morzaun. His uncle had confided in him a great deal today, and whatever reason he had for withholding the information had purpose. Zeeran would be patient. It had paid off thus far.

Draining the rest of his tea, Zeeran rose. "I should get back to my roof. It's nearly complete."

"I'm impressed. You've done well given your lack of experience." Morzaun stood and heaved a sigh. "My withholding of details has been frustrating for you, but know that I appreciate your loyalty. You and I will make a great team, and together we can bring peace to Virgamor. It will take time, but I'm confident we'll succeed."

Pride swelled within Zeeran's chest, and his lips lifted. "Indeed, we shall."

CHAPTER NINE

Threats Abounding

Zeeran focused on his tools, and blue light surrounded them. They lifted into the air, but it took more coaxing than he'd expected. After a day of working in the hot sun, exhaustion could be expected, though. He would need a long nap this afternoon.

Scooting toward the edge of the roof, Zeeran guided the tools to the ground. His cottage was finished, or at least the exterior was. He would still need to build himself some furniture–a bed, chairs, and table would make the place truly feel like a home. But at least the structure was sound, and he now had a place all his own.

Once the tools were safely on the ground, Zeeran did one last look over the roof. He'd never completed anything requiring so much work, and he was quite proud of how well he had done. Magic, of course, had assisted him, but he'd still been responsible for the planning and execution of the building. His home.

Zeeran climbed down the ladder, and loud claps met his ears when he hopped off the second to last rung and his feet hit the ground. He turned to find Morzaun grinning at him.

"Well done, Zeeran." His uncle's gaze roamed over the cottage, and he nodded appreciatively. "You should be proud."

"Thank you. I admit I've never been so tired."

Morzaun chuckled and gestured for Zeeran to follow him. "I'm certain that's true. Come, this calls for tea."

They entered Morzaun's cottage, and Zeeran took his usual place at the table while his uncle prepared their refreshment.

"I'll be spending some time away over the next few weeks," said Morzaun, passing Zeeran a cup. "After Sicarii returns, I intend to search for Eramus."

"Eramus?" Zeeran choked on the hot liquid. "But I thought—"

"He was dead? So did I." Morzaun's brows knitted together in a scowl. "Before I left the cave, your mother let it slip that she'd seen him wash ashore after the storm, a detail she kept to herself all these years." Pain overtook his features, and he heaved a sigh. "If I had known..."

A pang of sympathy struck Zeeran's heart. His uncle had lost his wife at the hands of Izarden's former king, Sytal. Senniva had died but not before she sent her son away with one of her handmaidens in an effort to protect him. Mama had seen the ship they boarded in one of her visions, the vessel tossed by a raging sea until it capsized into the dark depths. They had all assumed Eramus had died with the rest of the crew and passengers, but apparently his mother had seen more.

"I'm sorry," said Zeeran. "It was wrong of my mother not to tell you."

"I admit the confession was not well received. She lied to me for years—and those are years with my son I will never get back. But what's done is done. If Eramus is alive, I will find him."

"Where do you intend to start looking?"

"Olgetha. Yelene saw him wash ashore there after the storm. Perhaps the locals will know what became of him, and now that I have the amulet, traveling will be much faster."

Zeeran took a long drink of his tea. "Would you like me to go with you?"

"No. Not yet, at least. Once I've found Eramus, I may request your help. The people will not accept me as their king, but royalty flows through my son's veins. He would have a right to the throne should something happen to Delran."

The plan was sound. The people of Izarden would be far more likely to accept Eramus as their king given Morzaun's history. In his uncle's efforts to gain justice for Senniva, he'd decimated a large portion of Izarden's army. Such an act would not be forgiven easily by the people, if ever.

Morzaun had also killed Delran's father. Acts of treason were generally frowned upon even when they were committed against a tyrant.

"You'll want to put the rest of your plan"—whatever that was—"to the side for the time being, I presume?"

"In part, yes. Eramus is the key to taking Virgamor into our hands and establishing peace. The people will accept him. I will see my son on Izarden's throne."

Zeeran wasn't quite convinced that the people of Izarden would accept Eramus as their new king. His cousin would be able to wield magic, after all, and that immediately put him lower on the ladder of trust.

Zeeran sipped his tea. Having another person among them who could use magic was bound to assist in their plan, but if the kingdom opposed, even Zeeran and Eramus couldn't take down Izarden's army alone. Morzaun may have managed to nearly eliminate them on his own, but his power was more pure and stronger since it came directly from the Virgám itself. But then, Morzaun had a plan to regain his power. Should they succeed in that endeavor, Izarden would bow to their whims with or without acceptance.

"I wish you the best of luck in finding him," said Zeeran, "but I don't share in your belief that he is the *key* to our success. The people will never accept a warlock as their king whether he was involved in past events or not."

The muscles in Morzaun's jaw clenched. "Eramus will be king, regardless. I'll make sure of it."

"But even if you do find him, we have no way of knowing if he'll want to join us or—"

"Enough!" Morzaun sat his cup down on the table so hard the tea abandoned ship, creating an elongated puddle. "Eramus will join us. He is my son and your future king. Is that understood?"

Zeeran swallowed his annoyance. "Of course, Uncle."

"Good. Now, go. I have much preparation to do before I leave."

Deserting the remainder of his tea, Zeeran headed for the door.

Frustration bubbled within him. He understood his uncle's desire to find Eramus, but the man's attachment made him irrational. If they weren't careful, Eramus could hinder their plan rather than help, and Zeeran had given up too much to allow that to happen.

* * *

Zeeran lifted the thick log over his shoulder and shifted it until it settled more comfortably against his neck. His body ached from carrying the pieces back to his cottage, but if he was to carve out legs for his table, he would need four logs.

His steps traced the worn path back to the clearing, and with a grunt he added the log to the other two he'd already brought. One more, and then he could take some time to relax before he began removing the bark.

He trekked the path toward the woods again, but shouts emanating from Morzaun's cottage halted his progress. With the window slightly ajar, Morzaun's deep voice penetrated the air, his furious tone sending a shiver down Zeeran's spine. The man was a force to be reckoned with when he was angry.

Zeeran edged closer to the cottage wall and crouched beneath the window, his heart pounding. Perhaps he shouldn't eavesdrop on his uncle's conversations, but curiosity won out over his honor. He wanted to know the details Morzaun withheld from him, especially after the revelation that Zeeran's cousin would play an important role.

"Two failures is unacceptable!" The tap of Morzaun's boots as he paced across the floor filled the silence for several seconds. "After the training I've given you, I expected more."

"It wasn't my fault." Sicarii's voice came out timid, just above a whisper. Had she not been close to the window, Zeeran might not have heard her at all.

"Do tell. Who should I blame then?"

"The general's brother stepped in again. I fought him, but by the time I'd worn the man out, Aldeth and Yelene arrived."

Zeeran's stomach lurched. His parents had stopped Sicarii's mission? What had Morzaun ordered her to do?

A bellowing clatter echoed from the room as if someone had overturned a chair. Morzaun's voice dripped with venom. "Always in my way, the two of them. How much do they know?"

"Nothing, I swear it. I escaped before they could ask questions."

"Escaped without fulfilling your orders. Do not forget, Sicarii, I offered you my assistance in exchange for both your loyalty and obedience. If you are of no use to me, then—"

"I will not fail again. Please, give me another chance."

The plea in her voice was enough to scare Zeeran. Morzaun was certainly not a man to be trifled with, but surely he would not harm someone fighting by his side?

"Not with this," said Morzaun. "I cannot afford for you to make another attempt. Aldeth will likely return home with his family. There are other endeavors I may desire your assistance with, but I'm not certain you're up to the task."

"I am. I won't disappoint you."

Morzaun scoffed. "You have thoroughly done that already. Tell me, why would I give you the ability to wield magic when you can't even complete one simple task?" Taps against the floor announced Morzaun's approach of Sicarii and the window. Sicarii gasped, and Zeeran's pulse sped into a gallop. He lifted slightly, perching high enough on his toes to glimpse inside the cottage. His uncle stood directly in front of Sicarii, a jagged dagger held to her throat. He pressed the blade against her skin, and her body went rigid. "Perhaps I should see to things and rid myself of the excess baggage."

Zeeran scrambled away from the cottage and darted around the corner to the door. He threw it open without thought and rushed inside. "Stop!"

Morzaun dropped his hand and turned to face him with a scowl. Sicarii looked nothing short of relieved.

"What are you doing?" Morzaun said with a growl. "Were you listening?"

Zeeran swallowed. "Only long enough to hear you threaten her."

"This is none of your concern, Zeeran. Leave."

Zeeran crossed the room, his heart pounding. "She may have failed at whatever mission you assigned her, but she is still loyal to you. We haven't the benefit of many people on our side. To reduce our numbers further is unwise, wouldn't you agree?"

His uncle glared at him. "Sicarii, go. I need a word with my nephew."

Sicarii slipped past them, but Morzaun called to her before she could open the door. "Don't go too far. I have another assignment for you."

Zeeran released a breath of relief. Morzaun would not harm her while he still had tasks for her to complete. He would have liked to think his uncle hadn't intended to harm her at all, but he wasn't so sure.

The door closed with a soft thud, and Zeeran lifted his gaze to Morzaun. The man was still fuming, his features drawn tight and his dark eyes piercing.

Zeeran shifted on his feet. "I'm sorry for—"

"Never eavesdrop on my private conversations again. You are to keep your nose out of places it doesn't belong. If you think I'll offer you special treatment because you are of my blood, you're sorely mistaken. Do you understand?"

"Yes, Uncle." Zeeran bit his lip. "Why did you promise to give her magic? You know as well as I do it's impossible."

At least he believed so, but Morzaun had discovered spells Zeeran had never seen.

"It's *not* your concern. Let it go, Zeeran."

"It is if you're lying to her. Don't you think giving her false hope is—"

"What? Dishonorable?" Morzaun scoffed. "I will do what is necessary to achieve my goals. If bribery, however false the promises may be, is required, then so be it. You allow yourself too much attachment to the woman, and if you're not careful, it will be your undoing."

"And what's that supposed to mean? You think Sicarii will betray us?"

"I know she is plenty capable of it, and the closer you allow yourself to get to her, the more it will sting."

Zeeran shook his head. The loss of his aunt had pained Morzaun deeply, so much so that he became adamant that love was nothing more than a weakness. Perhaps he was right, but Zeeran wasn't *in love* with Sicarii. The woman had proven herself an asset, and they had few of those at the moment. She could only help with their plan, but Morzaun seemed incapable of seeing that.

"We all have to trust someone," said Zeeran. "I know my parents stabbed you in the back, but that doesn't mean everyone will doublecross you."

Morzaun pointed to the door. "We're finished discussing this. Out."

Zeeran left the cottage, frustration boiling his blood. He'd done everything he could, yet the man still didn't fully trust him. What mission had he sent Sicarii on, and how were his parents involved?

His feet halted outside Sicarii's home, and Zeeran wondered if she had gone inside or stormed off to find solitude in the forest. Would she leave them? He wouldn't blame her for considering the option after what had occurred.

He stepped to her door and drew a breath. She would hate him for patronizing her, but he needed to know she was all right.

Ridding himself of the last bit of hesitation, he tapped on the door.

CHAPTER TEN

New Life, New Mission

Movement inside the cottage alerted Zeeran to Sicarii's march to the door, but he still started when it parted from the frame and revealed her fierce eyes. She looked past him as if searching for Morzaun, and her expression softened when she found he was alone.

"What do you want?" She leaned against the door and crossed her arms. "Come for more of a show?"

"Show?" Zeeran took a step closer, and Sicarii tensed, the smugness disappearing from her features to something more weary. He placed his hand on the wooden frame and willed his shoulders to relax. The last thing he wanted was to corner her. "I intended to make sure you were alright."

Sicarii tilted her head and narrowed her eyes. "Why do you

care?"

"If you would prefer I didn't, then perhaps I'll go."

"Good. Go."

She gripped the knob, and Zeeran threw up his hand and stopped the swing of the door, the wood smacking against his palm with a clap. He didn't want to leave, not until he reassured himself of her well being, but her aloof nature made it difficult to keep his responses from the same hostility.

"You were leaving." One of her dark brows rose as if daring him to contradict the statement. Well, if she wanted him to go so badly, he had half a mind to do the exact opposite simply to irritate her.

"No. I wasn't."

"*Yes*, you were."

Zeeran leaned against the door when she tried to close it on him. The woman pushed, using all her body weight in an attempt to be rid of him. Sicarii may have been highly skilled with her daggers, but she hadn't the muscle to move him. He did enjoy watching her put every effort into the cause, though.

She released an exasperated groan, giving up the endeavor completely. "You are the worst sort of wart–the kind no one knows how to get rid of."

Zeeran chuckled. "I take that as a compliment."

"Of course you do. Leave, Zeeran. I have no desire to continue this."

"And here I thought we were having such a pleasant afternoon. I only want to talk."

Her nose wrinkled, pulling her scarred skin tighter. "Then go find a rock or a tree or even a squirrel. Any of those would make fine company for the likes of you."

Fine company... "The squirrel would be a far better conversationalist. At least it wouldn't throw daggers at me or bite my head off for attempting to be cordial."

"This is cordial?" She gestured between his form and the door.

"It would be if you weren't so stubborn."

Zeeran pushed the door open fully and crossed the threshold. Sicarii pursed her lips, backing up a step, and drew a fortifying breath likely meant to temper the anger glowing in her eyes. It didn't hide the fear, however, and Zeeran's frustration steamed as though someone had poured water on it.

He heaved a sigh. "I want to know—"

"I'm not telling you anything."

Zeeran took a step deeper into her cottage. Sicarii retreated several paces, fear stealing over her features and obliterating any evidence of other emotion. The soft light entering the window behind her cast a halo around her body and revealed a terror Zeeran didn't understand. And he had no wish to scare her.

With slow movements, he backed outside. This house was her sanctuary, and he would not steal her security. That was no way to earn her trust or approval.

Sicarii watched him intently, her breathing shallow. What had occurred in her past to make this woman tremble at his proximity?

"Sicarii, you don't have to tell me about the missions," he said, his voice barely more than a whisper. "I only wanted to make sure you weren't hurt. If I hadn't barged in—"

"What? You think you saved me?" She scoffed, but her restless shift on her feet spoke to her discomfort. "Do I owe you something for that? I could have handled things on my own."

"Owe me? Of course you don't owe me anything. Perhaps the concept is strange to you, but I was concerned. As your *friend*."

She shook her head. "I don't have friends, and I don't want them. Especially not you."

The words should have pierced him, but instead, Zeeran felt only sympathy. Her past trauma had left far greater wounds than the scars she bore, and that sort of healing took time. Perhaps she would never trust again, but he certainly wouldn't push her to try, no matter how much his heart yearned to help.

"Fine. I'll go, but know that my door is always open should you change your mind." He offered her a small smile. "Literally, now that I've finished my house."

She gave him a curt nod, but Zeeran didn't miss the slight twitch of her lips. Sicarii may claim to not want any friends, but he wouldn't take her words personally. She was still hurting, and people often chose to deal with pain on their own, even believed it was the easiest way. Though Zeeran would never admit it aloud, there had been many times when the loneliness of living on an island had overwhelmed him, but it was the company of his brother and sister who pulled him through it. His siblings were bright stars among a sea of bleakness, a guiding force that anchored him when the storms seemed too much to bear. Even the strongest of people needed such solid foundations to cling to on occasion.

Even Sicarii.

Zeeran said nothing more as he left her cottage. Sicarii could use a friend to confide in, someone to give her a spark of happiness when life inevitably became consumed with darkness. Zeeran needed that, too. Given that they lived in a forest with only Morzaun around, perhaps they could help each other. Perhaps, in time, Sicarii would feel comfortable enough to let him see the side of her she kept hidden.

* * *

The morning light from the eastern window illuminated the area perfectly, and a welcoming beam settled over his finished bed frame with enough brightness to coax him from a night of sleep.

At least it would once Zeeran had purchased a mattress and blankets.

For now he slept on the floor, but soon enough he would have a comfortable bed. Morzaun had taught him how to build traps and tan the hides of the fox and rabbits Zeeran had ensnared. After a month of living in the forest, Zeeran had a dozen pelts ready, and Morzaun had supplied him with information on where to sell them in Rowenport, had even praised his skill. Apparently he had a knack for hunting, one he never would have discovered had he remained with his parents.

He wouldn't be wealthy anytime soon, but the notion of making his own money satisfied him in ways he hadn't expected. Sure, on the island he'd worked, but the people of Verascene survived by bartering. Coin had little use there, nor were there any marketplaces at which to spend it.

Zeeran dressed and had a quick meal consisting of fruit and cooked oats before leaving his newly built refuge. The cool air chilled him, but not even the ending summer season could deter his excitement. With a sack over his shoulder, he repeated the incantation Morzaun had taught him weeks ago, and the world swirled around him, the colors of dawn blending into smears of yellow, pink, and orange.

He landed outside of Rowenport, upright and his breakfast still inside his stomach. Though it churned with a grumble, he kept everything down. That was success enough to call for celebration.

Which he would do once he actually had money to celebrate.

Zeeran followed the dirt road through the overlooking green hills down into the city. The marketplace was alive with movement and chatter in the early morning hours as shopkeepers began their day and merchants unloaded new merchandise from the incoming ships.

He followed the cobblestone path into the heart of the market to where Morzaun had instructed. Zeeran entered a stall with pelts of various colors and sizes dangling from the sides. A peddler with long brown hair ceased organizing his wares and turned to face him.

"Mornin'," he said. "Can I interest you in a fine hide?"

Zeeran shook his head. "No, quite the opposite actually. My uncle said you may be interested in purchasing some hides from me."

The man rubbed his chin. "Uncle, you say? And who might he be?"

"Morzaun."

The peddler clapped his hands together with an excited grin.

"Aye! If Morzaun sent you, then let's see what you have to offer."

Zeeran removed the sack from his shoulder and laid the hides out on the man's table. He watched his reaction with veiled anticipation. The peddler nodded slowly with a low hum. "These be fine pieces. You do the work yourself?"

"Yes. Morzaun taught me the proper technique."

"Aye. A good job he did, too." He held one up and the red fur caught the sunlight. "I'll take the lot, but I'll expect you to bring more soon."

Zeeran grinned. "That's a promise I'm happy to keep."

With a pouch of coin in hand, Zeeran made his way through the bustling crowd. A tune left his lips in a whistle. He entered a shop, and two heads of blonde hair glanced up at him. The ladies held swatches of linen in their laps, and their fingers stilled at the sight of him.

"Can we help you, sir?"

"Yes. I was hoping to place an order with you. I understand you take requests for blankets and such."

The older of the two women stood and placed her project on the seat of her chair. "Indeed. But we require part of the payment up front. If that suits you, we'd be happy to take down your request."

Zeeran nodded. "I'm happy to oblige."

He spent the next few minutes commissioning two blankets, one of heavy wool and a thinner one for warmer nights. Zeeran also requested a down pillow. A mattress could wait until he'd acquired more funds, but at least this was a start. He would return in a week to pay the rest and pick up his purchases.

With that settled, Zeeran headed back out onto the busy streets.

He filled his now empty sack with supplies and food. It would be nice not to rely on Morzaun for everything he needed, including dinner. The garden had provided him with some things, and the meat he brought in through trapping had certainly kept his stomach happy, but purchasing a few spices would make his meals far more satisfying.

Zeeran climbed the hill and turned to overlook the city. He threw his sack over his shoulder and smiled. He could get used to this life—depending on himself for what he needed, living on his own and visiting the city whenever he wanted. Magic made living far from the everyday bustle easy. He could enjoy a quiet life without sacrificing the benefits that living near the port could bring.

He closed his eyes and, with a deep inhale of the salty air, lifted his chin to the sun, basking in its warmth. The breeze tussled strands of his hair. This was far better than living on an island. Far better than being confined to a small village.

Zeeran opened his eyes and checked the area to make sure he was alone. He muttered the incantation to take him home. The world swirled around him, twisting and contorting, and then unraveled before him, the scene entirely different than the one he'd left behind. He stood in front of his cottage. His home.

"I see you've returned."

Zeeran spun around at the sound of Morzaun's voice. "Uncle."

Morzaun jutted his chin towards Zeeran's sack. "How did your visit to Rowenport go?"

"It went well. I sold all of my hides and brought back some supplies."

"Good. I'm glad you've taken the incentive to support yourself."

Morzaun placed a hand on Zeeran's shoulder. "I'm impressed with how well you've done the last few weeks."

Zeeran warmed under the man's praise. "Thank you, Uncle."

"Now that you've returned, I'd like you to come with me. I have an assignment for you and Sicarii."

Ignoring the way his heart lurched, Zeeran trotted after his uncle. "For both of us?"

"Yes. Magic will be useful for this—by way of transportation and completing the task."

What sort of task? He'd never been deemed worthy of an assignment before, though he'd seen Sicarii leave on Morzaun's errand several times. Did this mean his uncle had finally come to trust him? Zeeran bit his tongue to keep the questions from escaping. He wouldn't have Morzaun changing his mind because his nephew appeared overly eager.

Whatever the man wanted him to do, Zeeran would put forth his best effort. It was time he proved himself once and for all.

CHAPTER ELEVEN
The Fortuitous Inn

His uncle didn't elaborate any more about the so-called mission, but it became quite clear to Zeeran the moment he laid eyes on Sicarii that she was uncomfortable with the situation. Whether it was the mission itself or that Zeeran had been assigned to accompany her, he couldn't say.

"I have already given Sicarii the details," said Morzaun. "She can fill you in later." He handed Zeeran a square of parchment. "When I have found myself in need of a place to stay in Izarden, this establishment has proven exceptional. The owner knows me well enough to keep quiet about odd observations he makes of his guests."

What was that supposed to mean?

Morzaun chuckled, likely due to the confusion sweeping over

Zeeran's expression. "Hendricks knows I'm a wanted man, but he and I have an established business venture together, and he wouldn't do anything to put the hefty income at risk. Tell him I sent you, and he'll give you room and board for tonight."

Having a host who wouldn't ask questions came as a relief. After all, Zeeran was now a wanted man, too, and any display of magic, accidental or otherwise, would put a target on his back.

Zeeran tucked the parchment into his pocket. "And what will you do while we are away?"

"I will go search for Eramus. My last trip to Olgetha produced a few leads, and I intend to follow up on them. In all likelihood, I will not be here when you return but will expect a full report when I do." His gaze bounced between them. "Do not fail me. This mission will be essential to achieving our goal of overthrowing Delran."

"We won't let you down." Zeeran stole a glance at Sicarii, and she nodded in agreement.

Morzaun withdrew the amulet from beneath his tunic. "Good. I'll leave the two of you to it."

His uncle clenched the amulet and whispered the words Zeeran had become familiar with over the last few weeks. Morzaun's body faded, and Zeeran and Sicarii were left alone in the meadow.

Zeeran tapped a finger against his thigh. He hadn't spoken to Sicarii since the day Morzaun threatened her. She'd seemed content to avoid him, and not wanting to incur more of her wrath, he'd steered clear of her.

But they had no choice at the moment. They could hardly execute a mission together without speaking.

Zeeran cleared his throat. "Well, I suppose we should get going."

Sicarii shook her head. "I need to speak with you first."

"Oh?" He lifted a brow with a grin, careful with his tone to ensure she knew he meant to tease. "Is that so?"

She rolled her eyes, but her lips lifted. "Yes, alright, I deserved that." The amusement faded from her expression, and her gaze dropped to the ground. "I'm sorry about the other day...with how I reacted. I'm not used to someone bothering to offer me concern or sympathy."

Zeeran shrugged, hoping she wouldn't see through his façade – see how much he celebrated internally. "I shouldn't have assumed we were friends."

Sicarii bit her lip. "Perhaps not, but..."

"But?"

"But it wouldn't be so terrible."

He didn't bother to suppress his grin. "What wouldn't be terrible?"

Her fierce eyes darted to him, and she scowled. "Must I say it?"

He nodded, which brought her dark brows closer together. She released an exasperated groan. "*Fine*. I hope that you and I can be friends." She crossed her arms and gave him an expectant look.

The pose and sheer disdain in her expression made him chuckle, but he couldn't continue to tease her after how much effort the confession had required. "Yes, we can be friends."

Although the woman did her best to hide it, relief flickered over her features. The reaction, though subtle, pierced his heart. He would consider this a great victory. He hadn't won the war, but this battle would play an intricate part in the outcome.

"Shall we then?" asked Zeeran.

"Yes. We should go. Can you transport us close to Izarden—just outside the city? Preferably someplace where there is likely to be few people."

Zeeran thought on his time in Izarden. Before they had left Feya behind at the palace, she and Zeeran had hidden in a barn outside the city walls. The farmer who owned it was a friend of Papa's, and Zeeran could think of no better place to magically appear.

"I have a spot in mind." He took a step closer to Sicarii, and she responded as she always did, her body going rigid. She may not like this next part. "I need to hold onto you for this to work."

Her eyes rounded, but Sicarii made no attempt to move away from him. He could hold on to her tunic as he had with Morzaun, but that seemed awkward and would make the mounting tension between them worse.

That left his mind with only one option, and before fear could talk him out of it, Zeeran reached for her. She started with a gasp when his fingers curled around her hand, and her weary eyes met his. So many questions and concerns rampaged there, and he wanted nothing more than to smooth away her worries.

"It might make you sick," he whispered. "But I won't think less of you if it does."

"Does it…does it hurt?"

"Not at all. If anything it simply feels strange."

She wet her lips, and her gaze dropped to their hands. "And what happens if you let go."

Unfortunately, he had no answer for that particular question. He'd asked Morzaun the same thing, and his uncle hadn't felt it prudent to respond. "I won't let go. I promise."

Her fingers tightened around his, and a sharp jolt shot up his arm and into his chest. Sicarii pinned him with a glare. "Don't you dare let me die."

"There's no chance I'm letting you get away that easily. If you die, this wart is going with you."

"You intend to annoy me beyond the grave?"

"I'm afraid you're stuck with me even then."

The shy smile that claimed her lips did strange things to him. Sicarii was not a woman to show vulnerability, so to see a hint of her buried uncertainties and raw emotion only increased his desire to make her feel safe and protected in his company.

Zeeran took another step closer, and this time she didn't flinch at the reduced space between them. He lifted his free hand, and blue light emerged from his palm. "Let's go. We have a mission to complete."

* * *

The smell of animals, manure, and ash filled Zeeran's nose long before the world swirled into focus. Wooden stalls stretched before him, and dried straw littered the floor of the barn. Sicarii gasped next to him, and Zeeran wrapped an arm around her waist when her knees buckled.

"I've got you." He steadied her on her feet and led her to the stacked bales of hay in the back of the barn. "Sit down. Give yourself a minute."

She did as he instructed, clutching her stomach with a grimace. "I might be sick."

"It's a normal response. I threw up several times when Morzaun taught me the spell." He glanced around, and when his eyes settled upon a wooden pail, he sprinted to retrieve it. He returned to Sicarii's side in time to hand over the bucket. She spilled the contents of her stomach, and he turned away, the sight making his own stomach churn.

"I'm sorry," she muttered.

"Don't be. I would have been impressed if you hadn't thrown up." He took the pail from her with a careful eye. Was she finished? She looked less pale now.

Sicarii waved him away as if sensing his thoughts. "I'm fine. I don't think there's anything left in my stomach even if I weren't."

"You say that, but if we transported again, I promise you would be proven wrong." He had experience, after all.

"Thank goodness we won't be doing that until tomorrow then."

Zeeran cocked his head. "I know Morzaun insisted we stay at an inn tonight, but why not finish the mission now and go home? The longer we remain in Izarden, the more likely we are to be discovered. You may have anonymity, but I do not. As someone who has recently committed an act of treason, I'm more likely to be recognized."

She shook her head, but rather than frustration lining her features, Zeeran saw sympathy. "That would be sound, yes, but we can't do anything tonight. We must wait for the opportune moment, and that won't be until the nobility gathers in the courtyard for the celebration."

Zeeran's mind reeled. Celebration? The nobility? "What sort of mission has Morzaun asked of us?"

Sicarii grimaced. "I'll explain everything to you in the morning, but trust me when I say we can do nothing today. It's best we go to the inn and get settled for tonight."

His stomach knotted. It was hard to trust anyone when they kept secrets, but he had little choice at the moment. "Alright. We should get going then. Can you stand?"

The woman pushed herself from the hay bale. She wobbled a moment but seemed steady enough on her feet. They headed for the barn doors, and Zeeran noted char marks on part of the floor and a trail of ash leading to the ladder that ascended to the loft.

"It looks like something caught fire in here." He pointed to the blackened floor, and Sicarii shifted on her feet. She looked almost...guilty?

Strange.

She gave him no time to ask more, however, brushing past him with her shoulders squared. "Let's go."

Zeeran followed her to the door. Sicarii opened it a few inches and peered out through the narrow crack. "It seems clear." She glanced back at him, and her gaze wandered up and down his form. Zeeran stiffened, his chest constricting uncomfortably again.

"We should find you something better to wear. A cloak with a hood would be best." She said nothing more as she turned to peer through the gap one last time before pushing the door open further.

He couldn't argue against the suggestion. Remaining inconspicuous would be important, especially here in the kingdom's capital. Not many people would recognize him, of course, given that he had only been here once in the last two decades, but the soldiers of Izarden's army might. He had spent weeks in their company during their search for Morzaun, and there was a good chance Ivrin was here in the city.

Zeeran shuddered. He had no desire to ever see the general again. The memories of his bloodied form as he gasped for air penetrated Zeeran's mind. Ivrin would surely blame him for the near death experience. If Zeeran were captured, he may not even make it to trial given the man's propensity toward vengeance.

Sicarii led them through the city gates. Zeeran kept his chin tucked and his gaze to the ground, avoiding eye contact with the men standing guard. They passed through without incident, and Sicarii weaved through the crowds of people to a marketplace. They visited a stall selling cloaks, and Zeeran found one that would do for their purposes, though the fabric hung loose in places. Perhaps it would aid in his disguise.

"Let me see the parchment Morzaun gave you." Sicarii held out her hand, her brows raised in that expectant way he'd become accustomed to. Her eyes darted over the instructions, and she nodded. "I know where this is. Come on."

With less coin in his leather pouch, Zeeran followed Sicarii through the winding alleyways. She *did* seem to know where she was going, which left Zeeran to wonder how much time she had spent in these busy streets. How many missions had Morzaun given her? It occurred to him then that he didn't even know how long she'd been working for his uncle. They certainly didn't seem close, but that was hardly evidence for or against a long-term arrangement given how aloof the both of them were.

Sicarii came to a stop in front of a two-story building, and her brows furrowed. It only took a glance for him to understand why. The front alone looked shifty with its boarded windows, nevermind how much of the roof appeared patched with random discolored boards. Shredded linen fluttered out in places, too, caught by the soft breeze. Hopefully they wouldn't be staying on the second floor, because those guests were certain to be the first to know about a shift in weather.

"It looks worse than the last time I was here." Sicarii passed him a look of disgust. "But if Morzaun wanted us to stay at this establishment, then I suppose we shall."

Zeeran held open the door—the one that creaked and appeared ready to fall off its hinges—and allowed Sicarii to enter first. A musty smell assaulted him the moment he stepped inside, and it took great self control not to pinch his nose. And to keep breathing.

If the sure sign of rotting wood wasn't enough to make him queasy, the hint of body odor that mingled with the stuffy air was. Boisterous shouts echoed from the other side of the room where several men lifted tankards of ale. The first floor appeared to be both the entrance to the inn and a pub.

Zeeran sent his eyes heavenward. How fortuitous for them.

Sicarii did not fare nearly as well with hiding her disdain. She lifted her arm and coughed into her elbow.

"Welcome." A scratchy, old voice sounded from a few feet away, and Zeeran pivoted to face it. An elderly man with a hunched back and gray hair down to his waist smiled at them with a toothy grin. "You be lookin' for a place to stay?"

Zeeran stepped closer, keeping his voice low as he spoke. "Are you Hendricks?"

The man's eyes narrowed. "Aye, but who be askin'?"

Zeeran glanced around, leaning closer to the man, which was a mistake given the way he smelled, a mixture of stomach curling body odor and alcohol. "Morzaun sent us."

Hendricks cupped a hand to his ear. "What?"

"Morzaun said you would give us a place to spend the night," Zeeran responded, raising his voice a little.

"Speak up boy. These flaps don't work like they used to."

Sicarii rushed past Zeeran, and the man recoiled when she stuck her lips inches from his face. "He said, Morzaun sent us. Now give us two rooms."

Zeeran glanced around, his heart pounding, but no one in the pub seemed to have paid them any heed.

"Well, why didn't you say so to begin with." The elderly man sneered and yanked open a drawer in the desk he stood beside. He held up a brass ring with a key dangling from a short chain, the metal pinched between two fingertips. He jingled it in front of Sicarii's nose. "A room. Lucky you be."

Sicarii glared. "*Two* rooms."

The man shook his head, his lips pulled into a tight smirk. "I only got one. It's the celebration, see."

"And your fine establishment is completely full?" she crossed her arms and gave the man that raised brow—the one that said she didn't believe him.

"No, but half my rooms be...unfit for guests."

"Only half?"

The man scowled. Zeeran placed himself between the two of them. "Listen, Morzaun won't be happy if you don't provide us with what we need. As I understand it, the two of you are sound business partners, and you wouldn't want to irritate him. It's only one night."

The owner's bony shoulders lifted with a look of mock sympathy. "Irritation or not, I can't give you what I don't have. The roof leaks, you see. Only half the rooms keep the rain out to a bearable degree, and there's a storm comin'."

The skies hadn't looked the least bit cloudy, and Zeeran had no patience for this. "I'll take a room with the poor roof."

"Suit yourself." The man reached into his drawer, and after a few moments of fumbling, withdrew a second key. "Here you go. Last room at the end of the hall." He turned to Sicarii, and his toothy grin returned. "Yours be at the opposite end. That far enough apart for you?"

Sicarii rolled her eyes, and Zeeran grabbed the second key before following her up the stairs. They'd made it halfway when Hendricks' creaky voice pulled Zeeran to a stop.

"By the way, boy. I done took the beds out of the bad rooms, and I won't be supplying no blankets to be soaked by the rain, neither."

Zeeran clenched his jaw to keep a groan in. How fortuitous, indeed.

CHAPTER TWELVE
A Dance with an Assassin

Holding his breath could only work for so long. Zeeran inhaled and immediately regretted that he required air to live. The musty smell, though unaccompanied by the heavy scent of body odor, was worse in his assigned room. Sunlight illuminated the area, not from the boarded window but from the holes speckling the ceiling. It almost appeared as though someone had laid on the floor and shot at the sky with a miniature cannon.

Zeeran cocked his head. From where he stood, the little beams of light formed two eyes, a nose, and an extra wide smile on the warped wooden floorboards. He snorted. The room was certainly not deserving of a happy face.

He leaned against the door frame, not having the desire to actually step foot into the room. Every time he shifted, he stirred dust and who knew what else. He could taste the little particles dancing in the sunbeams, which prompted him to keep his mouth shut.

Yes, the less time he spent in there, the better. Tonight would be a long one.

The floor behind him creaked, and Zeeran glanced over his shoulder to see Sicarii approaching. She peered into the room and winced. "Well, this looks...quaint."

"I take it your room is in far better condition?"

She scoffed. "*Far* better would be an exaggeration." Her gaze darted to the useless ceiling. "Best I can tell, the roof is intact, though."

"Such good news." Zeeran ran a hand through his hair, not caring a wit how it looked once he had. "I propose we find dinner elsewhere. I don't trust anything from this establishment to enter my stomach."

"Agreed. I know someplace we can find a meal."

They wasted no time leaving the inn. The moment they cleared the front door, both of them drew in a deep breath. The streets were surprisingly busy, and it took a while to reach the destination Sicarii had in mind, but at least the outside of the building looked promising. The roof was in good shape, and the windows were clean enough to see through. There were even potted plants hanging below the sills.

When they entered, a spicy scent warmed his core. His stomach shared its anticipation with a loud grumble, and Sicarii chuckled. "The food is good. I ate here the last time I was in Izarden."

Zeeran wanted to understand more about her previous *visit,* but he knew better than to ask. Sicarii was as likely to offer details as Morzaun.

They settled into a corner nook, and not long after placing their order, bowls of stew and hot honey rolls sat before them. The liquid washed over Zeeran's tongue, and he groaned with pleasure. He would have to improve his cooking skills. Eating what he had the last few weeks paled in comparison to the work of an experienced cook. Perhaps he should have paid better heed to his mother when she'd made their meals.

Zeeran glanced around the place. Nearly every table was occupied, and the room was filled with chatter and laughter—not the same boisterous sort of the pub but rather an airy delight.

"You said there is a celebration tomorrow." He turned to Sicarii, and she met his gaze. She tilted her head and waited for him to continue. "What are the people of Izarden celebrating?"

"They call it Eve of Victory." She shifted on the chair. "It's the day the invading mercenaries were defeated."

"You mean the ones..." His voice trailed off as he looked around the room. Mercenaries had invaded nearly ten years before he was born. The invaders had destroyed much of the kingdom, including his mother and father's childhood home. It was that event that had sparked his parents' desire to help their people—to find a way to defeat those bent on destroying them.

And they had. Deep in the mountains of Aknar, legend spoke of a weapon unlike any other. The Virgám—the one salvation to save Izarden. His parents and uncle had found it, and the scepter had granted them the ability to wield magic.

Sicarii watched him carefully. "Yes, the ones your parents and Morzaun defeated."

Zeeran took a drink. His family had saved Izarden. *Magic* had saved the kingdom. Yet now magic and anyone with the power to wield it were despised. He shook his head. "I'm surprised they would celebrate such a thing given the reason for their *victory*."

"Well, they don't exactly mention how Izarden conquered them. In fact, they give credit to the army."

"Of course they do." Zeeran drummed his fingers against the table. He shouldn't allow something like this to niggle its way under his skin. The frustration would do no good—wouldn't change anything. How would they feel if they knew a magic wielder was celebrating with them? Not that he planned to celebrate.

"I suppose we should head back to the inn now," said Sicarii.

Zeeran grimaced. The thought of spending the remaining hours of evening and then an entire night in that room...

Perhaps joining the celebration wasn't such a bad idea.

"I'm not in a hurry to go back there," said Zeeran. "I think I'll check out the festivities. Would you like to join me?"

Sicarii's brows furrowed, and his heart took up a quickened pace. Why did waiting for her response fill him with such anxiety? He had asked without a second thought, but now his mind settled on fear. What if she said no? Did that mean she didn't want to spend time with him?

His stomach turned over. Worse yet—what if she said yes?

"Are you sure that's a good idea?" Sicarii asked, pulling him from his self-induced panic. "We have to lay low, especially you."

Zeeran shrugged, willing his expression to remain devoid of his internal chaos. "We have our cloaks, and as long as we steer clear of the soldiers, no one will recognize me."

"Alright. I suppose we can take a gander at things."

We.

"You don't have to sound so excited about spending time with me." Zeeran leaned forward. "If you don't want to come—"

"Do you remember how to get back to the inn?"

Zeeran opened his mouth but snapped it closed after a moment. In truth, he had no idea how to get back there.

Sicarii lifted a brow when he didn't answer. "I thought not. Seems I must go; otherwise, you'll get lost."

"I would find my way back eventually."

The other brow joined the first at the top of her forehead.

Zeeran scoffed. "Oh, fine. Please come with me so I don't get lost."

"As you wish, but you owe me."

The smug grin she displayed twisted his insides. Two unspoken confessions swam through Zeeran's mind, the first being that he felt relieved she'd agreed to come. He'd hoped she would say yes, and that raised a whole plethora of concerns he would need to evaluate later. Second, he didn't mind owing Sicarii in the slightest. In fact, he looked forward to returning the favor.

* * *

The streets were so full of people that maneuvering through the crowd grew impossible. Sicarii led Zeeran to one of the larger marketplaces where vendors had closed up early and most of the merchandise had been pushed to the edges of the street, leaving the walkway open for the hordes of people trekking to the central plaza.

There, the crowds gathered around a group of minstrels. Those on the outskirts seemed content to converse and sample the sweet delicacies sold by peddlers while a few brave souls took up dancing.

Zeeran watched the couples bounce and skip to the music, and a smile tugged at his lips. Mama had taught him to dance, though he'd found little occasion to use the skill. He wouldn't admit it out loud, but he'd always thought the exercise exhilarating.

"I don't see any soldiers," said Sicarii, her words difficult to hear above the hum of the music. "I think they'll stay closer to the palace. The festival is two nights long, but the king only celebrates the last night."

Zeeran shoved his cloak hood from his head, and Sicarii frowned. "You should leave that on in case."

"Do you honestly think they'd notice me in this crush? As long as I don't perform any spells, we'll be fine."

Her lips pulled to one side as she considered his logic. "Fine, but if we spot a single soldier, the hood goes back on. We can't jeopardize the mission."

The mission. He'd nearly forgotten the entire reason they were there. Sicarii had not given him the details of the assignment yet, but that hardly mattered. Whatever Morzaun had sent them to do, Zeeran would only earn his uncle's trust if he accomplished the task.

But he could worry about that tomorrow. Tonight he would simply enjoy a little distraction.

He glanced at Sicarii who was studying the ground, her tight expression revealing her unease. She could do with a bit of distraction as well.

"Would you care to dance?" asked Zeeran.

Her gaze snapped to him, a mixture of emotions in her eyes. "Dance?"

Zeeran chuckled. "Yes, you know, hopping around like a fool to music that is obnoxiously joyful."

"I know what dancing is."

"Wonderful. Would you care to participate?"

She opened her mouth, and her gaze darted to the people twirling around the minstrels. "I don't know if I remember how."

"That makes two of us, but I'm confident if we pretend to know what we're doing, no one will care terribly much." Zeeran scooped up her hand and gave it a squeeze. "I won't let you fall on your face."

She scowled. "Maybe I'll be the one to keep you from falling."

"How about we agree to keep each other upright?"

Sicarii heaved a sigh, but her fingers curled around his. "If you insist."

Zeeran led her through the crowd, and he could feel her increased trepidation with every step they took toward the musicians. He stopped where fewer people were engaged in dance and turned to face her. "Ready?"

Her expression said no, but to her credit, she nodded with firm resolve. Zeeran placed her arm in the crook of his elbow, and they locked each other in place. With the upbeat of the music, the two of them began skipping in a circle, and after two rounds, they switched arms and proceeded in the opposite direction. Zeeran's grin grew as Sicarii became more comfortable with each step they took, her lips lifting with pleasure. She bounced in time with the music, and he followed suit. They both remembered well enough, it seemed.

Zeeran gasped for air by the time the music stopped. Sicarii held her stomach, her shoulders rising and falling with her heavy breaths. The sunlight had faded, but between the light of the moon overhead and the numerous torches lit around the plaza, darkness stood no chance of consuming them.

"I admit that was fun," said Sicarii. "Thank you for talking me into it."

"Thank you for agreeing to be my dance partner even if I am a wart."

She laughed, and heat burst in his chest like a bloom opening to greet the morning light. The dancing torch flames illuminated her smile, her hair, her eyes—the genuine happiness exuding from every inch of her features. He wanted to keep it there. He'd seen Sicarii distraught and guarded more often than not, but this...*this* was the woman whose company he enjoyed.

This was the woman he was starting to—

A shout interrupted the thought. A burly man backed into Sicarii, and the collision thrust her forward. Zeeran caught her in his arms, steadying her against his chest, and tossed the man a glare over Sicarii's shoulder.

"Sorry," the man muttered, but there was no point in being angry with him, not with the glisten in his eyes that spoke to the ale he'd consumed.

"No problem," said Zeeran. But the man had already turned away. Zeeran watched him stagger through the crowd for several seconds before shifting his attention to Sicarii. His hands still rested on her waist, her body pressed against his. The realization sent fire through his veins.

"Are you alright?" he whispered.

Her lips parted as though to speak, but she only nodded. He'd steadied her. He could let go.

But his hands seemed unwilling to obey whatever logical promptings came from his mind. Instead, his gaze traced her face, every curve of her cheeks and freckle on her nose until settling on her eyes. They were a brilliant green, but until now—with her mere inches from his own face—he hadn't noticed the speckles of blue in them.

How warm they were, sparkling with the rays of moonbeams and torchlight. They beckoned him to draw closer. His hands tightened around her waist.

And then his gaze dropped to her full lips.

"Zeeran." Her soft voice, barely audible above the noise of the crowds, pulled him into focus. He looked up, his heart beating faster than necessary given they were standing still. Sicarii stared up at him with all the hesitancy and fear he'd seen when he entered her cottage. "Please stop looking at me like that."

He swallowed. "Like what?"

Her brows furrowed, and those green eyes darkened with new irritation. "Like I'm the most beautiful thing you've ever beheld."

"Maybe you are."

She gripped his wrists and removed his hold. His heart lurched when she took a step back, shaking her head. "Stop. I don't want your sympathy."

"Sympathy? Is that what you think..." He closed the gap she'd created between them and pulled her back against him. "This has nothing to do with sympathy."

"I won't fool myself into thinking you—or anyone—could find me attractive. I am *not* naïve, Zeeran. My face—"

He reached up and cupped her face between his hands. The action silenced her with a sharp inhale. Zeeran brushed his fingers over the red lines embedded in her skin. "There is nothing wrong with your face. I don't know who made you believe that these scars impact your beauty, but they're wrong."

Her lips lifted slightly. "Perhaps you are blind. Your aim isn't the best."

Zeeran threw his head back with a laugh and dropped his hands to settle them on her waist again. "I can see well enough. You're going to have to trust me."

Sicarii's eyes roamed his face as though considering his request, and he held his breath until she answered. "I do trust you."

The words sent a jolt through his chest. He'd worked hard to gain Morzaun's trust, and he still hadn't accomplished the feat. He never dreamed he'd earn Sicarii's either after the cold way she'd greeted him when he first arrived in the clearing. Having it now thrilled him in ways he couldn't explain.

Sicarii bit her lip, drawing Zeeran's attention to it. "I think we should both consider the consequences of where this is going."

"And what consequences might that be?" Surly none that would douse his desire. He could see nothing negative about holding her in his arms or tasting her lips as he so desperately wanted to do.

"We can't afford this." She gestured between them, her cheeks tinting a pale red. "Whatever this is. It's a distraction. A vulnerability I can't allow."

"Why?"

She scoffed at the simple question, and Zeeran tightened his hold around her. He brought her closer, and her hands lifted to rest on his shoulders. She wasn't wrong, but sometimes doing the wrong thing felt entirely right. He didn't want to ignore the feelings stirring within him but explore them. Sicarii was different–beautiful despite her belief otherwise. Something about her strong nature drew him in, but it was the gentleness and fear she buried that kept him there. He wanted to understand her.

"Morzaun says love is a weakness." She glanced at the people moving around them when the music started up again. "And I believe him. It has never brought me anything but pain, and I refuse to–"

Her mouth snapped closed, and she pulled away. This time Zeeran allowed her to slip out of his arms when she took a step back. What pain had love brought her? He desperately wanted to know, but pushing her never gave him good results. If Sicarii trusted him, she would tell him in time.

"I respect your opinion," said Zeeran, "but wholeheartedly disagree. It is, perhaps, one of the few beliefs I don't share with my uncle. Love makes us vulnerable, yes, but I don't think that it makes us weak. I look at my parents and see how much stronger they are as a team. My family has endured much, especially since gaining the ability to wield magic, and they faced it all together. Perhaps they could have done so alone, but it would have been far more difficult."

Zeeran ran a hand through his hair. "Living on an island my

entire life has not been easy. Sometimes I was lonely and hopeless. I wanted to leave, or maybe feel as though I *could* leave if I chose, but that was never an option with our powers. Verascene was the only place we were safe from Delran, and I often felt trapped. But my family kept the shadows away. My brother and sister were there whenever I needed help out of the darkness."

The confession stirred the guilt hiding in his soul. He'd left his family–abandoned them to help Morzaun. But that had been the right thing to do. Morzaun didn't deserve a trial that would end in his death. Zeeran had to take a stand even if his family wouldn't.

Didn't he?

He shook his head. "I love my family. Maybe that makes me weak, but I feel stronger knowing they have my back."

But did they any more? What if leaving had destroyed his connection to them?

His stomach twisted into a tight knot. Regret had not found him before, but now it ate away at his resolve. Homesickness flooded over him. Living on Verascene hadn't always been ideal, but at least his family had been there for him. Would Morzaun fill that role? Zeeran suspected his uncle wouldn't given how he opposed being close to anyone, and the thought of facing life's hardships without someone to lean on scared him.

Warmth enveloped his hands, and Zeeran glanced up to find Sicarii near again. She tilted her head, her dark brows furrowed with concern.

"I miss my family," he muttered. "Ladisias is as obnoxious as big brothers can be, but he never failed to offer me advice when I needed it. Even if I didn't *think* I needed it." A smile pulled at his lips. "And Feya always listened to me when I was a complete grouch. She made me laugh. Supported me when I couldn't stand on my own."

Sicarii released his hands and shifted on her feet. "They sound wonderful."

"They are, and I'm afraid...I'm afraid I've ruined any chance of ever having that support again."

The realization weighed on him like an anchor. Why did he feel as though he would sink to the bottom of the sea? He was a grown man. He could manage life without his family by his side, surely. Morzaun had coped well enough living on his own.

But his uncle had also turned rather bitter. He took pleasure in nothing, revenge filling every aspect of the man's life. Zeeran wasn't so sure he wanted to end up like Morzaun, but he couldn't stand up for his beliefs *and* have his family. There simply wasn't room for both.

"Are you going to ask me to dance again or not?"

Sicarii's voice stole his attention from the unsettling thoughts. She smiled, though it was hesitant. "Or we could always go back to the inn."

Zeeran shook his head vigorously. "No. Let's dance. I don't want to go back yet."

He took her hand and positioned it around his elbow. Dancing was a great distraction, and he had no desire to visit his troubling thoughts right now. There'd be plenty of time for that when sleep evaded him.

And Zeeran suspected tonight he wouldn't sleep a wink.

CHAPTER THIRTEEN
The Mission

Noise filled the busy streets long after sunset, and a starry sky appeared overhead. Zeeran walked alongside Sicarii as they headed back to the inn. Their pace remained slow; it seemed neither of them truly wanted to return to the smelly establishment, but if they were to accomplish whatever task Morzaun had given them, they would need to rest.

Or at least try.

Zeeran wasn't convinced he'd feel comfortable enough on the hard floor, especially with the dark, ominous clouds floating over the moon. The owner of the inn had mentioned rain, and Zeeran had brushed his forecast off like an annoying piece of lint. Now it appeared the man may have been correct in his predictions.

Zeeran's fingers brushed against Sicarii's, and the two of them glanced at each other. He hadn't meant to touch her, but the momentary connection with her skin sent a shiver up his arm. The constant flutter in his stomach when the woman was near simply wouldn't do. She'd made it clear she had no desire for anything to happen between them, and it would be best if he accepted her offer of friendship and leave the rest be. It wasn't as though he had his future planned. He couldn't offer her anything that would entice something more...

He stomped out the thought before it could finish. What was he doing? He and Sicarii were barely friends, and his mind thought to contemplate marri—

No. He wouldn't even think the word. For all the ridiculous notions he could conjure, that must be the worst.

They stopped outside the inn, both of them staring up at the building with a grimace. The idea of spending hours in that room filled Zeeran with dread. Were it not for having to pass several guards to leave and reenter the city, or the fact that magical transportation from here was risky, he might have considered staying in the barn instead.

"I suppose we should go inside," he muttered, his feet not the least bit convinced.

Sicarii nodded, offering him a sympathetic smile. Zeeran followed her into the inn and up the stairs, not bothering to spare a friendly glance at the owner. Sicarii stopped at her door and removed the keys from her cloak pocket.

"Goodnight," said Zeeran.

"Goodnight."

He continued down the long corridor to his room and inserted the key. Zeeran glanced over his shoulder to make sure Sicarii had gone inside her room only to find her staring at him. A loud rumble shook the walls and vibrated the floor.

Zeeran closed his eyes and released a heavy exhale. Of course there would be a storm.

As if he'd offered the leaky sky permission, patters sounded overhead. And inside his room.

Zeeran threw open the door, and it thudded off the wall. A steady drip of water fell from the ceiling, the wooden floor already home to several puddles that reflected the light flicking from the mounted candles next to the doorframe.

"You can't sleep in here."

He jumped at the sound of Sicarii's voice so near. She peered around him, her gaze darting from the ceiling to the lake forming in his room.

"Then where do you propose I sleep?" he asked, failing to restrain his irritation. "There aren't any other rooms according to the man downstairs."

Sicarii's lips pinched, and she studied him for several long moments before grabbing his hand. Zeeran's heart lurched, but he had little time to think on his reaction as she led him back down the corridor. Sicarii removed one of the mounted candles from the wall and tugged him into her room.

His heart doubled its efforts when she closed the door and flipped the metal latch into place. The candlelight danced over her features, highlighting the lines of her jaw and, unfortunately, her lips.

And he'd done so well not thinking about them after chiding himself the last time.

"My ceiling isn't leaking." Sicarii gestured upward as if giving him leave to check for himself. "You can sleep in here...on the floor. I'm not giving up the bed."

Zeeran grinned. "You won't share with me?"

She pinned him with a glare that looked more intimidating with the candle flames lighting parts of her face, the rest of her remaining shadowed. "You come anywhere near me tonight, and you'll be sleeping permanently."

He thought to ask if she slept with her daggers in jest, but something told Zeeran she probably *did* sleep with them. "Fair enough. I can't complain given that I will be dry, at least."

She gave a firm nod and marched toward the bed. Sicarii placed the candle on the nightstand and sunk onto the poorly padded mattress.

Zeeran sat down on the floor and leaned against the door. "Why do you suppose Morzaun had us come tonight—instead of in the morning, I mean?"

Sicarii shrugged. "There will be more soldiers roaming about tomorrow with the nobles joining the festivities. I suppose he thought it might be best. Less chance of you being spotted, especially entering town. There will be more men standing guard, and there's not much chance you could transport us inside the city without being noticed."

Zeeran grunted his agreement. It seemed sending them on a mission during a festival was risky, but perhaps that was the point.

They couldn't complete it otherwise. Zeeran suspected it involved Delran and his family, and what better way to achieve the mission than when they were drawn out of the palace.

"Here."

Zeeran glanced up in time to see the blanket hurtling toward him and caught the fabric before it crashed into his face. "What's this for?"

"Sleeping, obviously."

He narrowed his eyes. "And what about you?"

"I'll be fine." She removed her cloak and laid down, settling the material over her. "I have the bed. It's only fair for you to get the blanket."

Truthfully, it wasn't much of a blanket. The thin fabric would do little to preserve heat, and the square was barely big enough to cover him. Still, he smiled as he stretched it over himself. "Thank you, Sicarii."

She said nothing but leaned over to blow out the candle. Darkness and silence settled around them, and to Zeeran's surprise, his eyes drifted closed. Perhaps he would catch a little sleep after all.

* * *

A warm weight and slight shake to his shoulder pulled Zeeran from a dream—one where he held a certain woman in his arms and kissed her senseless. Heat ran up the back of his neck when he discovered that same woman standing over him, her hair woven into a single braid that dangled down her right shoulder and a beam of morning light casting a bright glow over her face.

"Did you sleep well?" she asked with a smirk.

He nodded dumbly, still reeling with the effort to separate dream and reality. Perhaps sleeping in the same room as Sicarii had been a bad idea.

"Good. Let's get going. We should have something to eat and then survey the area around the palace so we're more prepared for tonight."

Zeeran tossed the blanket across the floor and looked up at her. "And do you intend to give me the details of our mission before we begin?"

"Over breakfast." She offered him a hand, and Zeeran accepted it, though he placed his palm against the door to bear most of his weight as he stood. His body ached from spending the night on the floor, and he refused to let it show.

"I presume you have a place in mind for breakfast?" He adjusted his cloak and situated the hood over his messy hair. "I have no desire to eat whatever is cooking downstairs."

"Neither do I. We'd likely be too sick to accomplish anything." Sicarii unlatched the door and stepped into the corridor. Zeeran followed her down the stairs, the scent of burnt food wrinkling his nose.

The two of them returned their keys to a tired-looking Hendricks and headed out into the crisp morning air. The clouds had dissipated from overhead, but the glisten of water droplets on the cobblestone gave evidence to the storm that had rumbled through the night. Zeeran wondered what his room looked like after so many hours of rain, but at least he hadn't been required to find out first hand.

He glanced at Sicarii, who's gaze perused the street with focus. She seemed more tense today, and perhaps he would be too once he actually knew what Morzaun had sent them to do.

Zeeran ducked his chin when they passed a group of soldiers. There were many of them in the streets today, their black uniforms making them stand out in the crowd. He and Sicarii would not have leave to enjoy the festivities with so many of them about, not that they had the time.

Sicarii entered a pub and took a seat in a back corner away from the handful of other customers. Once plates of eggs and sausage lay before them, she leaned forward with her elbows on the table and met his gaze.

"Morzaun has asked us to infiltrate the palace," she said, her voice a hushed whisper.

Zeeran choked on the bit of egg in his mouth. "What?"

"He wants us to find Delran's heir." She glanced around as if to verify no one had close enough proximity to hear. "And eliminate him."

Eliminate him? Zeeran leaned forward, his brows drawn tight. "Morzaun wants us to *murder* Delran's heir? You cannot be serious."

Sicarii shrugged, though the way she bit her lip suggested she wasn't fond of the assignment, either. "Morzaun wants the boy out of the way. He intends to find his son—"

"And make him king." Zeeran sat back with a scoff and folded his arms. "I hate this plan. We have no idea if my uncle will ever find Eramus, nor do we know if he'll join us. It is foolish to risk so much on a chance."

“I don’t disagree, but I’m inclined to do as Morzaun asked, regardless.”

Zeeran narrowed his eyes, and she averted her gaze. When he first joined his uncle, Zeeran had believed Sicarii onboard with their cause, but there were times when he wondered if she was there of her own free will. Did she truly believe Morzaun belonged in a position of power, as he surely would be should Eramus take over as king? Or did her obedience stem from fear? He had never considered that his uncle might have manipulated her into doing his bidding, threatened her even.

But now was not the time to puzzle over such things. If they were going to follow through with this mission, they needed to focus. Murdering the future king of Izarden was not something to be taken lightly.

Zeeran rubbed a hand over his stubbled chin. “This doesn’t sit well with me. Not only is it risky, but I don’t feel right about it. Delran’s heir is young. Innocent. Killing Delran would be one thing, but a child...”

Sicarii stood, her green eyes fierce. “I don’t like it either, but I can’t disappoint Morzaun again. If you're questioning your loyalty, then you can incur his wrath by yourself. I can’t afford to do so.”

She marched toward the door, and Zeeran scrambled to his feet to follow. Images of Morzaun pressing his dagger to her throat filled his mind. His uncle had threatened her after the last failed mission, and Zeeran suspected that had not been the first time. The man must have something devastating to hold over her. Sicarii was not weak minded or meek.

His boots tapped against the street as he rushed to catch up with her. “Sicarii, please wait.” Zeeran grabbed her by the arm and gently pulled her to a halt. She wouldn’t look at him, and despite how she tried to hide her fear, he felt it emanating from her in waves. “What did my uncle threaten you with?”

She turned to him sharply, her features drawn in a scowl. “It isn’t your business. Worry about yourself.”

Zeeran took a step closer. “I don’t care whether it is or isn’t. I’m asking you to tell me–to *trust* me. You are not a woman who would simply do someone’s bidding without cause. What does he hold against you?”

Her expression crumbled, and she blinked back tears. “My past.”

Concern twisted his stomach, and he reached a hand to her cheek and traced one of the scars there. “My uncle...he didn’t do this, did he?”

Sicarii shook her head, and relief flooded over him. He didn’t want to believe his uncle capable of such a thing, but the man had ordered them to murder someone.

“I had those before I met Morzaun,” said Sicarii. “Your uncle had nothing to do with them.”

“Then what–”

She stepped backwards, leaving his hand suspended in midair. “It isn’t important, Zeeran. What matters right now is doing what we came here to do. I’m going to scout around the palace. If you aren’t up to this, then you can stay here.”

Sicarii spun around, and although everything within him resisted the idea of what they were about to do, Zeeran followed her.

Regardless of how he felt about the matter, he would not leave Sicarii to do this on her own. Too much could go wrong, and if she was determined to obey Morzaun's dangerous commands, he would make sure she came out of the mission alive.

CHAPTER FOURTEEN
To Murder Innocence

Hints of approaching dusk colored the sky, the clouds straddling the horizon turning a shade somewhere between pink and purple. Zeeran leaned against the marble palace wall, his chin tucked to avoid meeting the gazes of the soldiers passing by. He'd completed his scouting route, and waiting for Sicarii to return from hers left him anxious.

He had little reason to be concerned about her; she wouldn't attract the attention of Izarden's soldiers like he would. Still, he regretted having agreed to split up. Too much could go wrong.

Daring a quick glance, Zeeran peeked out from beneath his cloak and caught sight of Sicarii approaching. Strands of her red-dipped hair had come loose from her braid and now stuck out from beneath her brown hood, but she appeared relaxed, perhaps even more so than she had this morning.

He opened his mouth to greet her, but she grabbed his hand and pulled him behind her down the street. Ignoring the way her dainty fingers latched onto his prickling skin, Zeeran allowed her to guide him without resistance. She led him into a shadowed alleyway, far from the buzzing crowd and careful watch of soldiers.

"How did it go?" she asked once she had checked every dark spot someone could use as a hiding place.

"Well enough. There are five guards posted at the southern entrance, and at least three more patrolling the wall. What about you?"

Her lips lifted. "I gathered some useful information. Delran and his wife are enjoying the festivities in the courtyard, but their son isn't there. Apparently, he took ill some weeks ago and is still recovering. The king refuses to let him outside until he has regained his strength."

Zeeran's brows furrowed. "And why do you appear so happy about this turn of events?"

"Because getting close to the prince will be much easier if he's not surrounded by guards."

Zeeran threw his head back with a laugh. "And you think he won't be surrounded by guards if he's inside the palace? Sicarii, that's absurd. There's no way Delran doesn't keep his men posted at the boy's door, and besides, the odds of us slipping into the courtyard undetected are slim, let alone inside the palace itself."

"We don't need to slip in. That's why you're here."

His stomach lurched into his throat. "Me? You mean I'm to

transport us inside?"

Sicarii lifted her brows and nodded.

"That is a horrible idea." He kept his voice low but his tone didn't lack frustration. "Do you know how many things could go wrong? We could land in front of guards or impale ourselves on a dozen things. I'm not familiar with the inside of the palace enough for this."

Sicarii crossed her arms. "Morzaun said you entered the throne room when you came to Izarden."

Zeeran reared back. How had his uncle known that? Zeeran had gone into the palace when his father met with Delran. The original plan was for Zeeran to stay in the barn with Feya, but the king had demanded that all of them be present. Once Delran presented his offer for them to earn their pardon, he'd ordered them to go with General Ivrin to find Morzaun. The king had also demanded that Feya remain behind as *insurance* of their cooperation.

Zeeran glanced up at the palace, much of it hidden behind the marble wall in front of him. He didn't know what had become of his family. Was Feya safe? Had they returned to Verascene?

"There's not a chance we'll be able to walk in through the front gate," Sicarii's irritated voice pulled him from his musings, and he turned to face her. She poked a finger into his chest. "You have to use your magic to get us inside."

"And what were you planning to do if I hadn't agreed to come along this morning?"

"I've scaled the walls before. It isn't ideal, but I could do so again."

Scaled the walls? "You mean one of your previous missions had you sneaking into the palace?"

Her eyes widened, and she turned away from him. "It doesn't matter. The point is with your magic we can get in undetected and will have a better chance at success. The throne room may have men posted outside, but there will be no reason for them to be *inside* since Delran and the queen are in the courtyard."

Zeeran resisted the urge to remove his hood and run his hand through his hair. "This is a huge risk. I don't feel good about it."

"It's less risky than trying to sneak past all the guards."

He couldn't argue with that, but still. "What if you get sick again? Retching in the throne room is bound to give away our position."

Sicarii wrinkled her nose as if the memory alone disgusted her. "I can handle it, and Morzaun said you could put the guards to sleep. No one will even know we're there."

Zeeran shook his head, but he had little choice. Allowing Sicarii to scale the walls and do this on her own wasn't an option. Truthfully, transporting into the palace didn't bother him so much as the task that followed. He'd never murdered anyone, and although he supported dethroning Delran, killing a child to ensure power transferred to Eramus contorted his insides with guilt.

"Fine," said Zeeran. "I'll use the spell to get us inside, but I can't guarantee we won't be caught."

"I never expected you to promise anything." Sicarii glanced down the alleyway. "We'll go once it's dark. Perhaps by then many of the guards will be outside. The fewer you need to use magic on, the better."

"Once the sun has fully set, then." They would infiltrate the castle, and with any luck, things would go smoothly. Zeeran shoved down the unease threatening to drown him. He couldn't linger on what they were about to do, for if he did, he might very well change his mind.

* * *

The streets still buzzed with music and chatter, but the alley that had become their hideout was cold and empty. The entire city seemed to be celebrating, and part of Zeeran wished he could join them. Forgetting the reason for his venture to Izarden would provide a blissful reprieve; perhaps he and Sicarii could even dance again. It was a shame they were there on his uncle's errand.

"Zeeran." Sicarii's voice held an almost growl, and when Zeeran turned to face her, she scowled at him. "Are you listening? I asked if you were ready."

Oh. His thoughts had been a bit preoccupied, but he wasn't about to tell Sicarii what they consisted of–touching her, holding her close...kissing.

He shook his head to dislodge the images forming there. "Yes, I'm ready."

"Good. Maybe try acting like it. We can't lose focus for even a second. You may have magic, but that won't stop a soldier from running you through with a sword."

"I'm aware," he spat a little too loud, and she hushed him. Zeeran drew a deep breath. "Let's get this over with."

He closed his eyes and conjured his memories of the Great Hall which contained Delran's golden throne. He'd only been there once, but the details returned to him well enough to form a decent image. Zeeran could envision the rows of purple banners hanging from the ceiling and the long table near the windows. He could see the carved black eagle surrounding Delran's throne, its wings curled around the chair in a protective pose.

"I've got it," he muttered, keeping his eyes pinched closed.

Warmth surrounded his hand, Sicarii's dainty fingers threading between his. Zeeran's focus stuttered, and he nearly lost the image of the golden chair situated upon the dais. Pulling it back to the forefront of his mind, he recited the incantation. Sicarii gasped, and her hold tightened. A tingling sensation flooded through his body, accompanied by a sense of weightlessness.

And then it faded as quickly as it had come. The celebratory music of Izarden's citizens sounded muffled, and the smell of fresh bread and pastries vanished. Zeeran opened his eyes and glanced around the Great Hall, the dim light from the two sconces near the entry providing the only light and not nearly enough to fight the shadows.

Sicarii released his hand and crumbled to the floor holding her stomach. Zeeran crouched next to her and noted the paleness in her cheeks. He placed his hand on her shoulder with a whisper, "Are you well?"

She shook her head. "No. The guards posted by the door...go..."

When her mouth snapped closed and she lifted her hand to cover it, Zeeran rose and raced across the room. He peered around the edge of the arched doorway, pressing his back against the wall.

Two men stood sentinel over the empty corridor beyond, not another soldier visible in the flickering light of the sconces lining the marble walls.

Zeeran twirled his fingers until his blue aura appeared and then directed it away from him. It flowed to the floor and crawled along the woven rug until it met the guards' boots. Their knees buckled as it creeped up their legs, and Zeeran's spell guided them to the ground like feathers floating weightlessly through the air. They landed softly on the rug, and their peaceful expressions ensured his success. The men would sleep for an hour or so.

He spun around at the sound of Sicarii puking. She'd bent over a large, potted palm, clutching her stomach so tightly her knuckles turned white. Zeeran stepped behind her and gently rubbed circles on her back.

She moaned and spat into the dirt at the base of the plant. "I thought for sure I could manage it this time."

Zeeran chuckled. "It took me about twenty tries to keep my stomach contents *inside*. Don't be so hard on yourself. Besides, think how confused the servants will be when they come to water the plant."

Sicarii whacked his arm, but her grin still appeared. "Did you knock out the guards?"

"They're sleeping. We should have an hour, perhaps more."

"Plenty of time, I should think." Sicarii pressed a hand to her stomach. "Let's go. My stomach is empty now."

They exited the Great Hall, stepping over the sleeping men, and followed the decorative rug down the corridor. Zeeran's gaze roamed the walls—fell on every detailed painting and elaborate tapestry.

Izarden knew wealth and had for a long time. As the oldest kingdom in Virgamor, it had established a presence that few other kingdoms dared to oppose.

Mumbled voices sounded from the foyer, and Zeeran held out his hand in front of Sicarii. He gave her a look that said 'wait here' and tiptoed to the end of the rug. Slowly, he peeked around the corner. There were four guards stationed at the palace entry and all of them faced in his direction.

How would he use his spell without it being seen?

Zeeran backed away until he was at Sicarii's side again. "There's four of them, and they're too far away for me to use magic without my aura being noticed."

"Then we need them to come to us," she whispered back.

Good Virgamor. "What do you suggest?"

"Let me handle that. Just be ready when they approach."

They moved to the end of the corridor together. Zeeran peeked around the corner to make certain all four guards were still there and then gave Sicarii a firm nod. She cupped her hand to the side of her mouth, and a bird-like whistle reverberated through the air.

"What was that?" one of the men asked.

Zeeran pressed against the wall, Sicarii at his side.

"Sounded like a bird to me," said another man with a tone of nonchalance. "One probably got inside with all the movement in and out today."

Zeeran glanced at Sicarii, and she lifted her hand to her mouth again. This time she whistled much longer, not stopping until the shuffle of footsteps filled the foyer.

"Something's not right. Birds don't twitter after dark." The guard's voice came from mere feet away. Zeeran twirled his hand and quickly recited the incantation in his mind. He curled his aura around the cold marble wall, the blue light casting a glow on the smooth surface. A sharp gasp preceded a heavy thump.

"Miller?" another voice questioned from across the room. "Miller, this is no time for games."

Several long seconds passed before the other guard seemed to accept that Miller was not, in fact, playing a game. More than one set of footsteps drew closer, and when Zeeran was sure they were close, he sent a stream of magic around the corner again. This time two thumps followed his spell.

He turned to Sicarii, and she mouthed 'one more.'

"What are the three of you playing at!" The last guard's voice held a hint of fear. Meanwhile his companions had begun to snore, and Zeeran restrained a laugh. Sicarii whistled again, and the sound of metal scraping against a scabbard sent Zeeran's heart pounding.

Boots stomped against the pine floorboards, and Zeeran prepared his aura one last time. The blue light slithered along the floor, catching the light of the nearby sconces. The footsteps stopped. "What in Virga–"

The guard hit the floor, and his weapon clanked. Zeeran peered into the foyer and grinned.

"They're all out cold."

"Good. Let's go." Sicarii slipped past him and withdrew one of her daggers. "I know the way."

Zeeran followed her, brandishing his own sword. Morzaun had

given him the weapon for when they practiced, and although he had a more powerful one at his fingertips, he preferred to have a physical weapon handy.

Sicarii maneuvered through the carpeted corridors with focus. She never hesitated on her path, seeming to know the layout of the palace as though she'd been there more than once. She'd confessed to scaling the walls, and he wondered what mission Morzaun had sent her on to require that kind of bold invasion. Whatever it was, she'd failed to achieve what he sent her to do.

Is that why Zeeran had been asked to come this time? Sicarii had failed because she didn't have magic?

Sicarii halted at the end of a corridor and slowly looked around the corner before snapping back. "There's a guard outside the prince's chamber," she whispered.

"Only one?"

She nodded. "Probably thirty feet down. Do you think your spell can reach that far?"

Zeeran held back a chuckle. "My magic can reach much farther than thirty feet. It's whether the guard notices that will be the issue. Do you suppose there are more inside the chamber?"

"No. The last time I was here, I overheard the servants talking. There is a maid who looks after the boy, but no one else."

He didn't linger on the questions swarming his mind. They hadn't time for that at present, but when this was all over, Zeeran resolved to ask her more about her previous missions. She likely wouldn't confide the details, but he wanted to try. After all, Sicarii would have been in the palace at the same time as his sister. She may have even seen her.

Knowing how his sister fared would give his soul some relief.

"How would you like to handle this guard?" he asked.

Sicarii grinned, and without a word stepped around the corner. Zeeran reached for her, but she slipped through his fingers.

"Stop right there!" The guard's firm command turned Zeeran's blood to ice, but Sicarii didn't retreat.

"I believe I'm lost," she said, her tone feigning innocence.

Soft thuds indicated the man was coming toward them. Zeeran summoned his aura, and jumped into the center of the corridor. The guard halted, his eyes wide with surprise. Zeeran shot his spell at the man, and the blue light encompassed him in a matter of seconds.

The guard's eyes closed, and his body went limp. Zeeran rushed forward to catch him and guided his body to the floor.

"Next time warn me of your intentions." He turned a glare on Sicarii, who returned a smirk.

"It worked, didn't it?"

"Fortunately," Zeeran mumbled. "But I'd prefer not to alert the entire castle of our presence."

Sicarii approached the door and placed her hand carefully on the knob. "The maid likely heard the commotion." She twisted the handle and frowned. "And the door is locked. I doubt she'd let us in if we knocked. Can your magic get us inside?"

Zeeran shook his head. "I can't manipulate the latch without knowing what it looks like."

"Can't you just, I don't know, melt it or something."

He scowled at her. "Magic has limitations. I can't snap my fingers and make the door disappear."

"Then I guess we aren't using the door...or at least I'm not. Wait here."

He started to protest, but Sicarii rushed past him and opened the door to the room next to the prince's. She peered inside. "Empty. I'll be right back."

"Sicarii, don't–"

She shut the door behind herself, and Zeeran bit back a groan. Sometimes the woman was too fearless for her own good.

He leaned against the door, pressing his ear to the wood. No sound came from inside, but then, if the maid suspected danger, she would take the prince and hide. Would she be armed? What if Sicarii had been wrong about there not being any guards inside?

His stomach twisted, and the minutes seemed to drag on for hours. A sharp scream penetrated the air, and Zeeran's heart raced into a gallop. Voices and furniture scraping across floorboards sent his hand to the knob. He jiggled it, but the door remained locked. Zeeran bit his tongue to keep from shouting for Sicarii. He couldn't give away their position.

The latch clicked, and Zeeran backed away from the door. It parted from the frame to reveal a young woman with terrified blue eyes and blonde hair dangling over her shoulder in a thick braid. The glint of a blade drew his eyes to her neck.

"Back up slowly," Sicarii's familiar voice whispered, and the woman did as instructed. Three long strides brought Zeeran into the room, and he closed the door. At least if the woman screamed, the sound would be muffled somewhat.

There were two candles lit in the room, and the closest one

illuminated the maid's face to reveal her terror. Behind her, Sicarii's body remained engulfed in shadows, her face hidden beneath her cloak hood.

Sicarii leaned sideways, peering at him over the maid's shoulder, and nodded to the woman. "She could use some sleep."

At least he was getting plenty of practice with his sleeping spell.

With a flash of blue light, the woman collapsed, and Sicarii leaned her against the wall. Zeeran studied the room, searching for their target. He could see little in the dimly lit space, but the soft sobs emanating from beside the bed gave away the prince's position. He and Sicarii approached, and Zeeran cast the *illustris*, conjuring an orb of light that hovered above his palm.

The shadows evaporated, revealing a boy with dark hair and brown eyes, his features much like the kings but for his youthful, chubby cheeks. He sat against the wall, his arms tightly wrapped around his knees. He couldn't have been more than seven.

If Zeeran's stomach hadn't been in a tangle of knots before, it certainly was now. How was he supposed to kill someone so innocent? He would never forget those eyes if he went through with it. This boy was not his enemy, and taking his life when he had done nothing wrong went against everything Zeeran believed. Had he not protected Morzaun for this very reason? Because he believed the man didn't deserve to be executed?

Yet he'd come here with the intention of ensuring the young prince's last breath. Why should his uncle receive mercy and not the child? He couldn't help who his father was, nor had he ever done anything to deserve such punishment.

Sicarii shifted at Zeeran's side, her brows drawn tight. She gripped a dagger, her hand shaking. Perhaps she was hesitant to complete this mission, too.

"W-who are you?" the boy whispered. "What do you want?"

Zeeran's heart turned to ice at the fear in his voice. The young lad didn't understand—he never would. Eliminating the heir of Izarden was the only way to ensure Eramus could claim the throne, but...

Sicarii took two steps forward, lifting the dagger, and the boy's eyes widened.

No. They couldn't do this. He wouldn't allow the child to die.

Sicarii lunged, and Zeeran did the same.

CHAPTER FIFTEEN

The Forgetful Prince

The boy screamed and ducked his head into his arms. Zeeran caught Sicarii by the wrist and pivoted her away from the child. She staggered, and the dagger sliced across Zeeran's forearm. He gritted his teeth but did not release her.

"What are you doing!" Sicarii attempted to yank her hand away, but Zeeran held fast. He'd sensed her hesitation. She didn't want to kill the child anymore than he did.

"We can't do this." Zeeran glanced at the boy who's sobs filled the room. With the wave of his free hand, he cast his sleeping spell one last time. The sobs ceased, and the prince slumped over, his breaths evening. "We can't kill him. He's innocent."

Sicarii's scowl faltered. "I know that, Zeeran, but we were given an order."

They had been, and Morzaun would not be happy if they failed to follow through, but Zeeran couldn't bring himself to do this. It was wrong, plain and simple, and he wanted no part in it.

He released his hold on Sicarii's wrist and positioned his hand over the wound on his arm. He muttered his healing spell and watched as his skin stitched itself back together. "My uncle is right about many things—about Delran and removing him from the throne—but this...I can't condone this. He's a child." Zeeran shook his head. "He doesn't deserve death merely because of who's blood runs in his veins."

"If we don't do this, Morzaun will have our heads. You don't understand. We can't contradict his orders. I can't."

Fear shone in her green eyes. The situation wasn't simple. Morzaun would be more than angry if they came home without eliminating this obstacle, but perhaps there was a way around the command. "What exactly did Morzaun say...when he gave you the order?"

She thought for a moment. "He said that we were to remove Delran's heir from the picture. Get rid of him."

Well, that left things open for interpretation, didn't it?

"Then we'll do that," said Zeeran. "We can get rid of him in a way that doesn't involve murder."

"You know full well what your uncle meant. He won't be pleased."

"So we don't tell him."

Sicarii scoffed. "Don't tell him? You must be insane. How do you propose we keep this from him? You think he won't notice when word of the prince's death doesn't travel through every village and town?"

"Not if we do this right. We can make the prince disappear. Morzaun will believe we've killed him, but the boy will get to live."

She folded her arms and fixed him with an incredulous look. "And how do we make him disappear? You realize that if we kidnap the child and then leave him somewhere, he'll still find his way back to the palace. He's royalty, Zeeran. The minute he tells someone who he is, he'll be rescued and we'll be dead for defying Morzaun's orders."

Zeeran's stomach clenched. He'd suspected Morzaun had threatened Sicarii, but he'd held onto hope that his uncle wasn't quick to murderous intentions. If the orders in regards to the prince didn't prove it, the look in Sicarii's eyes did.

The confirmation troubled him but would have to be analyzed later. The longer they remained in the palace, the higher the odds of being caught. They needed to make a decision quickly.

"He won't tell anyone who he is if he doesn't remember." Zeeran tucked his chin, shame already flowing over him, eroding away his resolve like a stormy wave eating at the shore. But this would be better than death. It would be better if the boy were raised by someone who wouldn't corrupt his innocence.

"You can do that?" asked Sicarii. "You can make him forget who he is?"

Zeeran nodded. "I know the spell. It's quite simple, one my mother used to help us practice incantations as children. We would whisper in each other's ears and take turns making one another forget. It was a game."

"This isn't a game, Zeeran. If it doesn't work and Morzaun finds out–"

"I know, but I can't live with killing the boy. Can you?"

Sicarii averted her gaze, her eyes glossy with unshed tears. "Of course I don't want to kill him, but it would be a lie if I said I wasn't afraid. Your uncle is not someone to trifle with on the best of days."

Zeeran scooped up her hands, drawing her attention back to him. "You said you trusted me; I'm asking you to do so now. Morzaun will never know, and this child will have the opportunity to grow up someplace safe. You and I can make sure of that."

Sicarii sighed as if the weight of Virgamor rested on her shoulders but then stepped closer. She rested her forehead against his chest, and his heart responded with a happy lurch.

"Alright," she whispered. "Let's find him a new home."

* * *

Zeeran laid the young prince down on the soft grass, the trickle of moonlight between the clouds and trees his only guide in the darkness. He stood at the edge of a clearing, nestled among a forest of pine and birch, hidden from view. Across the plain of tall grass, flickers of fire and candlelight shimmered like stars in the night. His family had passed through this village when they first arrived in Izarden, and Zeeran knew the people here were kind. They had offered them respite from their travels, and the village's isolation in the thick forest away from the kingdom's capital made it an ideal location to leave the prince.

He glanced down at the boy resting peacefully at his feet. This place would be better for him; Zeeran truly believed that. Delran would only corrupt the lad, mold the child into a version of himself. The prince would become another tyrant, ambitious and merciless.

Blue light encompassed Zeeran's fingertips. The boy would never remember his noble bloodline. Morzaun would never know the prince was alive, thus giving him a chance to live. The situation wasn't ideal, perhaps, but this was the only solution Zeeran could conjure that satisfied both his uncle's demands and his conscience.

His aura flowed over the prince, surrounding him in a soft blue glow. Zeeran muttered the incantation, and as memories pulled from the boy's mind, the images barreled through his thoughts. Time slowed, and in those moments Zeeran learned who the prince was—his likes and dislikes, every injury he'd incurred, each time his mother had wrapped him in a loving embrace.

Zeeran's chest constricted and tears pricked at his eyes. No, the situation was far from perfect, and bringing the boy here—knowing this was the only option to protect him—did little to ease the guilt.

The spell ended, and Zeeran heaved a sigh. The task was done, and he couldn't change it now.

A branch snapped behind him, and he jumped in response, turning to face the shadows. Sicarii pushed through the low branches, and the moonlight illuminated her pale skin as she stepped out of the trees.

"I don't understand how I can be sick when I lost everything in my stomach the first time."

Zeeran grinned. "I warned you."

"You did, and now I'm dreading doing this again."

He scooped up her hand and gave it a squeeze. "The more you travel with me, the easier it will be."

Sicarii lifted one of her dark brows. "Do you anticipate me traveling with you much once we've completed our task?"

Zeeran shrugged. "I can hope. You could accompany me on trips to Rowenport. Perhaps one day I could even take you to Verascene."

Her eyes widened. "To the island where your family lives? I don't think that's a good idea."

"I didn't say to meet *them*. My plan included only the two of us on a beach with a picnic lunch, though I wouldn't mind introducing you to my family someday."

Sicarii pulled her hand away and brushed past him. "Perhaps someday." She turned to face him after a few paces and smiled, but Zeeran sensed her words were not genuine. Something about meeting his family unsettled her, that much was clear, but he had no intention of pushing the matter. Besides, he needed to reconcile before even attempting such a thing.

"Where should we leave him?" Sicarii gestured to the prince. "We need to do this before he wakes up."

"I have a house in mind. The people of this village are generally kind, but there is a family I feel confident will take him in."

Sicarii turned toward the village and swept her braid over her shoulder. "It's late. I suspect most of them have retired for the night. We shouldn't have any problem leaving him without being seen."

Zeeran nodded and bent over to scoop the boy into his arms. He lifted him with a grunt. "Let's go."

They followed a dirt path across the plain and into the tiny community which consisted of a dozen cottages and several animal pens. Many of the flickering candles were now extinguished, and their black cloaks allowed them to blend in with the shadows. Zeeran stopped in front of one of the larger cottages and carefully laid the young prince on the ground near the door. The boy's entire life had changed tonight, and Zeeran would never forget his hand in it. The reminder that the child would be better off here was the only thing that kept his somewhat guilt suppressed.

Zeeran grabbed Sicarii's hand and led her around the corner of the cottage.

"What now?" she whispered.

"We need to alert them so he isn't out here all night." Zeeran glanced around until his gaze fell on a tin pail. That would do.

He reached sideways, grabbed the metal bucket, and shuffled to the corner of the cottage. With the snap of his arm, the pail flew toward the cottage door and clanked against the ground.

Movement sounded from inside the cottage, and Zeeran held his breath, peering around the wall. The door opened with a creak, and a woman wearing a nightdress and holding a candle stepped outside. She gasped when her gaze landed on the prince and quickly crouched at his side.

The concern in her expression was enough to reassure Zeeran. The lad would be well taken care of here.

"Beth? What's wrong?" A deep voice penetrated the darkness, and a second figure joined the woman. "Who is this?"

"I don't know," Beth replied. "I've never seen him before, but we can't leave him. Let's bring him inside, and we'll figure out where he came from once he wakes."

Zeeran leaned back against the wall and breathed a sigh of relief.

"We should go," Sicarii whispered.

He nodded and, taking her hand, led her through the village and back down the dirt path to the forest. Once they had reached the cover of the trees, he stopped and turned to face her. "Ready to go home?"

The moonlight caught her green eyes as they searched his face. "Yes, but first I want to thank you."

"For what? I haven't done anything."

Sicarii shook her head and withdrew one of her daggers. She ran her finger over the blade, her brows drawn into a tight line. "For stopping me from using this. I would have regretted it the rest of my life, but I didn't see another way. When Morzaun gives an order, I've learned to obey. I've seen what becomes of those who do not keep their word to him."

"What do you mean?"

"It doesn't matter. My point is I'm glad you were here. I'm glad you came up with this idea." She shifted on her feet several times, and with an abruptness that startled him, leaned forward and kissed his cheek.

Zeeran's face heated, and his body thrummed with energy, ready to explode. Sicarii backed up a step, averting her gaze. "We should go now."

"Are you sure you don't want to thank me some more?"

She narrowed her eyes, but he didn't miss the slight raise of her lips.

“I think that’s quite enough for the time being. I wouldn’t want it to go to your head.”

Zeeran stepped forward and took her hand, threading his fingers between hers. “It isn’t my head I’m concerned about.” He tapped a finger against his chest. “This organ is far more susceptible to your charms and much harder to heal, even with magic.”

“I suppose I’d better be careful then.” She tilted her chin up, bringing her lips closer—close enough that it would take nothing more than for him to lean forward to capture them. How would she react if he did? The desire to kiss Sicarii had threatened him before, and the only thing that maintained his restraint was the discomfort she exhibited.

But that discomfort seemed to vanish more with each passing day. Perhaps he wouldn’t kiss Sicarii tonight, but one day he would, and Zeeran suspected it would be the grandest victory he would ever know.

CHAPTER SIXTEEN

Subtle Threats

Morning came far too early for Zeeran. Birdsong that he normally greeted with a smile only made him duck beneath his covers and wish to block out the sound. He and Sicarii had returned mere hours before sunrise, and after sleeping on the floor at the inn and seeing to a day full of risky missions and high emotions, he remained exhausted.

Perhaps he should sleep in.

His mind wandered to the prince. How did the boy fare? Part of Zeeran wished to return to the village to be certain the child was in good hands, but he trusted his instincts. The family he'd chosen to leave the boy with were good people, and they'd see to his needs.

On the other hand, he wished to visit the palace if for no other reason than to see the panic on Delran's face when he discovered his son and only heir had disappeared. The entire city was likely abuzz with the news.

Zeeran sat up and stretched his arms over his head. He and Sicarii had made quite the team yesterday. The woman's beauty had drawn him in the moment they met, despite the scars lining her face, but it was her mysterious past that kept him intrigued. The more he learned about her, the more he liked her. She displayed a tough exterior, one many would find intimidating, but beneath her hard façade was another person altogether. She had a gentle side—a vulnerable side that he wished to know.

And their time together during the mission had given him that opportunity. He still didn't know how Sicarii had received her scars, but he understood the fear he so often saw in her emerald gaze was linked to them. She'd stated his uncle was not responsible for the markings, which had come as a relief, but Zeeran suspected *some* man was. It explained the unease he saw her exhibit whenever he'd drawn near at first.

However, Sicarii seemed to have overcome her wariness in tandem with trusting him. She had kissed him on the cheek, after all.

The same heat he'd felt last night rushed to the tip of his ears. On second thought, he didn't require more sleep—not when he had the opportunity to spend time with Sicarii while his uncle was away.

Zeeran slipped off his makeshift cot and dressed. The morning light greeted him when he left the cottage, and although his heart tugged him in the direction of Sicarii's cottage, he needed to check his traps before indulging his desire to see her. Winter would soon be upon them, and the cold weather meant an ebb in opportunity. He needed to sell enough pelts to hold him over until spring.

He checked and reset each of his traps within an hour and brought in two foxes to skin. His stomach grumbled by the time he had them hung, and with no sign of Sicarii, he decided a light breakfast would be his next course.

After slicing some bread, Zeeran sat at the table tapping his finger against the wood. Why did he feel so anxious? He had spent time with Sicarii the last two days, even slept in the same room as her, and not once felt this nervous. Her kiss, while only a simple gesture of gratitude, had changed everything. They had entered some strange place where their relationship had gone beyond friendship but not quite grown into more.

And he wanted more, but taking things slowly with the woman was important. She had a past he'd yet to unravel, and whatever trauma she'd experience would affect her future.

A knock sounded from the door, and Zeeran pushed off his stool so abruptly it toppled over. He scolded his feet for carrying him with such haste that his breathing grew heavy. This was ridiculous. He needed to get a handle on himself. Sicarii wasn't the type to be charmed by an enamored man.

Not that he was enamored.

Zeeran opened the door, and the moment his eyes settled on the dark-haired beauty his lips lifted without permission.

"Good morning," she said. "I thought you might sleep in, but it seems you've been busy." Sicarii gestured to the two foxes hanging from a wooden beam next to his cottage.

Zeeran leaned against the doorframe. "If I finish my chores early, I have more time to relax in the afternoon."

Her gaze dropped to the ground. "Of course you would want to relax after yesterday. I should probably do the same. Morzaun may have another mission for us once he's returned."

"Possibly." Zeeran reached out and took her chin between his thumb and forefinger. He lifted until her green eyes met his. "We could relax together. *Or*, I believe someone promised to assist in my training."

A smile brightened her expression, and Zeeran's stomach somersaulted. He dropped his hand and cleared his throat. "That is, if you still think you can manage my obvious skills."

She chuckled, and her gaze wandered over him appraisingly. "Unless you've improved greatly since last time, I imagine it will take little."

"I don't believe my skill could have gotten worse, put it that way."

"That would have been difficult, indeed."

Zeeran threw his head back and laughed. "How cruel of you to agree with me. Surely I wasn't so bad?"

She tilted her head from side to side with a smug grin. "I suppose I've seen worse...from children."

He pursed his lips and gripped the doorframe to keep from lunging forward and scooping the woman into his arms. "You're lucky you came armed; otherwise, I would have to repay your insults with a bit of revenge."

"I'm motivating you to give me your best. Grab your sword and meet me outside."

Zeeran flourished his hand and bowed. "As you wish."

Minutes later, he stood across from Sicarii, sword held at the ready. The two of them danced across the meadow, and although the woman bested him every single round, Zeeran found he didn't mind. His pride remained intact because he'd accepted Sicarii's skill far outmatched his own a long time ago. She moved with a grace and agility that he would likely never possess, and watching her do so captivated him.

"Are you even trying?" Sicarii asked when she disarmed him for what had to be the fiftieth time. "Or have I exhausted you completely."

"I believe the problem is a mixture of lack of skill and exhaustion," said Zeeran. "Likely more the former, though."

"Then perhaps it's time to fine tune your movements." She sheathed her dagger and stepped closer, immediately drawing a reaction from his heart. She guided his sword to the sheath at his waist, and Zeeran slipped it inside. Then, her dainty fingers positioned his arm in a pose meant for blocking. She grabbed his waist and angled it before moving on to his feet. Each touch disarmed him further, and his mind forgot all notion of fighting.

When Sicarii straightened, she met his gaze. One sweep over his expression drew her brows together. "What's the matter?"

A surge of hesitation gave him time to consider the desire urging his muscles to move. It was a difficult thing to ride the line between his wants and moving too quickly. If he made Sicarii uncomfortable, he might well lose her altogether, including her friendship.

Slowly, Zeeran wrapped his arm around her waist and pulled her closer. Her breath hitched when his fingers splayed over her lower back, her hands lifting to his chest. For several moments, he seemed capable of nothing more than staring into her eyes.

Her lips parted, but no words came out, which was fine by Zeeran as he planned to take them for himself. He leaned closer, tilting his head to one side, and Sicarii gripped his coat in her fists, pulling him in.

"Well. I hadn't expected this."

The sound of Morzaun's voice doused the elation building inside Zeeran's chest. Sicarii relinquished her hold of him and flew out of his arms. Her cheeks tinted a deep red, and she turned her gaze to the forest.

Zeeran faced his uncle and offered the man a nod of acknowledgement while pushing down his frustration. "Uncle, how was your trip?"

Morzaun's gaze bounced between Zeeran and Sicarii, and his eyes narrowed. "It went well. I found precisely who I was looking for."

Zeeran's brows shot to the top of his forehead. "You found Eramus? Did he wish to join us?"

His uncle chuckled. "I didn't speak to him. My son barely knew me before the shipwreck. Dropping into his life without a bit of observation would be unwise. I intend to approach him, but not before I have learned more about him–about the life he has lived since leaving the palace."

"That seems wise," said Zeeran, "but what of his magic? Surely those around him don't trust it."

"Best I can tell, the people in the village where he lives are unaware of his powers, which also explains how Delran has yet to find him. The king never ceased searching, and if the boy's powers were known, someone would likely have passed on that information."

Zeeran nodded. The people of Izarden despised magic wielders. That Eramus had survived this long without revealing his ability was impressive. Zeeran recalled when magic first took hold of him. Control was difficult, and often his emotions had drawn out his aura without permission.

Perhaps his cousin was possessed of a milder temperament.

"When will you return?" asked Zeeran.

"Soon, but that is of no concern to you at present. I want to know whether the two of you found success."

Sicarii tensed, and her pleading expression encouraged Zeeran to take charge.

"We were successful," he answered coolly.

Morzaun's expression brightened. "The prince is no longer an obstacle, then?"

Perhaps he shouldn't have been irritated with his uncle's reaction, but the feeling rooted in Zeeran's core. Did the man truly take no issue with the murder of an innocent child? Zeeran fisted his hands, his nails digging into his palm. "The boy will not stand in the way of our plans. Delran has lost his heir."

"Bravo. This is good news. I confess my confidence in your ability to succeed was lacking. But this...this proves you both capable. Now we are well on our way to dethroning Delran and establishing real peace in Virgamor."

Zeeran forced a smile. Murder didn't feel much like peace.

His uncle cocked his head, studying him. Could he sense Zeeran's bubbling frustration?

"Sicarii, I need a moment with my nephew," said Morzaun. "You and I will talk later about your next assignment."

With one quick look of concern aimed at Zeeran, Sicarii left them alone in the clearing. Morzaun didn't speak until the thud of her cottage door filled the silence. "What's bothering you?"

"You sent me on a mission to murder someone—a *child*. Am I not allowed to be frustrated with that?"

"The boy was in the way of our plans, Zeeran. Murdering the innocent is never ideal, but we must do what is best for the greater good. Eramus will sit on the throne of Izarden. We will have the respect we deserve, and the kingdom will finally be at peace. That is our goal. The loss of the child is...regrettable, but necessary."

No. Not necessary. Zeeran had found a way around Morzaun's command that preserved the child's life while still removing him from the man's path. There were ways to accomplish their goals without stealing the life of those who had done nothing wrong. But Zeeran would never reveal what had transpired last night, for Morzaun would never approve. Sicarii was right to fear the man if he could so easily dismiss the guilt of taking a young boy's life, and it gave Zeeran cause to wonder—cause to reconsider the allegiance he'd pledged.

He wanted Delran removed from the throne. Anyone might be a better ruler than the current king. But how they achieved their goal was just as important, and Zeeran wasn't so sure he shared his uncle's philosophy.

Zeeran stepped closer to Morzaun and dropped his voice to a low but firm tone. "Don't ever ask me to do that again. I want justice. I want peace. But that is not the way I wish to obtain them."

Morzaun's expression turned dark. "I'm not asking you to agree with my methods, Zeeran, but if you wish to be a part of this, then you will obey my instruction whether it goes against every naïve, misplaced moral in your bones. You are a traitor to Izarden, and do not think for one moment Delran would offer you an ounce of mercy." He pressed a finger to Zeeran's chest. "Delran will have you executed without a second thought. He doesn't tolerate those who betray him, just as I do not."

The warning, though subtle, penetrated Zeeran's soul like a dagger of ice. Chills stormed over his skin, the threat of danger almost tangible. Weeks ago, he wouldn't have thought his uncle capable of harming his family despite what had occurred between the man and Zeeran's parents. Now, he knew better, and fear settled over him, an ominous cloud waiting to unleash its fury.

But there was little he could do to change the circumstances. Saving Morzaun had marked him a traitor. His family would never take him back, and he would be a hunted man the rest of his days if Delran was not dealt with.

"I understand," Zeeran whispered.

Morzaun pulled away, seemingly satisfied. “Good, because we have a great deal of work to do.”

CHAPTER SEVENTEEN

Meeting Family

Several months later…

Soft thuds joined the quiet sound of bubbling water as Zeeran drummed his fingers against the table. Morzaun stood next to the hearth, leaning against the stone chimney. Exhaustion left Zeeran's eyes droopy, and although there was much to do now that the weather had begun to warm, he struggled to find the motivation. Every day dragged on with the same monotony.

"How soon will Sicarii return with word about Dunivear?" he asked.

Morzaun chuckled, removing the pot from the fire and proceeding to make their morning tea. Zeeran joined his uncle with each sunrise now. At first, he'd welcomed the offer, believing their time together would amount to more trust, but the two of them spoke little about Morzaun's plan. His uncle remained as closed off as ever, and anytime Zeeran prodded for information Morzaun responded with less than enthusiasm.

So, Zeeran had steered clear of asking for details with the exception of one frequent topic in particular: Sicarii and her missions.

Morzaun had kept her busy with his orders in the months following their escapade with the prince. She never spent more than a few days at her home in the clearing before Morzaun sent her off on yet another mission, often someplace far away. Weeks would pass before Zeeran would see her again, but she always gave him a large portion of her time when she came home despite the exhaustion he noted in her features. Perhaps that was what worried him most–that Morzaun was pushing her to a breaking point.

"I don't expect Sicarii back for some time," said Morzaun. "I've sent her to make observations...among other things. She'll return once I'm satisfied with the information she's collected."

Zeeran bit his tongue. Morzaun had used the amulet to check in on her every few days, and Zeeran had requested to do the same–had even asked to assist her with *the mission.* But Morzaun refused to tell him Sicarii's precise location, and since Zeeran had never traveled to Dunivear, he couldn't transport there himself. The entire situation was maddening.

"Relax, Zeeran." Morzaun sat two cups of tea down on the table and joined Zeeran in the chair across from him. "Sicarii is fine. You should focus less on her and more on your training."

"My training has gone awry. It seems the more I practice with the sword, the more my magic struggles. I can't understand it."

His power had declined over the last few months. Some days his spells performed normally while others he struggled with even the simplest of incantations. His parents and brother had never experienced difficulty or lapses in their power, but Feya had. His family had always believed Feya's lack of ability stemmed from fear of her own power, but now Zeeran wondered if there was more to it than that. He had no fear of magic, after all.

Morzaun's forefinger rubbed circles on his cup. "Are you certain you are taking care of yourself? Adequate sleep, eating properly—"

"It isn't that." Zeeran tempered his frustration. His uncle didn't understand. The man's power had been ripped from him by someone else. He'd never had to worry about slowly losing his abilities and wondering *why* they seemed to be diminishing. The notion of not having magic scared Zeeran. It had been a constant companion since he was ten years old, and having such power at his fingertips offered a comfort and protection he didn't want to live without.

Zeeran sipped his tea, and the liquid warmed him from his core. "I don't know how to describe it. I can feel the presence of my power, but it's as though I don't have access to it, at least not completely."

"I see. And your spells? You can still summon them?"

"Yes, but often with far less power. Once I summon my aura, I can generally coax it into submission, but sometimes it doesn't want to appear. It's much like lighting a fire in the rain."

"And only your power seems to be affected?"

Zeeran shook his head. "No. I often feel exhausted, and no matter how much I sleep, it doesn't go away."

Morzaun hummed. "Interesting."

Zeeran glanced up at his uncle and studied his contemplative expression. "Do you have any idea what could be causing it?"

The man's dark eyes settled on him, and for several moments he said nothing. "Afraid not." Morzaun finished his tea in three big gulps and pushed the cup aside. "You should get some rest. In a few days, I hope to visit Eramus again, and I want you to come with me."

"Come with you? For what purpose?" Zeeran wasn't against leaving; in fact, he was happy to be given the option of tagging along. He'd spent a great deal of time alone with Sicarii away and Morzaun off watching, and finally speaking to, his son. But his uncle would never ask Zeeran to accompany him without purpose, and Zeeran wanted to know the reason before agreeing to go.

"Eramus has kept his power hidden for years," said Morzaun. "He has decent control, but the strength of his spells has not reached its full potential. My son needs training, and there is only so much I can do without my powers, but you can help him in ways I can't."

Zeeran drank his remaining tea and sighed. "Very well, I'll come with you, but I don't know how much training I can help with given my current difficulties."

"With some rest, I imagine you'll be up for it," said Morzaun. "I'm confident that's all you need. We'll go in a few days."

"I hope you're right." Because without his power, Zeeran felt vulnerable. Without his power, his usefulness to Morzaun evaporated.

* * *

Zeeran stood outside his cottage, his face to the sun, allowing the warmth to chase away the early morning chill. At least the temperature would be more pleasant where he and Morzaun were going. Izarden fared well during the winter, ignorant to the difficulty of living through the heavy snowstorms that often raged within Selvenor. It had certainly taken Zeeran time to adjust to the harsh weather given his life on the island had not acclimated him to snow or temperatures that made him feel much like the shards of ice that dangled from his roof the last few months.

The thought sent a shiver down Zeeran's spine, and he rubbed his hands together vigorously. Perhaps he should take a few days to visit Verascene. He'd considered the idea for months, but the thought of seeing his family—of discovering that they had no desire to see *him*—had kept his feet firmly on Selvenor's soil.

Morzaun's cottage door swung open, and the man crossed the clearing. He stopped in front of Zeeran and tugged at the black cloak hugging his shoulders. "Ready?"

"I suppose. It's not as though I need much preparation. You've spoken to Eramus on several occasions now, so my magic won't be a shock to him."

"I have spoken to him about a great many things, but there is much he doesn't know." Morzaun drew closer, and his eyes flashed with a dark look that nearly made Zeeran shudder. "You will not reveal that I'm his father."

"If that's your wish, but I don't understand why—"

"Understanding is not required." Morzaun's clipped words struck Zeeran in the chest. If he'd learned anything since joining his uncle, it was that the man had little patience and was quick to anger. Zeeran had no desire to test either attribute.

"I won't reveal anything."

Morzaun gave a curt nod and backed away a pace. "Good. Then we can depart."

Zeeran reached out and gripped his uncle by the cloak near the man's shoulder. Morzaun had taken him to the forest outside of Eramus's village weeks ago so that Zeeran would know the location and be capable of transporting there should the need arise. The village was secluded, which had certainly aided in Eramus remaining safely hidden from the king of Izarden, and according to Morzaun, the villagers had only recently become aware that a magic wielder lived among them. How long it would take for word to reach Delran was anyone's guess.

"Have you considered asking him yet?" Zeeran shifted on his feet and winced, wishing he could tuck the question back into his mind.

"When I decide to ask Eramus to join us is of no concern to you. He's not ready at present. Let that suffice."

"Yes, Uncle."

Zeeran drew a deep breath and began muttering the incantation, but his words were cut short when Morzaun ripped from his grasp. Following the man's gaze, Zeeran's eyes found the source of his interrupted spell. Sicarii strode toward them, her black hair flowing freely in the shallow breeze, her skin paler than he remembered. The woman's cheeks had thinned and lost the warm pallor they once possessed, and her clothes hung loosely against her frame.

Her condition twisted Zeeran's stomach into knots. He'd been right to worry his uncle pushed her too hard, and if the man insisted on sending her away again, he would give his protests.

But for now, Zeeran focused on restraining himself from darting forward and sweeping Sicarii into his arms. Though they remained only friends, his heart yearned for more. Perhaps if Morzaun allowed her to rest from her travels, they would have enough time together to sort out their strange relationship.

"I wasn't expecting you back so soon," said Morzaun, his brows drawing tight.

"The guards began to take notice of my presence. I thought it best to remove myself from Dunivear for a time. I'm no good as a spy if they become suspicious of me. Besides, I could use the respite."

She shifted on her feet as if the confession wounded her pride. Zeeran suspected it did. Sicarii was never one to admit weakness, especially not to Morzaun.

His uncle looked her over, his head tilted in contemplation. "You and I should discuss things now." Morzaun turned to Zeeran. "I sense Eramus is in need of me, but not in *dire* need. You will go to him. Let him know I will be along shortly."

Zeeran opened his mouth, but Morzaun held up his hand. "Go. I won't be long. And be cautious. Eramus isn't likely to trust you."

Going to see Eramus intrigued Zeeran, but he had no desire to leave Sicarii when she'd just arrived. He wanted to speak with her—to ensure she was well. But more importantly, he wanted to step in if Morzaun sent her back to Dunivear or anywhere else for that matter. She clearly needed a break, and Zeeran didn't trust his uncle to give her one.

"There are things I wish to discuss with Sicarii as well." Zeeran crossed his arms. "I'd like some reassurance that she'll still be here when I get back."

Morzaun's expression twisted with annoyance. "She shall. Now, go."

Zeeran glanced at Sicarii, and she offered him a small smile that eased the tension in his chest. They could talk once he returned.

Whirling his hands through the air, blue light erupted from his palms. The familiar incantation fell from his mouth, and the world around him contorted into a smear of color before righting itself again. A shadowed forest surrounded Zeeran, along with the soft sounds of wildlife deep in a melodic performance. The birds whistled in the canopy of green leaves above him, and the stir of smaller creatures rustled the branches and dried leaves littering the forest floor. It was a peaceful place, one that welcomed anyone in need of solitude. Perhaps he would bring Sicarii here someday, if for no other reason than to ensure they could have a discussion entirely undisturbed.

As he left the coverage of the forest to enter a nearby meadow, Zeeran inhaled the warm air. The sweet scent of flowers filled him, and he found himself wishing summer would soon arrive in Selvenor. He leaned against the thick trunk of an oak at the edge of the clearing and stared out over the grassy plain. He could barely make out the dirt path leading into the forest on the opposite side, a narrow trail that wove to the village where his cousin had spent the last decade of his life.

Many questions had consumed Zeeran the moment Morzaun mentioned he'd found Eramus. Why would a boy, the son of a princess, come to this secluded village after he'd washed ashore following a storm? Had he feared Delran even as a child?

Morzaun had answered those questions in time, no doubt curious himself. Although the storm hadn't claimed Eramus's life, it had stolen his memory. His name was the only thing he *could* remember from his life before the shipwreck.

A pang of sympathy flooded over Zeeran. He couldn't imagine forgetting himself in such a way, losing all memory of his family and childhood. Those memories were precious treasures, ones that, if removed from the safe depths of his mind, haunted him. Called to him. Fueled his longing for home.

Soft muttering drew him out of his thoughts. Zeeran scanned the meadow, and his gaze landed on the man stalking into the tall grass. Although Zeeran had never met his cousin, he knew him at once. With his dark hair and eyes, Eramus looked much like his father.

Eramus came to a stop mere yards from Zeeran and stooped over to pluck a yellow flower from the grass. He stared at it with a contemplative expression that quickly turned into a scowl. "It isn't fair. I've done nothing to deserve him hunting me like some animal."

A grin pulled at Zeeran's lips. Irritation about being hunted was something he could understand. With amusement in his tone, he folded his arms and announced his presence. "Life is rarely fair."

CHAPTER EIGHTEEN

The Oath

Eramus spun around, and his eyes searched the meadow until they found Zeeran. His cousin's brows puckered with clear confusion.

Zeeran pushed away from the oak tree and stepped toward him. "Born with the abilities the likes of which the world has never seen, the power to save Virgamor from the destruction of selfish men, and yet we are the ones hunted. Hated. They will never appreciate us for what we are. Respect and acceptance...they are meaningless to people like us."

"Who are you?"

The caution in Eramus's tone made Zeeran chuckle. He couldn't hold him at fault for being leery, of course, but it was entertaining all the same. "He said you would be suspicious. I suppose I can't blame you for that, not with the way your people have treated you."

"He? You mean Morzaun?"

"Yes. He'll be joining us soon, but I think he sensed you needed guidance." Though how exactly Morzaun could sense such a thing, Zeeran didn't know. Was it some sort of paternal instinct? Did his parents ever sense his wavering allegiance to Morzaun or the loneliness that gripped him into the late hours of the night?

Zeeran shook the questions away. "Unfortunately, Morzaun thought I would make a suitable substitute until he could come himself, but I'm no good at this sort of thing."

Eramus's lips pulled to one side with his barely concealed scowl. "Why would he send you in the first place?"

"We're family. That must count for something." Zeeran held out his hand in greeting. "The name's Zeeran."

For several moments, Eramus simply stared at the gesture. His gaze lifted, and he left Zeeran's empty hand hovering in the air as he spoke. "You can use magic. My mother spoke of you."

That took Zeeran by surprise, but he didn't allow it to show in his expression. Eramus had supposedly lost his memories after the shipwreck. Curious. Perhaps he ought to utilize the opportunity to get a feel for his cousin's loyalties. "She spoke of me? Nice things, I hope. I always liked Aunt Senniva. Shame I didn't come to know her better before...well, you understand. Boils my blood, what happened, but Sytal got what he deserved in the end."

Rather than take the bait with a response, Eramus massaged his temple. "My mother was your aunt?"

"That is how the whole cousin deal works."

"You're my cousin?"

Zeeran lifted a brow and looked the man over again. Perhaps Morzaun had made a mistake in hoping to place his son on the throne. He certainly didn't seem very bright, unless...

Had Morzaun not mentioned Zeeran's family? His uncle had told him he'd explained the origins of magic to his son. While he may not have revealed himself as Eramus's father, surely he had spoken of Zeeran's parents? He could think of no reason that bit of information should be withheld.

Zeeran heaved a frustrated sigh. "Yes, Eramus. I was under the impression Morzaun had discussed this with you, but it appears I'm mistaken. Your father and my mother were siblings. You were told about the three children who found the Virgám, were you not?"

Eramus nodded, and Zeeran continued, "Right. So, there was your father and both of my parents. They are the original wielders of magic. Passed their abilities on to us, although we are not nearly as strong as they are. Bit frustrating, that."

"Yelene and Aldeth are your parents?"

Zeeran narrowed his eyes. How could Eramus, who had only just learned of their connection, know his parents' names? "That's correct, but how did you–"

A soft whizzing cut him off as Morzaun's body materialized before them. His fingers clenched the round amulet hanging from his neck, and the blue glow emanating from the gem in its center faded once the black dust swirled into Morzaun's familiar form.

Morzaun blinked, likely in an effort to force the melded colors into clarity. "Ah, Eramus. I was hoping Zeeran would find you."

"He showed up a few minutes after I did," said Zeeran.

"Very good. I've wished for the two of you to meet for a while."

Eramus turned to face his father fully. "Then why didn't you mention him or my aunt and uncle? Why does it feel as though you are hiding things from me?"

Morzaun sighed. "I never wanted to overwhelm you. Between training and the details of your past, I feared it would be too much to tell you everything at once. Forgive me. I only have your best interests at heart."

Zeeran crossed his arms and bit down on his lip. Morzaun had never shown him that sort of patience when he asked questions. Any effort to get answers about the plan to overthrow Delran were met with orders of silence or glares that achieved it without words. Zeeran had spent months working to earn Morzaun's trust, and Eramus seemed to have garnered it despite the suspicion in his tone. Despite his lack of knowledge. Why could Zeeran not earn the same respect from his uncle?

"I thought Zeeran could assist with training today." Morzaun stepped closer to them, his lips turned upward in a smile. "Unlike me, he can wield magic, and spells are much easier to learn when you have a proper example."

A *proper* example? Zeeran held in a scoff. Well, if Morzaun wanted him to teach Eramus properly, he would do so. He moved to stand opposite them. "Where should we start? Oh, I know." He held his palms up, facing them directly in Eramus's path. Blue light flickered around Zeeran's fingers. "The *impetras* will do."

"Zeeran." A growl of warning rumbled from Morzaun's throat.

"Just a bit of fun. I'll go easy on him."

Or not. For the first time in weeks, Zeeran felt completely in control of his magic. And it felt *good.*

His aura bent to his will with little thought, and a wave of blue light barreled across the empty space between him and Eramus. The spell crashed into his cousin's chest, sending his body hurling backwards at least a dozen yards. Eramus landed on the ground, and he gasped as though the collision had knocked the air from his lungs.

A hint of guilt prodded at Zeeran's stomach. Perhaps he'd been slightly overzealous.

"Zeeran!" Morzaun grabbed him by the collar and yanked him closer, his dark eyes glaring with fury. "This isn't a game. Eramus isn't ready for that kind of duel."

"And the best way to get him ready is to knock him down a few times. I recall it being great motivation for me."

"You had your father and I to guide you. And your brother." Morzaun released him with a shove. "Don't do it again."

Zeeran clenched his fists, watching his uncle turn and walk away, the breeze catching the tail of his black cape. Eramus didn't need to be coddled. If Morzaun wanted his son on the throne, they should make sure he could handle the position, not baby him with soft training and mercy. Eramus was a part of their plan, and if he proved too weak, he might ruin it completely.

"I don't recall you being so overprotective when you trained Ladisias," said Zeeran. "You certainly haven't shown me such gentleness the last few months. But of course you would go easy on *him.*"

Morzaun spun around, the look of warning in his eyes a near tangible threat. “If you don’t like the way I do things, then go back to Verascene.”

Back to Verascene? His uncle knew he couldn’t simply run home. Zeeran had betrayed his family. He’d abandoned them to fight at Morzaun’s side. Yet despite the sacrifices Zeeran had made, Morzaun seemed perfectly content to dismiss him.

Zeeran turned away from them as Morzaun assisted Eramus from the ground, muttering encouragement about defensive spells. He shouldn’t allow the exchange to irritate him further, but he found himself unable to lock the emotion away.

“Conjure your shield,” said Morzaun, “and Zeeran can send a small wave of magic toward you.”

Zeeran met Morzaun’s threatening gaze and huffed. “Whatever you say.” He waved his hands, summoning his aura, and fired a stream of magical energy at his cousin, suppressing his power into a beam barely visible in the afternoon light. It crashed into Eramus’s shield. His cousin gasped, but the shield held.

Morzaun clapped in support and congratulated his son, the pride in his voice fueling Zeeran’s frustration into something more palpable. His spell responded to the shift in emotion, and more energy flowed across the meadow. The force of the attack ate away at Eramus’s shield, and the blue dome dissipated.

Once again, Eramus was tossed onto his back, gasping for air.

“I told you that’s enough!” Morzaun shouted.

His uncle started forward, but before he could take more than a few steps, a flash of blue light halted his feet. It shot past him and smacked Zeeran square in the chest, throwing him to the ground with a hard thud. Zeeran groaned.

Eramus had some fight in him after all.

Zeeran clambered to his feet. He would not be made a fool by someone who had little experience with magic. He whirled his hands, but movement across the meadow stole his attention. Zeeran dropped his hands to his side and squinted at the approaching figure.

A woman with long golden hair drifted over the grass as though she walked on air, her steps light and a warm glow on her cheeks. Both Eramus and Morzaun followed Zeeran's gaze, and the latter scowled when his eyes fell upon the woman.

She came to a stop next to Eramus and smiled. "Hello. I'm sorry for interrupting your training, but I was hoping to steal you for the afternoon." She leaned closer to him and whispered something more that Zeeran couldn't hear. Whatever it was, Eramus responded with his own whispered words and a crooked grin.

"Eramus's training is of the greatest importance," said Morzaun, his tone doing little to hide how he felt about the young woman's presence. "I'm afraid I insist he stays."

The look Eramus pinned him with nearly made Zeeran chuckle. His cousin didn't take kindly to Morzaun's demands. "I will stay, but with Evree. I think I've had enough training for today."

The wrinkle of Morzaun's nose drew out Zeeran's laughter. He wrapped his arms around his stomach, and it took him several seconds to gain control of himself enough to speak. "Looks like he'd rather spend time with her than you. Not that I blame him."

He winked at Evree, and her cheeks turned rosy again. She

ducked behind Eramus, who glared at Zeeran with a scowl even more deadly than Morzaun's. "Leave her alone."

Zeeran held up his hands. "Don't worry. I've no interest in your friend." And he didn't. The woman was lovely, but she didn't possess dark hair and eyes that haunted his thoughts. She didn't emanate a strength, hard won through a past full of secrets. What was Sicarii doing right now? Was she anxiously awaiting his return? Did she anticipate their time together as much as he did?

"Leave, Zeeran." Morzaun's cold voice pulled Zeeran's thoughts away from Sicarii.

"With pleasure," he muttered under his breath. If his uncle wanted to deal with Eramus on his own, he would happily oblige. Watching them infuriated him, and though he was loath to admit it, Zeeran recognized the burning sensation in his chest as jealousy. He'd worked hard to earn Morzaun's trust, and it seemed no matter what he did, it was never enough.

With the wave of his hands, blue light surrounded him. The world contorted in a smear of color, and the meadow faded from his view.

* * *

Zeeran stood outside Sicarii's door, his fist raised to the wood. He hesitated to knock, not because he didn't wish to, but because a bout of uncertainty filled his stomach. He hadn't seen the woman in months, and yet one glimpse of her had sent his heart into a pace more fit for running than standing still. He cared for her, that much he could admit, but was confessing the growing depths of his affections wise? What if Sicarii didn't reciprocate his feelings?

A deep breath did little to calm his nerves. He had told himself countless times there was no reason to rush things. He wanted to give Sicarii the time and space she needed, but they had only continued to build on their friendship.

When Morzaun didn't have her off on a mission, that was.

Before his uncle sent Sicarii away again, he needed clarity. He needed to know if she longed for more than their casual acquaintance. Part of him feared rejection, but an even greater part feared Sicarii cared for him. He'd never given a moment of consideration to finding a wife and settling down, at least not until he and Sicarii had gone to Izarden on Morzaun's orders. Was he truly prepared for such a life? One where he became a husband—possibly a father?

The warmth that settled in his chest at the images his mind conjured suggested he *was* ready for those things. He could clearly see himself in a quaint cottage with Sicarii by his side and a few children causing mischief. It seemed an ideal life—a quiet one devoid of missions, kings, and schemes of revenge.

But he couldn't have that life. Not yet. Delran posed a threat not only to those who could wield magic, but to all of Virgamor. The man wanted power and might never be satisfied to rule only Izarden. He'd already proven his intentions, making attacks on Dunivear and blaming them on other invaders. Many saw through the tactics, but as Izarden remained the kingdom with the most military presence in Virgamor, no one was willing to stand against them.

Until Delran was removed from the throne, Virgamor would

never know peace, and while Zeeran could leave the people to fight the battle on their own, he had no desire to spend the rest of his life in hiding. He wanted freedom, and that only came with the fall of the king.

His knuckles rapped against the door, and the shuffle of muffled footsteps sounded from inside. He held his breath until the door swung open and Sicarii stood before him. Her green eyes brightened, the sunlight catching on them like emerald gems. Her lips lifted, and the skin around her eyes crinkled.

"Come inside, Zeeran." She shifted out of the way, making room for him to enter. His heart skipped several beats. In all the time he'd known her, she'd never welcomed him into her cottage. They had spent countless hours in the meadow or forest, but never in such an intimate location as her refuge.

"Thank you," he whispered, pausing in front of her for a moment before moving deeper inside. He stopped in the center of the room and took in the details. A fire glowed in the little stone hearth, casting a warm glow over the walls, which were mostly bare but for a few feet of space where dozens of weapons hung. Daggers, javelins, swords—Sicarii had an entire arsenal of sharpened blades.

He smiled. He would have expected nothing less from her.

"How was your...trip?" Zeeran asked.

"I take it Morzaun has not given you any details." She swept past him and removed a kettle from the hearth. "Tea?"

"Yes, please."

She gestured to the table, and he crossed the room to take a seat. "No, Morzaun has not told me anything about your mission to

Dunivear, and I don't expect you to discuss it. I only wanted to know how you are doing."

Curiosity about the orders his uncle had given Sicarii did reside within him, but that was not his priority at the moment. Sicarii's face retained a pale color, and her clothes hung loosely about her arms and waist. It was clear to him that she hadn't lived in the healthiest of states the last few months, and the realization irritated him. There was no way his uncle hadn't noticed, which meant he'd allowed her to continue despite the effect the mission had on her health.

"I'm fine." She handed him a steaming cup and sat down on the chair to his left. "A bit of rest, and I'll be good as new."

"Of course." Zeeran forced a smile. He didn't want to overwhelm her with his concerns. Sicarii took pride in her solitude, in her ability to provide and care for herself, but how long should he wait before stepping in? The woman might wither away to nothing before confessing her health had deteriorated, and something told Zeeran his uncle would never worry over her. "Are you to stay for a while?"

She shook her head. "Morzaun wants me to spend some time in Izarden. I'm not sure how soon he plans to make a move against Delran, but the more information we have about the king, his guards—all of it—the better our chance of success."

"But you just got here. Surely he intends to give you time to rest."

Sicarii sipped her drink, lifting her shoulder with lazy nonchalance, but she failed to hide the furrow of her brows. "I'll stay for a few days before heading out."

"That's not enough. You've been at his beck and call for months. He can give you a few weeks to recover."

"What do you expect me to do, Zeeran? Of course I'd love to stay here for a few weeks, but if I defy him...you know how he feels about those who become worthless to him. If I'm not gathering information, spying, doing his bidding, then what value do I have?"

She looked away, moisture gleaming in her eyes. Zeeran reached over and wrapped her hand in his own. "You have value whether you are on a mission or sitting here in this cottage staring at the walls. Perhaps not to my uncle, but to me."

Sicarii squeezed his hand, and her whispered voice enveloped him like a soft summer breeze. "I know, but if I don't prove my worth to him, it could be my life on the line."

He wanted to deny it, to reassure her that his uncle would never harm her in any way, but he was no longer sure. After Morzaun had ordered them to murder an innocent child, doubt and regret had been Zeeran's constant companions. He'd lost track of how many times he'd wondered if joining Morzaun had been the right choice. He didn't regret saving the man from Ivrin and Izarden's gallows, but choosing his side...

He just didn't know anymore, and the confusion constricted his chest.

"Have you ever thought about leaving?" Sicarii whispered as though she sensed his thoughts. She glanced at him, her eyes cautious, as if the topic they'd breeched were forbidden. In a way, it was. Should Morzaun ever hear them speaking of desertion, he would be furious.

"Yes," he answered. "I think about it, but as much as I'd like to go, I would never be free. As long as Delran reigns, I'll be hunted. Living like that isn't what I want. Freedom is worth fighting for, isn't it?"

"Is that what we're really fighting for? Freedom?" She slipped her hand away and sighed. "Delran is a monster, but sometimes I wonder if Morzaun will be any better."

"Then why do you stay? You haven't betrayed Izarden. You could leave and start a new life."

Sicarii remained quiet for a minute, her fingers caressing her cup of tea. "I swore an oath to your uncle. I can't break it." Her green eyes met his. "He may not have direct access to magic, but he has his relics. I'm duty bound to him, Zeeran. Leaving isn't an option for me, but you...you still have a chance to find a fresh start."

He wanted to argue against her statement, to remind her that starting fresh was out of the question for him. The moment people learned of his abilities, he would be shunned—or worse. But his mind ignored the desire to argue that point, focusing instead on Sicarii's revelation. "What happens if you break your oath?"

Her chair scraped against the wood floor with a wail. She stood and crossed her arms over her chest. "You should go."

"Sicarii."

"Go."

The order was firm. Authoritative. But Zeeran also heard the pain in it. She didn't want him to leave, but discussing the oath with his uncle made her uncomfortable. Or, perhaps, left her on dangerous ground. The sort of scheming Morzaun was involved in required secrecy and loyalty. What better way to ensure those participating in his traitorous activity held their tongues than to bind them with magic. Zeeran still wasn't sure how his uncle had done it. The gems possessed abilities that none of them entirely understood.

But perhaps Morzaun had discovered their secrets. More than he let on.

Zeeran stood and gently touched her arm. "I'll go, but may I see you tomorrow? We don't have to discuss any of this again. I promise."

She studied his face for several moments before nodding her acceptance. Zeeran left her cottage, his emotions a chaotic mixture of frustration, rage, and fear. He considered confronting his uncle, but that would only put Sicarii in the crosshairs.

Still, a conversation with the man needed to be had. He wouldn't ask Morzaun about Sicarii's oath, but he wouldn't let him send her away again, either.

CHAPTER NINETEEN

Time and Change

An herbal smell filled Morzaun's cottage, the kettle dangling in the hearth shrieking as it exhaled a puff of steam. Zeeran had come by before the sun rose, determined to have a discussion with the man about Sicarii. His uncle seemed to understand the purpose of the visit and ordered him to take a seat at the table while he prepared tea. Perhaps a drink was not a bad idea given how anxious Zeeran felt. Morzaun's herbal concoction always calmed him, almost as if severing him from his emotions for a time.

Morzaun had said little since inviting him inside, and Zeeran wondered if he were angry about yesterday. Training Eramus had, admittedly, ignited a spark of jealousy that pushed him to unleash his spells without restraint, and while Zeeran entertained some remorse for taking his emotions out on his cousin, it had also felt good to feel fully in control of his power again. He still had no understanding of why his magic seemed to ebb and flow like a tide. He'd never had an issue with his power before, which led him to believe there was some outside force hampering it.

At least, his mind clung to the notion. The alternative–that his abilities were fading–seemed a far worse conclusion and one he refused to embrace.

"Will you be going to see Eramus today?" asked Zeeran.

"No, not for a few days. I decided to take matters into my own hands. Eramus has a distraction that needs to be handled before we can ask him to join us."

"A distraction? You mean the pretty girl who came to the meadow?"

Morzaun dropped a cup, and it rattled against the floor. He stooped to pick it up, mumbling. "Yes, that one."

"And how exactly do you plan to *handle* that distraction?" Zeeran folded his arms, glaring at his uncle's back as the man poured hot water into two cups. "Eramus seemed rather attached to her. He isn't likely to let her go on your order."

"Which is why I've hired someone to take care of the problem." Morzaun crossed the room, placed a steaming cup in front of Zeeran, and settled onto a chair. "Once she's out of the way, I'm quite certain Eramus will take no issue in joining our cause, especially if he believes Delran is responsible for the girl's demise."

Zeeran swallowed against the lump forming in his throat.

"Demise? You intend to kill her?"

"No, I'm paying someone else to do that. In fact, my plan should be well underway by now."

"But she's innocent. She has done nothing to deserve such a fate."

"The woman is in my way, simple as that." His uncle glanced at him. "Don't concern yourself over it, Zeeran. You have your own distraction. Luckily for you, Sicarii is on our side and remains valuable to me."

Zeeran's hands curled into fists beneath the table. He was no longer under any illusion that his uncle valued life. The man didn't hesitate to eliminate anyone in his way, and no one was exempt. Sicarii was there because her skills were useful, and Morzaun had allowed Zeeran to join him for the same reason. They were tools to be used and wielded, nothing more.

"If you want her to remain valuable," Zeeran began with some hesitation, "then give her some time to recover from her mission in Dunivear. She's exhausted. You can see it as well as I can."

Morzaun studied him for several long moments before heaving a sigh. "If it will put you at ease, then I will grant her permission to stay for a few weeks. By then, we'll have Eramus on board and can strategize our move against Delran."

The tension in Zeeran's shoulders released. He hadn't believed his uncle would give in to the request so easily. The decision likely wasn't made out of sympathy or concern, but the man had agreed, and regardless of the reason, Zeeran was grateful.

He took a deep drink of tea, and the liquid warmed him from the inside out, immediately soothing him in its odd euphoric way. "Am I to accompany you on your next visit with Eramus?"

"That depends. Can you control your temper and restrain your impulses?"

"I confess to getting carried away. I'll do better."

Morzaun's black brows rose. "You will. I take any attack on my son seriously."

His uncle smiled, but there was a clear warning in the man's expression. Zeeran supposed he couldn't blame him for favoring Eramus. Morzaun had been kept from his son for a long time, and after losing his wife, had become overly protective of his child. Perhaps it was natural instinct, fueled further by Morzaun's desire to see Eramus on the throne in Delran's place.

Regardless, Eramus had done nothing to Zeeran, and he would put aside his foolish jealousy. Besides, the more Morzaun threatened Sicarii, the less he wanted to remain in his uncle's company. Once they had succeeded in overthrowing Delran, he would leave the man and his son to their lives.

Yesterday, Zeeran had wrestled with his thoughts late into the night, but the sleepless hours had brought him to one conclusion. When he left, he hoped to not do so alone. All he needed now was to convince Sicarii to come with him once all this was over, and something told him he stood a real chance of convincing her to agree.

* * *

With every drop of the ax, Zeeran's muscles grew weaker. He'd already stacked a pile of firewood large enough to heat his home for the next two months, which was largely unnecessary given the last of the cold weather had started to fade, but he'd needed the distraction. After his discussion with Morzaun that morning, he'd hoped to spend the day with Sicarii. His plan had been thwarted, however, when his uncle requested to speak with her first. They'd been inside the man's cottage for nearly two hours now, and Zeeran's patience had worn thin.

Morzaun had agreed to allow Sicarii to remain a few weeks, but Zeeran found trusting the man's word more difficult than he used to. Knowing how far his uncle would go to enact their plan had opened his eyes, and all the warnings offered by his parents and brother flooded back to him. They had been right all along. Morzaun wanted revenge and would do anything to have it. Zeeran still couldn't blame him for hating Delran, but he'd joined the cause to prevent his uncle from suffering an undeserved fate.

The problem was Morzaun seemed more than content to deal punishment and suffering to those who didn't deserve it, the very thing Zeeran thought he was fighting against. His allegiance to his uncle was, in a sense, hypocritical, and he wondered more and more whether achieving freedom was worth the cost he was increasingly asked to pay.

The door to Morzaun's cottage swung open, and Sicarii caught his gaze. She smiled, which relieved him in some strange way he couldn't explain, and she marched toward him, her midnight hair tossing over her shoulders in the breeze.

She stopped in front of him as he straightened and rested the ax on the ground, her arms folded and a look of false irritation in her expression. "Someone has been meddling in my business."

Zeeran glanced around, putting on his own façade of confusion before pointing to himself. "Me? No, I'd never meddle in an assassin's business. You don't think me so foolish, do you?"

"Not only do I think it, I *know* it. You told Morzaun I needed to rest."

He shrugged. "So I told the truth...or part of the truth."

"What do you mean? There's more truth?"

"I left out the bit about you staying so I could spend time with you."

A soft rosiness filled her cheeks, but Sicarii looked pleased by the declaration. "I'm not certain you have Morzaun fooled on that front. He seems well aware, especially after..." She turned away, the tint in her face deepening to a dark red.

"Especially after my kiss was rudely interrupted?" he asked, unable to contain the smirk spreading over his lips.

"You were...were you truly going to kiss me?"

The cautious way she asked was so unlike the woman who wielded daggers. Sicarii could be entirely fearless, strong, and intimidating. But this side of her, the one that cracked with vulnerability, was the puzzle he'd worked to unravel. He still didn't have all the pieces, for she kept many of them hidden from view, but the picture he'd thus far assembled was beautiful. Each piece he connected only made him wish to complete the entire thing, to fully witness every part of her.

He took a step forward, tilting his head as he studied her. "I've wanted to kiss you for a while, but I won't do so unless it's what you want, too. I know your past haunts you, and the last thing I want is to push you someplace you aren't comfortable, to make you resent me."

"You know, when my wart says things like that it's really difficult to dislike him."

He grinned. "*Your* wart? Does that mean you finally claim me?"

"No one in their right mind would claim a wart." She shook her head, and her dark brows knitted together, but the twinkle in her green eyes betrayed the ruse. Sicarii grabbed his hand and interlocked their fingers, sending a zing up his arm.

Zeeran released the ax handle, and it thudded against the ground. He yanked on Sicarii's hand, drawing her closer, and wrapped his arm around her waist. She gasped, and her free hand slid up his chest and over his shoulder. He could kiss her now without concern she'd pull away. Everything suggested she wanted him—her firm hold on his coat, her body pressing against him, and certainly the way her eyes dropped to his lips.

But he would not kiss her yet, not until he had eliminated all doubt. He wanted the woman in his arms to feel as certain about this as he felt, and that might require more time.

Not terribly much more, though, given the ways she was currently looking at him.

Zeeran leaned forward and left a soft kiss on her nose. She closed her eyes, and her lips parted as if in anticipation. He held in a chuckle when after several moments her eyes flew open, a hint of disappointment furrowing her brows.

It wasn't his intention to tease her, and the reaction boded well for his efforts, but he would not rush things between them. Sicarii wanted him, but there were times when he still sensed her fear. It faded more with each passing day and would hopefully soon disappear completely. Until then, he would prove his devotion and continue garnering her trust.

"What do you say to spending the day in Rowenport with me?" he asked. "I have a few pelts to turn in and some shopping to do."

"That certainly sounds like the kind of resting I should be doing." She released his hand and slid both around his waist. Zeeran held her close, and Sicarii rested her head against his chest, her whispered words soft with gratitude. "Thank you for giving me time, Zeeran. I'd love to spend my days with you."

Days. Not day. His heart and stomach flopped in sync. He took Sicarii by both hands, his elation contorting his face into something sure to look embarrassingly giddy, but he found he didn't care. "Then let's go, love. We have a lot of time to make up."

CHAPTER TWENTY

Royalty Found

Zeeran leaned against the brick wall of a nearby pub while Sicarii perused a stall displaying leather belts and sheaths. Her expression held a light that had been absent upon her return from Dunivear, and he wanted to believe he'd played a part in its reappearance. She seemed at ease walking the streets of Rowenport with him today, and for a moment, he could picture a quiet life with her—one where they could visit the city for occasional necessities and spend the remainder of their time far away from the bustling crowds.

Far away from Morzaun.

Since joining his uncle, Zeeran had hoped they could eliminate Delran as a threat, thus providing all magic wielders with a sense of safety. He wanted the security for himself, but even more than that, he wanted it for his family. They'd lived on Verascene for nearly two decades, trapped on an island with few people but safe from the king of Izarden's threats. He didn't condemn his parents for choosing to raise their children in such a remote location. They had the best intentions. But he longed for freedom, for the ability to explore and live wherever he wanted without fear.

Those hopes had slowly faded, however. He still wanted those things, of course, but such security came with a price. Morzaun was not the man Zeeran remembered—not the strong, moralistic person he'd idolized for most of his life. The man had a darkness about him, a nature Zeeran had been blind to for so many years. His family had seen it. They'd tried to help him see it, too, and now he regretted ever abandoning them to join his uncle's cause.

He glanced at Sicarii and watched a smile reach her eyes as she engaged in conversation with the shopkeeper. No, he could not regret his decisions. Joining Morzaun had given him the opportunity to meet Sicarii, and that was something he would never resent. But he worried about *her* safety now more than his own. She'd made an oath with his uncle, and he needed to understand what all the exchange entailed.

Sicarii crossed the cobblestone street with a new sheath in hand. He grinned and jutted his chin toward it. "Did you truly need another one? How many weapons do you carry at a time, anyway?"

She leaned close to him, bringing a soft floral scent to his nose, and her whispered breath tickled his ear. "That's not a secret I'd reveal, but perhaps someday you can count while you remove them yourself."

His skin prickled at the implication of her words. She studied his wide-eyed expression and smirked, seemingly satisfied with the chaos she'd created in his mind.

"Shall we continue?" She gestured down the street to the few stalls that remained for them to visit, but he had half a mind to take her home right then and there. His thoughts certainly didn't revolve around shopping any longer.

"Onward, then." He pushed away from the pub, reining in his wayward thoughts, but the moment he lost the support of the solid brick wall, the world spun. The loud chatter of vendors and their customers muffled into a low rumble. His balance faltered, and he reached for the wall, clawing at the air for purchase.

"Zeeran?" Sicarii steadied him, and his fingers scraped over the rough brick exterior of the pub. Her warm hands held his trembling shoulders until the world righted itself. "Are you alright? You look so pale."

"Fine. I don't...that was odd. For a moment I felt dizzy." He rubbed a hand over his face and blinked. Whatever had ailed him seemed to have gone as quickly as it had come. Were it not for Sicarii's worried expression, he might have thought the entire thing an illusion created by his jumbled thoughts.

"Are you sure? Your color is still off."

"My color?" He chuckled and scooped up her hand. "You have my color memorized, do you?"

She gave him an incredulous look. "Don't do that, Zeeran. I'm being serious. You scared me. We should go home."

"Perhaps I overexerted myself chopping wood this morning. I have felt rather exhausted." Which was true, but what he wouldn't tell her was that his body had felt heavy and sluggish even before splitting those logs. He focused on his power, and as he suspected, something was affecting it. His aura refused to manifest.

"It's settled then," said Sicarii. "We're going back. I need to purchase one more thing before we go. Do you think you can manage a few minutes without me?"

He released her hand to fold his arms. "I'd prefer not to *manage without you*, but I think I can survive a few minutes away from your company."

She looked him over, her dark brows furrowed with concern. "Very well, but don't go anywhere. The apothecary is only a few stalls down."

"The apothecary?"

"Yes, there's an herb I need." She turned and took three steps before pausing to look over her shoulder. "Stay right there."

"Yes, love."

Her cheeks tinted, and she marched away with haste. Zeeran slumped against the wall, his shirt snagging on the brick as he slid to the ground. He closed his eyes and pulled in a deep breath. Whatever was hindering his magic had a strong effect on his stamina as well.

Not having access to his power was one thing, but zapped energy made him an easy target and useless with assisting in the plan to overthrow Delran.

Sicarii returned several minutes later, and the worry on her brow deepened when she took note of his position on the ground. She offered him her hand, and Zeeran struggled to his feet, his muscles protesting the movement.

"We need to leave," she said, her voice hushed. "I overheard some people talking inside the apothecary. The prince has been located."

Zeeran turned to her sharply. "What?"

"Word of his disappearance has spread through the kingdom the last few months. Everyone would have heard by now. The villagers we left him with must have suspected...it doesn't matter. He's been returned to Izarden, and the king believes magic was involved."

Zeeran groaned, resting his head against the wall. "If word has reached Rowenport, then it's only a matter of time before my uncle learns of it."

Sicarii nodded. "We should go home and tell him before he finds out on his own. I don't know that it will temper his wrath, but it won't make things any worse."

Her reasoning was sound, but the idea of facing Morzaun after he discovered they'd directly disobeyed his orders sent a chill slithering down his spine. He didn't worry for himself, for Morzaun would be a fool to attack when Zeeran had magic. But Sicarii didn't have that luxury.

Zeeran extended his arm and focused on the magic coursing through his veins. A blue flame appeared above his palm, sputtering as it struggled to remain ignited. "I agree. It would be best to tell Morzaun ourselves. There's just one problem—my magic is too weak to transport us right now."

She watched the tiny flame until his exhaustion extinguished it. "Then we spend the night and tell him first thing in the morning."

"First thing tomorrow," agreed Zeeran. He could only hope his power returned with the rise of the sun.

* * *

When morning arrived, Zeeran's body thrummed with a dull ache. He lay on his bed, staring up at the ceiling as light filled the room. He'd slept well given how worn the inn's mattress was, and some of his energy had returned. A bit of breakfast would help put him to rights, and then they could go home.

He held up his hand and focused on the magical energy flowing through him. A bright blue flame flickered over his palm, stronger than yesterday, albeit weaker than normal. It was enough, though, to transport them to Selvenor. The spell would likely drain him completely, but at least he could then recover in his own bed.

Unless, of course, Morzaun demanded he leave. Facing his uncle and confessing he'd disobeyed orders created a niggle of concern within him. The man didn't tolerate betrayal well, as evident by the way he spoke of Zeeran's parents.

Regardless, Zeeran held no regrets about how he and Sicarii had handled the mission. Killing an innocent child, even if the boy were Delran's heir, went against everything Zeeran believed. He understood Morzaun's need for revenge. No one could blame the man for his hatred after everything that had happened, but what right did they have to take another's life who had done nothing to them? How did murdering an innocent child make them any better than Delran?

He dressed, and a knock sounded at the door as he tugged on one of his boots. "Come in!"

The door opened partially, and Sicarii peeked inside. "How are you feeling today?"

"Well enough to travel." He slipped his foot inside the other boot and stood. "My magic is much stronger, but I imagine I'll need time to rest once we've returned."

She entered the room fully and closed the door behind her. The furrow in her brows eluded to concern, and he suspected he knew the cause. "What's the matter?"

"I went downstairs for a moment, and there's an entire crowd having breakfast."

Zeeran chuckled, shoving his arms into his coat. "And you don't like people so you scurried back up here?"

Sicarii folded her arms, pinning him with a glare. "I don't mind *some* people, but that isn't the issue. They were discussing the prince."

"And?"

"And the boy was found well over a month ago."

A month? When Sicarii had mentioned the boy's discovery yesterday, he'd thought the event had occurred only a couple weeks ago. News took time to travel, but if that much time had passed since the prince was found, the entire kingdom likely knew.

And if the entire kingdom knew, his uncle may already be aware.

"We should go," said Zeeran. "We need to speak with my uncle right away."

She nodded and crossed the room to his side. "I agree, but are you sure you're well enough?"

"To get us home? Yes. After that, you may have to drag me to my cottage."

"That's not very reassuring."

He sighed and wrapped an arm around her waist, pulling her close. "Perhaps not, but it's the truth. Something is affecting my power, Sicarii, and until I understand the cause, these episodes of exhaustion will likely continue. I won't lie to you, tell you I'm completely well when that isn't the case, but I can sense my magic and its limitations. I have enough energy to get us home safely. You can trust that."

"It isn't a lack of trust but an overabundance of concern." She lifted her hand, and her dainty finger grazed over his cheek. "I don't want anything to happen to you."

Zeeran covered her hand, pressing it into his skin and tilting his head to leave a kiss on the inside of her wrist. "I'll feel much better once we've spoken to my uncle. I confess his reaction is more concerning at the moment than my power."

"Maybe we should have listened to him."

Moisture filled her eyes, and he tightened his hold around her. "We made the right choice, and if my uncle questions our loyalty, I will do everything I can to protect you from his wrath. You have my word. Now"—he scooped up her hands and squeezed them gently—"let's go home."

CHAPTER TWENTY ONE

An Unknown Power

The meadow swirled into view, the grass a lush green with the recent spring rains. Zeeran's knees buckled, and he fell to the ground, Sicarii's hand still clutching his. She crouched and slid her arm across his shoulders, concern lining her face as deeply as her faded scars.

She glanced at the dark sky, and her brows furrowed. "We should get you inside. The weather is about to turn."

Zeeran shook his head. "We must speak with my uncle. Putting it off will not help our case, love."

"You're right. I just..." She turned back to him, and her green eyes traced over his body. "You need to rest. If he tries something, and you're too exhausted to fight back–"

"Morzaun may threaten me, but I'm his family. I don't believe he would harm me without reason. We disobeyed his orders, but we still achieved our goal of removing the prince."

Sicarii tilted her head, her expression chiding. "But we *didn't* achieve it. The prince has been located and returned to Izarden. And besides, you shouldn't have so much trust in your uncle." Her gaze dropped to the ground. "He's capable of more than you know."

He scratched the back of his head. She had a point, but they had *thought* wiping the prince's memory and taking him far from the palace would prove successful. Intentions made a difference, didn't they? Regardless, Morzaun would be a fool to try anything against someone with magic, even *exhausted* magic.

"I know you're worried," he said, "but I'm fine. Promise."

Sicarii heaved a sigh. "Alright, let's get this over with. You're coming to my cottage afterwards where I can keep an eye on you. Make sure you eat and rest."

"Is that all you intend to make me do?"

She whacked his arm, and he flinched, chuckling. Sicarii helped him from the ground, and although his legs wobbled at first, he found his footing. A long nap sounded rather appealing, especially if it involved snuggling with the woman currently clutching his arm as though she believed he might collapse at any moment. It had taken months for Sicarii to open up to him, and while she still held secrets, the remainder of her walls would eventually crumble.

They stopped in front of Morzaun's door, and Sicarii withdrew one of her daggers from the belt around her waist. Zeeran lifted a brow, and she shrugged. "Just in case."

"Do me a favor and keep it tucked at your side. There's no sense in adding to the tension."

Her grip on the hilt tightened, turning her knuckles white, but she allowed the weapon and her arm to dangle at her side. Truthfully, being prepared to take the offensive wasn't a bad idea. Morzaun would not respond well to the information they were about to deliver.

Zeeran tapped on the door, and his uncle answered a few seconds later, his expression dark. "Finally back, are you?" His eyes darted between them, and he opened the door farther with a gesture ordering them inside. "We've some things to discuss."

Morzaun knew. There was no denying the fury buried just below the surface. It laced his tone and expression, but whether this was worse than telling him themselves, Zeeran couldn't say. He did as instructed and stepped into his uncle's cottage, Sicarii tight on his heels. She sat down next to him, her dagger unsheathed and pressed against her thigh.

"The prince is alive," spat Morzaun. "The two of you failed. What I don't know is whether it was deliberate or simply poor execution."

"Both, if you would like the truth." Zeeran shifted on his chair but held Morzaun's gaze. "I refused to kill an innocent child. I stopped Sicarii from murdering him. Dethroning Delran is essential to our plan, but there are ways to go about it without harming those who have done nothing to us. I erased the boy's memories and took him to a remote village near the coast. I thought it would be enough."

Morzaun crossed his arms. "Clearly not. The boy has returned to Izarden—to Delran! You've done nothing but prolong his inevitable fate, and now it will be far more difficult to get to him."

"He's a child. Don't you think an alternative was worthy of a chance?"

"We don't have room for alternatives and mistakes, Zeeran. We're at war, and I will not sacrifice the plan I've worked tirelessly to enact to preserve the life of one boy!"

The chair screeched against the floor when Zeeran thrust himself from the seat, his fists clenched. The room spun, but he fought against the pressing exhaustion. "What makes you any better than the king! I believe in removing Delran from power as much as you do, but I will not become him in the process. We seek a better ruler–a better life for those who possess magic and those who don't. But I am not an assassin for hire, Uncle. I will not do your bidding when it boasts of *everything* we are fighting to change."

Morzaun stepped forward and gripped Zeeran's coat. Sunlight cascading in from the window glinted off of metal, the gleam catching Zeeran's eye as Morzaun raised his dagger. The cold blade settled against Zeeran's throat, and he searched within for his magic. It hummed, dim and weak, too deep for him to access.

"You know how I feel about those who betray me," said Morzaun, his words an almost growl.

"I want the same thing you do." Zeeran swallowed, and the blade dug into his skin. "But we can do this the right way. We can take Izarden by showing the people who Delran really is. I won't turn into a monster. I don't think that's what you want, either."

Morzaun's nostrils flared, but Zeeran's legs gave out beneath him before his uncle could respond. His body went limp. Confusion filled Morzaun's face, and his hold loosened enough for Zeeran to slip from his grasp. He smacked against the floor, Sicarii's shouts filling his ears.

"Zeeran!" She kneeled next to him, and he blinked against the darkness filling his vision.

"How long has he been this way?" asked Morzaun.

"Since yesterday afternoon," answered Sicarii. "We couldn't return last night. He was too exhausted to use the transportation spell. I think coming home drained him again."

"I'm fine," Zeeran muttered. "Need to rest."

"Indeed." Morzaun crouched and lifted Zeeran's arm around his shoulder. "We will continue this discussion once you've recovered."

There was little more to discuss, but Zeeran could offer no protest. Morzaun lifted him to his feet, and the shadows encroached on his vision, shrinking his view until darkness completely overtook him.

* * *

Three days of rest gave Zeeran's body plenty of time to recover. He spent much of it inside his cottage despite the amount of work waiting to be done. His traps needed to be checked and his wood stockpile shrank with each cold night, but Sicarii had threatened to knock him unconscious if he saw to any of those chores.

And he took her threats seriously.

He smiled as he added boiling water to his bowl of oats, the typical staple of his morning meal. Sicarii typically joined him after breakfast, and he looked forward to their time together each day. They spent a great deal of it talking, reading, or napping, which consisted of him holding her until they both dozed off. She feigned annoyance every time he drew her close, but the way she snuggled against him and sighed contentedly spoke to her true feelings.

Sicarii cared for him; he knew that well enough. His attachment to her continued to grow, and he wasn't sure how much longer he could refrain from telling her so. His actions surely spoke for themselves, but he wanted to say the words aloud.

He loved her.

Zeeran jumped to his feet when a knock sounded on the door. He swung it open with a wide grin, but it faltered when both Sicarii and his uncle stood before him. Morzaun had promised a continuation of their discussion, an event Zeeran had not looked forward to. It seemed his uncle had decided the resting period had concluded.

"I'm going to visit Eramus in one hour, and you are to join me," said Morzaun. He glanced at Sicarii. "So get whatever is going on between the two of you out of your system now. I need you to focus today."

That was it? No lecture or discussion? Zeeran wouldn't complain, but it did strike him as odd. Morzaun had been furious about their disobedience, and for the first time, he'd wondered if Sicarii was right to be so concerned. He hadn't believed his uncle would harm his own blood relation, but...

"I'll come to your cottage in ten minutes," said Zeeran.

Morzaun gave him one firm nod and marched away. Zeeran grabbed Sicarii's hand and tugged her inside, closing the door behind them.

"That went better than I expected," she said, attempting to pull out of his grasp.

Zeeran held her tighter, and one tug brought her flush against him. "I certainly expected a lecture, but it seems I'm still needed. Now that my powers have fully recovered, Morzaun likely wishes to resume Eramus's training."

"Are you sure you're well enough?"

"Yes, though I wish I weren't. Spending another day in your company is far more appealing than training my cousin." He stroked a finger along her cheek, and Sicarii shuddered, pressing into his touch. He smiled and leaned forward to leave a soft kiss on her longer scar. "You are much easier on my eyes than him, too."

"I think you're too charming for your own good," she said, her tone light with amusement. "And quite possibly a little blind."

"It's the rest of the world who is blind if they cannot see the value of the gem before me, but I'm quite grateful they remain ignorant. I selfishly wish to keep you all to myself."

Her face crumpled with emotion, and Zeeran placed a long kiss on her forehead. "I'll come find you once we've returned."

They bid one another farewell, and Zeeran trudged to Morzaun's cottage. They spoke little, even after Zeeran transported them to the familiar meadow near Eramus's small village.

"Did he know you were coming today?" asked Zeeran.

"Not today specifically, but I suspect he can sense my presence as I can his. I never have to wait long."

Zeeran kicked at the ground to disperse his irritation. He would rather not waste time standing in the meadow when he could be wooing a certain woman in his cottage or catching up on his neglected chores, but given Morzaun's mood, he wouldn't voice his frustration.

Fortunately, his uncle seemed correct in Eramus's ability to sense him. The man stormed across the meadow, his gaze dark. Morzaun wasn't the only one in a foul mood.

"Eramus," said Morzaun when his son stopped in front of them. "How are you?"

The concern in his uncle's voice was obvious, but Zeeran held little sympathy for him. He didn't agree with keeping so much from his cousin, especially in regards to Morzaun's relationship to the man. Eramus deserved to know the truth, but more than that, he was unlikely to trust them if Morzaun continued to keep secrets. That placed their plan at risk, which made his uncle a hypocrite for lecturing him about saving the young prince.

"I'm glad you're here," said Eramus. "We have some things to discuss."

Zeeran snapped a twig from a dangling branch, drawing Eramus's gaze to him. His cousin narrowed his eyes. "Preferably alone."

"I'm certainly not leaving now." He shouldn't antagonize the man but for some reason couldn't help himself. "I want to hear this discussion."

"Are you so desperate for Morzaun's attention that you must make a nuisance of yourself?"

Zeeran dropped the twig and stomped forward. He jabbed a finger into his cousin's chest. "I'm not desperate for anything." Certainly not Morzaun's attention. Perhaps at one time that had been true, but no longer.

"You're clearly jealous."

Zeeran shoved Eramus backwards. "Of what, you? Why would I be jealous of a man who can't even use his power properly? You wouldn't last one minute in a duel against me."

"Zeeran, that's enough," said Morzaun, his tone full of warning.

He ignored him. "Why don't we settle this right now, Eramus?"

His cousin glared at him, seeming to deliberate the option. "I don't want to fight you, and after I speak with my *father*, he's all yours. I don't want anything to do with either of you."

The color drained from Morzaun's face. Zeeran backed away, grinning at the unexpected development. How would his uncle handle this? Deny it? There seemed little chance of that given the determined look in Eramus's eyes.

"Perhaps I'll let the two of you have your discussion," said Zeeran, continuing his retreat.

"Don't go far," Morzaun ordered. "I need you here."

Needed him? Ah, yes. Eramus possessed magic. Morzaun didn't feel safe without someone to defend him. A wave of satisfaction washed over him at the realization. "Afraid of your own son? Can't say I blame you. The last duel you participated in didn't end well, did it?"

Morzaun grabbed his coat, yanking him close, and pressed his jagged dagger to Zeeran's cheek. Perhaps he had gone too far with his taunts. Why he couldn't control his words when Eramus was around, he didn't know, but he needed to calm his tongue or he might lose it altogether.

"Watch yourself, Zeeran. I may not have my magic, but that doesn't mean I can't defend myself. You know this dagger is capable of more than ripping flesh."

His heart skipped several beats. Morzaun had divulged what the other relics were capable of, at least in part, but never the dagger. Zeeran had thought his uncle had yet to discover the gem's abilities, but that presumption had been a mistake. Morzaun knew–Zeeran could see that in the man's threatening, dark eyes–and the lack of knowledge filled him with fear.

He swallowed. "Forgive me, Uncle. I won't disappoint you again."

And he wouldn't, because instinct told him his life might depend upon it.

CHAPTER TWENTY TWO

The War Begins

Morzaun returned his dagger to the inside of his cloak and shifted his attention to Eramus. "How did you find out?"

As the two of them fell into a heated conversation, Zeeran retreated several paces into the shadows of the woods. His heart beat rapidly with his lingering fear. Sicarii had said she didn't know what his uncle was capable of, and for the first time, he wondered if perhaps she knew of more egregious actions the man had committed. Zeeran had never believed Morzaun deserved death—he still didn't—but his uncle had clearly become unhinged, so desperate to enact his revenge he would hurt anyone who stood in his way.

Even his family.

Zeeran touched the place on his neck where Morzaun's dagger had grazed his skin, leaving a shallow cut. Perhaps King Sytal had deserved the fate Morzaun handed him, but putting his uncle on the throne was out of the question. Instinct told him this madness would not end with Delran's demise.

He glanced at his cousin, now in a deep argument with Morzaun. Eramus seemed to sense what Zeeran had been blind to all along. There was more to Morzaun's plan than bringing about justice. A darkness consumed the man, and Zeeran no longer wished to be a part of it.

Blue light illuminated around Eramus's hands, his expression twisted with rage. Morzaun retreated until he stood only feet in front of Zeeran.

"I won't let you do this," said Eramus, his magic intensifying.

Morzaun glanced over his shoulder at Zeeran, expectation clear in his dark eyes. He would no longer participate in his uncle's schemes, but he'd also not have the man's death on his conscience. He lifted his hands and summoned his aura. Eramus snapped his wrists, sending a beam of magical energy hurtling toward his father.

Zeeran darted in front of Morzaun, a shield of blue light appearing to catch Eramus's spell. When the magic dissipated, Eramus glared at him with clenched fists.

"I won't allow you to attack him," said Zeeran.

"Why have you chosen his side? You have a family who loves you, yet you abandon them to follow a path of darkness. How can you believe murdering the innocent will lead to peace?"

An icy sensation washed over Zeeran, but he kept the effort of Eramus's words from his expression. He didn't agree with killing the innocent–it was that disbelief that had gotten him into this mess in the first place. He had thought his ideals aligned with his uncle's. How wrong he'd been. And while he wanted nothing more than to make amends with his family, he couldn't allow Morzaun to continue with his plan unchecked. The man would do anything to see Delran's demise, and he possessed relics that gave him access to magic.

Relics Zeeran needed to relieve him of. They weren't safe with Morzaun. *Virgamor* wasn't safe so long as his uncle had magic. His parents had been right all along.

Blue light encircled Zeeran's hands. If he had any hope of stealing the dagger, amulet, and ring, he would need a convincing façade . Morzaun would never allow him close enough if he believed Zeeran's loyalties still wavered.

"What do you know of my family?" Zeeran spat. "Keep your nose out of my business."

"I know they care about you. Worry over you."

Morzaun stepped forward, his lips curling into a smirk. "Ah, so my sister and her husband came to see you. It was them who told you the truth. Tell me, are they still here? I'd like a few words with them myself."

"You won't go anywhere near them. You or your guard dog."

Zeeran threw his palms forward, ignoring every ounce of guilt growing within him. He had no desire to hurt Eramus, but his uncle would see the act as one of loyalty. Eramus conjured a shield, and it caught the beam of magic, dispersing it to either side of him. Zeeran pressed harder, and his cousin's defense stuttered until the beam of light pushed through. It collided against Eramus's chest, knocking him to the ground with a groan.

It took him a minute to find his strength, but Eramus stood and whirled his hands with renewed determination. He fired another wave of magic, and Zeeran blocked before sending the *impetras* back at him. Eramus dove to the ground, the spell flowing over his head. If the man would stay down, they could be done with this, but anger seemed to fuel his cousin as it did his uncle.

Zeeran prepared another spell. He didn't want to harm Eramus, but unless his cousin surrendered, he had no choice. With the wave of his hand, jagged shards emerged from his blue aura, and he took aim.

"Zeeran!"

Morzaun's shout faded as Zeeran focused on his spell. The shards flew forward. Eramus raised his shield, and the daggers bombarded him. The shield faltered, and Zeeran willed the edges of his magic to dull just before they ripped through the last of Eramus's defense. They sliced through his clothes and slashed his skin, and although capable of damage, the lethality of the spell had diminished.

Eramus moaned in agony, blood coating his tunic. Morzaun started forward, concern on his brow, but Zeeran halted him in place with a spell. "Stay out of this."

His uncle glared, but Zeeran darted toward Eramus before he could respond, ready to mend any life-threatening damage. The healing incantation fell from his cousin's lips before he could reach him, and a beam of magical energy shot forward. It crashed into Zeeran's torso and flung him backwards. He rolled across the ground several times before the world stilled, his ears ringing.

At least his cousin had good aim.

Shouts brought him to his senses. Zeeran sat up, blinking to bring his surroundings into focus. Morzaun had Eramus pinned to the ground, and his cousin writhed in an attempt to free himself.

"Zeeran! Come!" Morzaun demanded.

Zeeran pushed himself from the ground, his chest heaving, and crossed the meadow. Eramus glanced up at him, a mixture of anger and pleading in his eyes.

"You got one lucky shot," said Zeeran. And though he was loathed to admit it, the force behind the spell had been impressive.

"Enough," Morzaun said with a growl. "Use the *soporia* on him. He's coming with us whether he wants to or not."

His heart pounded. He needed Morzaun to believe he remained loyal to him, but at what cost? If Eramus came with them and continued in his refusal to join their cause, Morzaun might...

Well, the man was unpredictable at best, and putting his cousin's life in jeopardy didn't really fit into Zeeran's plans.

"What are you waiting for?" Morzaun grunted, shifting his weight to keep Eramus pinned.

Zeeran summoned his aura, his mind searching for an alternative–anything he could do to keep Eramus out of Morzaun's grasp.

As if in answer to his silent plea, two figures ran towards them from across the meadow. Zeeran doused his spell. "We've got company."

Morzaun glanced up briefly and then returned his attention to his son, releasing him. "Get rid of them and come with us, or I'll end them right now."

Eramus rolled onto his side and scrambled to his feet. The two men halted a few yards shy of them, their similar features a clear indication they shared the same bloodline. The taller of the two spoke first, his tone deep and commanding. "Forgive our intrusion, but we've come to speak with Eramus. I'm afraid we haven't made your acquaintance."

"Pleasantries are unnecessary," said Morzaun. "We won't be here long enough for them to matter."

The man's eyes narrowed. "I'd prefer to know regardless of how long you intend to stay. The three of you were engaged in quite the tussle when we entered the meadow. Of course, Eramus knows there are plenty in the village willing to offer him assistance should he need it."

Morzaun scoffed. "The only thing I've seen them offer is banishment when they discovered he could wield magic." He turned to the second man. "A banishment suggested by *you.*"

Clearly, there was drama between these men, and Zeeran lacked the patience to deal with it at present. He wanted to return home. The sooner he could devise a plan to acquire the relics from Morzaun, the sooner he could be done with it all.

And he would take Sicarii with him.

"Your desire to speak with Eramus must be dire"—Morzaun lifted his chin to take in the darkening sky—"to bring you out in this impending storm."

"The army of Izarden was spotted east of the village," said the taller man. "Hundreds of soldiers march toward the meadow as we speak."

"The army," Eramus stuttered. "King Delran is here?"

That was not good. His uncle and Delran in the same meadow would mean an all out battle, and it was the small village who would suffer for it. Them and the soldiers who dared stand with their king. Zeeran would be expected to eliminate them. Morzaun would demand he fight.

"What of the others?" the villager asked Eramus. "Your aunt and uncle would surely help protect us."

Zeeran's attention snapped to the man. His parents were still here?

"How amusing." A smirk filled Morzaun's expression, and Zeeran's gut twisted. His uncle had a vendetta against his family, one the man would not hesitate to act on. They weren't safe.

"We should go," said Zeeran. "Let them deal with Delran. This isn't our fight."

"Not our fight?" The glare in Morzaun's expression pierced him. "This has always been our fight!"

Zeeran shook his head. "This has become more than a fight against Delran."

Morzaun opened his mouth to argue further, but Eramus's mumbled words cut him off. "I don't understand how he found me."

Zeeran raked a hand through his hair, his thoughts drifting away from the conversation between the other men. When had he lost control of his life? He'd left his parents, determined to find his place—to eliminate the threat against magic wielders. Living in peace, having freedom—those things would remain forever out of his grasp as long as Delran sat on the throne. For so long, he'd poured all of his focus into making an idealistic hope a reality, and he still clung to his dream for a brighter future, but this was not the way forward. Morzaun's path did not wind through an open plain of opportunity but slashed through a jungle of tough decisions, ones that brought harm to anything and everyone in its path, regardless of their innocence.

Morzaun's scream shook Zeeran from his thoughts. His uncle launched forward, gripping one of the villagers around the neck. Eramus rushed forward to intervene, and Zeeran fired a spell. It collided with his cousin, sending him rolling over the soft grass.

"Stay out of this, Eramus," Zeeran said through gritted teeth. Magic or no, Eramus would wind up hurt if he interfered. Morzaun was not a man to be trifled with, and Zeeran needed to step in for everyone's sake.

The second villager darted forward as Morzaun and his opponent exchanged fists. Zeeran aimed his palm, planning to topple the other before he could reach the duel, but Eramus's shield appeared to block the attempt.

Eramus shouted to the man, ordering him to return to the village, his voice strained with the effort of maintaining his spell. The villager refused. Perhaps if Zeeran convinced him, they would return to the safety of their cottages. Keeping so many people alive was becoming quite strenuous.

He whirled his hands, and his aura took the shape of jagged shards. Thrusting his palms forward, the spell shot across the meadow. The shards ripped through flesh and cloth. Eramus fell to the ground, writhing as he screamed.

Guilt flooded over Zeeran, but he needed his cousin to believe his threats. He approached him and the villager, who'd crouched at his side. "I don't know why he insists on you joining us. We don't need you. Go *home*, Eramus."

His cousin muttered the healing spells, and blue light settled over him. Bloody gashes stitched themselves back together, the process slow and doing little to abate the man's pain. Zeeran summoned his aura, and while he forced a menacing expression onto his face, he coaxed a subtle amount of his power down his leg and through the long grass until it found Eramus's body. The wounds began to heal faster.

A flash of light lit the meadow in a warm glow. Zeeran spun around moments before a burning ball of fire landed a few yards from them. The collision with the ground hurtled him backwards, and he landed with a hard thud. Smoke doused the area, constricting his lungs, and Zeeran coughed as another fiery projectile soared through the sky and landed in the forest behind him.

Zeeran sat up and squinted as he peered through the thickening smoke. At the edge of the forest, Izarden's army—what must be more than a thousand men—stood ready for war.

Definitely not good. He possessed magic, but not enough to stand against so many on his own, and whether Morzaun commanded him to or not, he had no intention of putting his life in jeopardy with such a narrow chance of success.

Zeeran pushed himself to stand, his muscles protesting, and ran toward Morzaun, who had knocked the villager to the ground. He halted feet short of where his uncle crouched next to the man, his jagged dagger hovering over him, blood-stained.

Bile filled Zeeran's throat at the sight of the crimson-drenched clothing. The villager's chest remained still, the life gone from his body. Morzaun turned to look at him over his shoulder, fire in his dark eyes.

"We have to go," said Zeeran, his throat dry and his voice hoarse. "Delran has arrived, and I cannot fight them all."

"I won't leave...not when I have the opportunity—"

Zeeran gripped his uncle by the coat and yanked him to his feet. "I won't fight an army for you! Not when I know it will end with both of our bodies cold."

Delran's command boomed from across the field. The trebuchets launched more fiery stones, and Zeeran conjured his shield. The spell protected them from the blast, but smoke continued to engulf them. It burned his lungs and eyes. They needed to get out of there.

Coughing, he dragged Morzaun to the edge of the clearing where the smoke was less thick. "We have to leave—"

"Eramus!"

Zeeran stilled at the sound of his father's voice. Through the haze, several figures raced toward his cousin, who now crouched at the dead villager's side. Delran commanded another attack, and more stones of fire rained from the sky. His father summoned a wall of green light, and Zeeran commanded his own power to do the same.

Attack after attack bombarded them. Exhaustion wore at his strength, but the desire to leave suddenly had an opponent—a longing to see his family, to hear their voices and remain until he knew they were safe. How could he abandon them a second time?

The sound of Izarden's battle cry rent the air as soldiers stormed across the meadow. Arrows fell from the sky, battering his shield.

"Zeeran!"

The feminine cry drew his attention. He turned to see his mother, her skirts lifted as she ran toward him. His father called for her to come back, but she ignored him.

Zeeran glanced heavenward when a soft whistle filled his ears. A flurry of arrows cut through the darkened sky and angled toward them. Before he could react, a heavy wind swept past him, tussling his hair. The harsh air followed his father's command, rising over the meadow and impeding the army's arrows from reaching them. They dropped to the ground like rain, each one creating a soft thump when it hit the grass.

Zeeran breathed a sigh of relief. His father had saved them.

His mother's choked sob drew his attention. She stood a few yards away, and he barely constrained his own tears at the pain in her expression. Sadness mingled with hope—she was happy to see him, but hesitant and uncertain. He wanted nothing more than to rush into her embrace and reassure her.

Her lip quivered. "Zeeran, please come home."

He closed his eyes. Whatever concern he'd had about being welcomed back on Verascene with his family evaporated, but he couldn't accept the invitation. Not yet. "I can't."

"Of course you can! We love you. All we want is for you to come home." She gestured over the field. "This isn't who you are. You're my sweet little boy who hates parsnips and enjoys jumping in mud puddles and–"

"He isn't a child anymore," Morzaun interjected, his harsh words making Zeeran jump. He'd forgotten his uncle was next to him. "He can think for himself and make his own decisions. Just because he views the world differently than you doesn't make him evil."

"Murder is wrong, Morzaun, no matter the reason. We once promised to stop the evil threatening our people, and you've become the very thing we wanted to protect them from. I know Senniva's death–"

"Don't say her name!" Morzaun's chest heaved, and his mother's shoulders slumped with sympathy that overtook her expression. Morzaun shifted closer to Zeeran and placed a hand on his shoulder. "Come. It's time for us to leave."

Zeeran stared at his mother while Morzaun stepped aside and addressed his son one last time. She begged him with her eyes and outstretched hand. How he hated to cause her so much pain, to make her believe he no longer wanted her comfort and guidance. But he had a mission to achieve, though very different from the last time he'd abandoned his family.

Blue light cascaded over Morzaun, and his uncle disappeared. Zeeran lifted his hands, his aura encompassing them, and mouthed 'I love you'. It wasn't much for reassurance, but it was the best he could offer his mother right now. He barely caught her crumpled expression before the world around him contorted, and the meadow faded and sounds of battle faded.

CHAPTER TWENTY THREE

A Haunting Past

Zeeran collapsed to the ground, his breathing heavy. Tremors wracked his body, and he clenched fistfuls of grass, willing himself to calm. Images of the battle filled his mind, but the memory that haunted him most was the devastation in his mother's expression. He'd seen in her eyes all the pain he'd caused over the last few months, and mingling with her sadness was a desperate plea for him to come back to her.

To come home.

He wanted that more than anything, but despite the desire to dive into her arms and return to Verascene, he had a mission to accomplish. Dethroning Delran was no longer his focus. The king of Izarden needed to be replaced, yes, but Zeeran no longer believed Morzaun should take his place. His uncle was a danger to Virgamor, a man consumed by the lust for revenge. But more than that, he still had access to magic, and Zeeran needed to relieve him of the relics—the very objects he'd helped his uncle obtain.

Zeeran glanced up to find Morzaun bent over with his hands on his knees. The man's chest heaved beneath his black, leather armor, and strands of his long hair stuck out in all directions. Beneath his tunic rested the amulet capable of transporting him via magic, and somewhere tucked within Morzaun's cloak was the jagged dagger. The third relic, a ring, adorned the man's finger.

While Zeeran remained ignorant of all their abilities, one thing was certain. He needed to get the relics away from his uncle and return them to his parents. Morzaun could not be trusted with magic of any kind.

"So close," Morzaun muttered. "We had the perfect opportunity to take down Delran, and we failed."

"Perfect opportunity?" Zeeran scoffed and shook his head. "We were severely outnumbered. I may have magic, but I can't take on an army alone."

His uncle stared down at him, calculating and stoic. "No, you could not have."

Zeeran's gut twisted with irritation. Morzaun had once faced the army of Izarden on his own and found victory, but the power he'd possessed—the power Zeeran's parents possessed—was far greater than their children's. The three original wielders of magic had gained their abilities directly from the Virgám, and that connection served to strengthen their spells. Zeeran would have never defeated so many by himself, and his lack of desire to attack Izarden's army hadn't helped. Magic was linked to their emotions, and if his power sensed hesitation, it would be reflected in the spells he cast.

He clambered to his feet and brushed the dirt from his trousers. "I need to rest. It's been a long day."

Morzaun nodded, and although Zeeran suspected he still wished to discuss things with him, the man did not stop him from leaving. A warm breeze swept through his hair as he made his way through the tall grass to his cottage. He paused briefly at the door, glancing at the building across from his home, but decided against paying Sicarii a visit. He wanted to see her—needed to, really—but his mind required focus. He had much to sort out.

A scheme to steal the relics from Morzaun could not be implemented without careful and thorough planning. Zeeran could utilize his magic, of course, but using his power against his uncle was trickier than it sounded. The man had a strange second sense, a fact given how in tune Morzaun was with Eramus. His only chance of success would be to take him by surprise.

Zeeran entered his cottage and crossed the room to the table. The sun settled low on the horizon as he continued to pour ideas onto paper late into the night. When the sky illuminated, a new day would begin, and with any luck, his plan would be ready.

* * *

A dull ache throbbed in his lower back. Being tossed around during his duel with Eramus had left Zeeran with a few bruises, and the amount of time he'd spent in the wooden chair did nothing to help matters. He'd barely left the cottage the last week, claiming the need to rest and recover the one time Morzaun had stopped by. The man seemed surprisingly calm despite all that had happened. Perhaps Eramus's adamant decision to never join their cause had shaken him into a state of melancholy.

Regardless, the solitude had not given Zeeran a clear path forward. Obtaining the relics was no easy task, and despite his determination, a solid plan remained elusive. Morzaun had disposed of the ring and amulet, hiding them shortly after their return. Whether the action came from suspicion of Zeeran's failing loyalty or simple caution after their encounter with his parents, Zeeran couldn't say. Additionally, part of him feared the betrayal. Should Morzaun suspect his intentions, he would not hesitate to retaliate. Zeeran could defend himself, but what of the people he cared about? It would be foolish for his uncle to go anywhere near his family, but Sicarii was not as fortunate. Once he had a firm plan, he would take her far beyond Morzaun's reach, someplace she would be safe until he completed his mission. Perhaps his family would be willing to watch over her.

Sicarii had visited him over the last few days, and each time he welcomed her into his home. Every moment spent in her company fueled his growing affection, and it had been difficult to keep his scheming from her. She had earned his trust, but she would be safer not knowing of his intentions for now.

He would tell her the truth and then transport her to Verascene. She could take refuge deep in the thick forest of the island if she felt uncomfortable meeting his family. Eventually, he would introduce her to them, but he wouldn't push her. It had taken a long time to earn her trust, and besides, Zeeran had some amends to make himself first.

Thoughts of his family sent a sharp pain through his heart. He missed them, but more than anything, he wished to beg for their forgiveness. He had betrayed them, and until he witnessed his mother's tears, had wondered if they would welcome him home. All doubt had fled with her pleas.

A knock sounded at the door, and Zeeran heaved a sigh as his chair slid over the wooden floor. He scooped up the papers and tucked them beneath his bed covers before crossing the room. He opened the door, expecting to find Morzaun given they had never finished their discussion, but it was Sicarii's beautiful green eyes staring back at him. His lips immediately lifted, and warmth spread through his body the way a fire heated a room, the sensation growing in strength until it consumed him.

Sicarii returned his smile, but it lacked enthusiasm.

"Is something wrong?" he asked.

She shook her head and held up a bottle of wine. "May I come in?"

"Of course, but what's that for?"

She shifted on her feet, avoiding his gaze for a moment before stepping inside. Zeeran closed the door, and Sicarii crossed the room to place the bottle on the table. "To celebrate."

"And what exactly are we celebrating?"

"Whatever you would like. I only wanted an excuse to see you."

Zeeran took her by the wrists and drew her closer, settling her hands on his chest and freeing his own to wrap around her waist. "You don't need an excuse to see me. I'd welcome you into my home anytime." He rested his forehead against hers. "You've already found a place in my heart, Sicarii. I would prefer to be with you always."

Her eyes glazed, and she absently fiddled with the collar of his tunic.

"Perhaps that is what we should celebrate," he continued, lowering his voice. "Love."

"Love?" Her fingers stopped.

"Yes. Surely by now you must know how I feel about you."

He dropped one hand to reach for the wine bottle, but Sicarii grabbed his arm, her expression laced with panic. "Wait. Maybe...let's..."

He tilted his head, giving her a questioning look. "Something *is* wrong. You can tell me whatever it is."

Sicarii shook her head and stepped out of his arms. "I thought I loved someone once. I'm afraid to do it again."

Deep pain filled the lines in her forehead, and a tear slid over her scared cheek. His heart squeezed, and he restrained the urge to wrap her in a protective embrace. Love had hurt this woman before, not just a man. He could sense it in the way she hesitated. Sicarii cared for him; he knew that with surety, but something held her back, haunting memories that terrified her.

He stepped forward, closing the distance between them again, and lifted his hand to her face. She winced, but didn't pull away, her eyes closing as she leaned into his touch.

"Tell me how you got these," he whispered, gently running his finger over the marks. He traced them across her cheek and over her nose and forehead. They were faded, but the pain she'd incurred still existed and he wanted to be the one to heal her wounds.

"I was so young." Her voice shook with emotion, but she pushed past the strain. "I believed myself in love, and I thought..." She swallowed, her eyes fluttering open. "I thought he loved me, too."

"He?"

"His name was Aneer. He lived in the village where I grew up." Her hand lifted to cover his, and she sighed. "Aneer began courting me when I was eighteen. He was...charming and kind. Flattered me with sweet words and made me promises of a life I couldn't refuse. So when he asked for my hand, I accepted."

"You were married?"

She nodded, her throat bobbing with a hard swallow. "Our marriage was good at first, but a month after the wedding, I began to notice things—small things that I hadn't given thought to before. The way he questioned me after every visit to the village. The looks of distrust in his eyes, though brief. I chose to ignore those things, infatuated with him as I was.

"One afternoon, I spent some time in the village visiting my family. Night had fallen by the time I arrived home, and he...Aneer began to question me. He wanted every minute accounted for, and when I stumbled over my words, he accused me of—"

A sob cut her off, and it took a moment for her to regain control over her emotions enough to continue. "He believed I had been with another man. That was the first night he laid a hand on me."

Zeeran clenched his jaw. *First* night, which implied there had been more. As if the scars weren't enough evidence. Fury ignited in his gut. Sicarii was no longer attached to this man, but it did nothing to douse the fire.

"Over time, I learned to stay home as much as I could, but Aneer's paranoia continued to grow. He began accusing me of inviting men to our home, and when we lost our unborn child, he blamed me for that as well, despite the bruises I had to suggest another cause.

"One day, we ran out of candles, so I went to the village to purchase some. I was gone not more than an hour, but he snapped. He said I belonged to him and would make sure no one else ever wanted me." She pointed to her face and gave him a wry smile.

Zeeran rubbed a hand over his chin. He shouldn't ask, but couldn't stop himself. "Is he still alive?" Virgamor help him if he was.

"No. I met your uncle shortly after that incident. He offered to train me—teach me to defend myself. But I wanted more than that. I was desperate, Zeeran. I couldn't go to my family for fear of what Aneer would do to them. Running away wasn't an option; I had nothing. So, I accepted Morzaun's offer. I am indebted to him, though I wish I were not. If I'd known..."

Tears broke over her cheeks as if they were a flood held back by a broken dam. Zeeran swept her into his arms, holding her tightly against him. She'd endured so much, only to be trapped in his uncle's grasp, and he wanted nothing more than to free her.

And he would.

"I killed him, Zeeran," she said between sobs. "I killed my husband to escape. Morzaun knows, and he has sealed my allegiance to him with a multitude of threats. Sealed them with magic and consequences I simply can't face."

Gently, he pulled Sicarii away from him enough to look into her eyes. He wiped away her lingering tears and held her face, his thumb caressing over the marks that served as a constant reminder of the past. "I have a few things to say, but first, I want you to know that these scars do *not* make you any less beautiful. They are nothing more than a sorry attempt for a madman to lay claim on you, to exert power over you. If you allow his words to become your thoughts, then you have let him win." He smiled and tucked a wayward strand of her hair behind her ear. "And I know how much you hate to lose."

She chuckled lightly and nodded. "I won't let Aneer's words get to me anymore."

"Good. Second, I don't know the details of this allegiance you've sworn to my uncle, but I won't let him harm you. I'm leaving, Sicarii. I can't be a part of his scheme anymore, and I'm taking you with me."

Her face paled, and Zeeran kissed her furrowed forehead. "Don't worry, love. We'll go to Verascene. My family will protect you from Morzaun. We can leave all this behind us."

"I can't. There is so much you don't understand, and I can't tell you." Her face wrinkled, her body shook with frustration. "I want to tell you, but if I do..."

"If we leave, he won't be able to hurt you. Threaten you."

"Even if that were true, your family would never accept me, Zeeran. You should go without me."

No. He wouldn't leave her behind. He had to convince her. Whatever shame or guilt she felt could be overcome. His family wouldn't condemn her for working with Morzaun, just as they were willing to forgive him. "Come with me. You'll see."

"I can't, but you *must* go see them. Please." She grabbed his face when he shook his head, and with fiery determination, her lips pressed against his.

CHAPTER TWENTY FOUR

Truth Revealed

One touch of Sicarii's lips unraveled him completely. Zeeran wrapped his arms around her and pulled her flush against him. His mouth moved in time to hers, each kiss fueling his passion into a sensation all too consuming. He focused on her every touch and movement. She was his world, and nothing else existed beyond the two of them.

His hands wandered over her body, and he tilted his head to deepen his display of affection. So many months of waiting had all led to this moment, and the fire he felt far exceeded his expectations. It threatened to turn him to ash in her hold. He was entirely hers.

"Come with me," he whispered against her lips. "I can't leave you behind. I won't."

She pressed her forehead to his and gripped his coat. "I can't,

Zeeran. Go home to your family. You'll understand, then. I promise."

His brows furrowed, and when she pulled away, he tightened his hold around her. "What do you mean?"

Her eyes glazed, making the pools of emerald shimmer. "You asked me to trust you, now I must ask the same. I promise going home will give you the clarity I simply can't offer, no matter how much I want to."

"Then I will return for you. Besides, there is more I must do." He lowered his voice to a whisper. "I must obtain the relics from Morzaun. I didn't want to tell you, but leaving without them....I don't trust my uncle with magic. He's lost himself, and no amount of justice for one person is worth the things he wishes to achieve, the harm he will cause."

She remained quiet, seemingly deep within her thoughts. He brushed his knuckles over her cheek, and Sicarii sighed. "I can see convincing you to leave me is beyond my capability. Go, then. And come back." She smiled, but it was laced with sadness and what he could only assume was disbelief, as if she had resigned herself to never seeing him again.

But he would prove her wrong. He would return. For her. For the relics. To put an end to Morzaun's scheming.

Zeeran leaned forward and placed a soft kiss on her lips. "I love you, Sicarii, and you should know that I have no intention of ever living without you."

Emotion raged in her expression, but she removed herself from his arms. "Go. Now, before you lose your chance."

He wanted to ask again what she meant by her words, but she

passed him a silent answer, one that ensured he would receive no more detail than what had already been given. The woman before him was every bit as complicated as the day they'd met, but with the mystery surrounding her past unveiled, she had allowed him into her heart.

Fully. And he wanted nothing more than to stay there, to reassure her he would never hurt her the way Aneer had. Sicarii was the most unexpected part of his life, and he would not lose her after fighting so hard, waiting so patiently. She deserved to be treasured, to be treated with respect.

Zeeran backed away from her and focused on his magic. Blue light encompassed his hands, illuminating the room with a soft glow. His eyes trailed over Sicarii and settled on her sad expression. He didn't understand her hesitation, but he trusted her, and if visiting his family was what it took to keep her in his life, then he would do so. He would ask them to welcome her, take them under their protective wing. And when Morzaun's threats were doused, he would ask her to marry him.

"I will come back for you," he said with firm resolve.

She nodded with a faint smile. Words to the transportation spell sounded through his thoughts, and the room contorted. Sicarii's emerald gaze held his, and as his cottage faded before him, her soft words penetrated his heart. "I love you, Zeeran."

* * *

Shades of green swirled around him, the smudged colors

transforming into trees and shrubs. Large leaves bigger than his hand brushed against him from all sides, the thick island vegetation a familiar sight. A light breeze rustled the canopy above, bringing with it the scent of the sea, and the warm air enfolded him like a blanket.

He was home.

His heart pounded, excitement and anticipation brewing in his chest. He had missed this place despite how desperately he'd wanted to escape before. It had taken nearly a year in Morzaun's company for him to understand what he'd left behind, all that he had given up to pursue a path of vengeance. Now he comprehended both his own folly and his uncle's.

A feminine wail startled him out of his musing, and Zeeran pushed through the brush toward the sound. On an island inhabited by so few people, there was a good chance he knew the person in distress. As he drew near, the woman's familiar voice jolted his heart, halting him in his tracks.

Feya. His little sister. The last time he'd seen her, Delran had demanded she remain behind. He'd worried over her safety for months until Morzaun reassured him his family had all returned to Verascene.

As Zeeran drew closer, his ears caught the low, soothing tone of a man. Perhaps Ladisias was with her. It was difficult to tell from the soft mutterings. He pushed his way through two boxwood shrubs, shoving the branches away from him as he went.

"Zeeran?"

He glanced up to meet his sister's shocked expression, but his gaze immediately bounced to the man at her side, a man Zeeran recognized as one of the guards from the palace, and then back to Feya...or to her rather round belly, to be exact.

Fury ignited within him. “You! What did you do to her!”

“Nothing!” The man’s eyes rounded as he seemed to realize what Zeeran referred to. “Well I did do that, but it’s not—”

“How dare you lay a hand on her.” Zeeran sprung forward and grabbed the man by the collar, and with one hard yank, the Izarden soldier stumbled away from Feya. Zeeran reared back his arm, ready to punch the daylights out of him, but Feya’s groan stole his attention before the assault could be thrown. She leaned against the tree, her fingers digging into the bark as she hissed.

Zeeran rushed to her side, followed by the soldier, who at least had the decency to appear concerned. “What’s wrong, Feya?”

The soldier swatted Zeeran’s shoulder with a scowl. “She’s in labor.”

Clearly, and the cause of her pain would certainly be dealt with. Blue light surrounded Zeeran’s hands, and the soldier went rigid.

“Taking her prisoner wasn’t enough? You had to defile her as well. I’ll kill you!”

To Zeeran’s surprise, the soldier only sidled closer to Feya. “Then get in line behind your father, but I don’t think your sister will appreciate you murdering her husband.”

“Husband?” Had he heard the man properly?

Feya moaned, both hands clutching her stomach. “I’ll kill you both myself if you don’t stop arguing.”

The soldier swept his arm under her knees and tucked her against his chest. She squeaked in response, but her head gingerly fell against him. The man turned toward the dirt path. “If you still want to kill me, fine, but at least wait until I’ve taken care of your sister. I need to get her home.”

Dousing his aura, he watched him haul Feya away, quite stunned by the entire situation. What confused him most was his sister’s content expression when the soldier placed a gentle kiss on her forehead. Why would she willingly accept being in *that* man’s arms? He didn’t understand it and could only follow them to ensure she was well.

Husband? What in Virgamor happened while she stayed at the palace in Izarden?

Zeeran followed them to a newly built cottage not far from his family home. The soldier carried Feya across the large open room and into a bedchamber. Zeeran stopped at the entry, watching the man gently place her on the bed and sit down on the edge. He brushed Feya’s long golden hair away from her face, the concern in his expression genuine.

Zeeran didn’t know the details of Feya’s time in Izarden, but he couldn’t deny this palace guard cared for his sister. It was obvious in the way he held her hand and whispered soft reassuring words.

“I’ll go get Evree and your mother,” said the soldier. “Hang on, love.”

Evree? The woman Eramus had been infatuated with?

The man stood, and his eyes fell on Zeeran, a hint of uncertainty in their blue depths.

“It’s fine, Strauth,” said Feya. “My brother won’t hurt me. Please hurry.”

She groaned, and the sound seemed to snap the man out of his hesitation. He darted to the door, and Zeeran had to duck out of his way to avoid being trampled. Once Strauth had disappeared, he crossed the room and sat down on the edge of the bed.

"Talk to me," she whispered.

"About what?" He certainly had a plethora of questions, but now didn't seem like the best time to ask them.

"Anything. I need a distraction. Why did you come home?"

He shifted. Telling his family his plan would only complicate matters. He didn't want them involved, especially given Feya's current condition. "I've come to visit. Not stay. How long have you been married?"

"Nearly a year, which you would know if you hadn't been gone so long." The way she chided reminded him of their mother, and it brought a smile to his face.

But it faltered with his next question. "And did he force you—"

"Virgamor, Zeeran! No, Strauth didn't *force* me to do anything. I love him."

A wave of relief flowed over him, and his shoulders relaxed. "It seems I've missed a great deal. I can't believe you fell in love with the man holding you hostage."

His sister pinned him with a pointed look, and Zeeran chuckled.

"I'm glad you're here, but won't you consider staying? You shouldn't return to our uncle—"

Another contraction stole her breath, and Zeeran held her hand until the pain faded. "I never saw things the way you do—the way our parents do. I believed Morzaun was justified in his desire for revenge after everything Sytal did. I can't blame him for ending the man's life."

"And mine?" she whispered. "Was he justified in attempting to end my life?"

"Yours? What are you talking about?"

She shook her head, her brows pinched with frustration. "Of course he wouldn't tell you. Uncle Morzaun hired an assassin to kill me while I stayed at the palace."

"What? That's not funny. Don't joke about—"

"It isn't a joke. I nearly died twice! Were it not for Strauth, I certainly wouldn't be alive."

"You must be mistaken. Why would our uncle hire someone to kill you?"

He waited patiently for her to answer as another contraction shook her petite frame. She inhaled and then released the breath slowly. "I'm not mistaken. The assassin told me herself, and she had Uncle Morzaun's dagger. She said I had something he needed."

She? An icy chill slivered through his bones. Morzaun had sent an assassin to kill Feya, and he could think of only one female with the skill to accomplish such a task, a woman who had directly confessed to having entered the palace before. Morzaun had sent Sicarii on several missions to Izarden, and one of those had been with the sole purpose of murdering a member of his family.

"She had the dagger?" he asked, the words struggling against the lump in his throat.

"Yes, why?"

He rose from the bed and marched toward the door. Fire boiled his blood, his chest burning with a mixture of rage and hurt. He'd trusted Morzaun—he'd trusted Sicarii—and they had both betrayed him. And while knowing the woman he loved was involved pained him deeply, what concerned him most was what Morzaun had intended for Sicarii to do with the dagger. Those relics each possessed unique abilities, and having her use it specifically wasn't coincidence. The man was scheming something, and Zeeran would find out what.

"Zeeran, please don't go!"

Feya's plea stopped him a foot beyond her chamber, and he turned to look at her. He hated to leave her alone in this condition, but Strauth would soon return with his mother. She would not face this on her own.

He smiled, though certain the attempt was poor. "There's something I need to take care of, but I'll come back as soon as I have. I think it's time I came home.

Her lip quivered. "Please stay. I don't want you to get hurt."

Zeeran returned to her side and wrapped her in a hug. The anger stirring in his heart dissipated as she squeezed him back, and he was loathed to release her. But he had a mission to accomplish. "I promise I'll be back soon. Don't worry about me. You have more important matters to focus on."

He pulled away, and Feya opened her mouth to protest, but another wave of pain prevented her pleas. He slipped from the room and out the front door, glancing toward the other cottages to make sure none of his family was in sight. He'd hoped to see them all, to offer his apologies and beg for their forgiveness, but it would have to wait. Morzaun had some questions to answer.

CHAPTER TWENTY FIVE

The True Enemy

Zeeran followed the dirt path out of the village. He needed to transport home but didn't dare use his magic where he might be seen. The villagers on Verascene would think nothing of it, of course, but if his family noticed, they might attempt to prevent him from leaving.

He wasn't sure what he intended to do upon confronting Morzaun, but he wouldn't allow this newly acquired information to simply settle. According to Feya, their uncle had hired Sicarii to kill her, and the more Zeeran thought on the matter, the more he knew without doubt it was the truth.

But what had Feya meant by *she had something he needed*? What could Morzaun possibly want from her?

He began muttering the words to his spell, but a shout interrupted him. "Zeeran, wait!"

Zeeran spun to face his brother, who stopped in front of him. "What are you doing, Ladisias? Feya needs support. You should be with her."

"And that doesn't apply to you as well? You're her brother, same as I am."

Zeeran raked a hand through his hair. "It isn't that I don't wish to be, but I must face our uncle. Feya told me what happened, and I..." He swallowed. It was one thing to feel the anger surging within him, and another to confess his role in it. He hadn't assisted Sicarii or even known of Morzaun's scheme against his sister, but he'd joined the man, promised to aid him in his plans to dethrone Delran. Only now did he understand Morzaun's unwillingness to share all of the details with him. His uncle knew Zeeran would have never agreed to placing any member of his family in harm's way even if it meant their success.

"I never should have left." The words came out strangled, regret and shame making his body tremble. "Perhaps if I hadn't, none of this would have happened."

"That isn't true." Ladisias stepped forward and placed a hand on Zeeran's shoulder. "Morzaun had that planned before you joined him."

"How do you know?"

Ladisias heaved a sigh. "Because General Ivrin and his brother were planning to kill all of us and hired the same assassin to do the job. Or they thought they did. She was never actually working for them, but Ivrin's plan gave her access to the palace without having to worry about the guards."

Zeeran rubbed a hand over his chin, his anger kindled into an unbearable flame. How could he have been so blind? Sicarii had been working with his uncle all along to hurt a member of his family. She'd allowed him to believe they were friends, and then continually lied to him. She may as well have stabbed him through the heart.

I want to tell you, but I can't. Her words echoed in his mind. Sicarii had practically begged him to visit his family. Why would she do that, knowing they would reveal the truth—reveal her betrayal? Unless...

"She wanted me to know." He shook his head. "Sicarii wanted me to know the truth about Feya, about Uncle Morzaun...all of it. That's why she told me to go home."

Ladisias tilted his head. "Sicarii?"

"I won't blame you for thinking poorly of this assassin, but she is not as she seems. Sicarii told me on numerous occasions that she is bound to our uncle. I suspect he's used magic to seal her loyalty somehow."

"You believe she obeyed his commands because she had no choice?"

Did he believe it? Sicarii had never given him the precise details regarding her commitment to Morzaun, but the lack of honesty had seemed to bother her. She'd wanted to tell him everything. He could sense it, even now as his mind skimmed through months of memories. But something—or someone, rather—had prevented her from divulging the information.

"I do think that's what happened. Morzaun has threatened her; I've seen it with my own eyes. Her disobedience has consequences,

Ladisias. I don't know what will happen if she betrays the man, but it was enough to leave her stricken with fear."

Ladisias studied him for a moment. "You've spent a great deal of time with this woman."

It wasn't a question, and accusation laced his tone, though whether it was disapproval or simply curiosity, Zeeran couldn't say.

"All that matters now is that you return to Feya," said Zeeran. "I'll deal with Morzaun. You can expect me home in a few day's time to meet my niece or nephew."

"Absolutely not. You won't be facing Morzaun on your own." He paused, his brows furrowing. "How did you get here, anyway?"

It wasn't a surprising question. Zeeran's family had no understanding of Morzaun's ability to transport via magic, through spell or relic. Perhaps he should teach them when he returned. It would certainly make their lives easier, even give them the opportunity to leave the island for short errands. The waters surrounding Verascene limited their travel and required a great deal of preparation to maneuver.

"Magic," Zeeran answered. "I'll explain later. Right now I have more than one reason to return home." He paused. The meadow with the cottage he'd constructed with his own hands was no longer his home. In truth, he'd never belonged there. He'd been blinded by the idea of freedom, by Morzaun's words and the way he painted the future. The possibilities of a better life had lured him in, and only now did he wonder if the entire thing had been a trap.

Morzaun had used him.

"I have to go." The fire in his chest would not be quenched until he confronted the man.

"Not on your own, Zeeran. Our uncle is dangerous. I'm coming with you."

"No." Zeeran pointed to himself. "I have wrongs to right. This situation is mine to resolve."

"Why? Because you abandoned us? Because you brought our uncle here and stole the relics?"

Zeeran swallowed. "Yes. How can I beg for your forgiveness if I do not first fix what I've broken?"

"I didn't say you shouldn't fix it. I said you weren't doing this alone."

His chest warmed at his brother's insistence. Ladisias still trusted him—loved him—despite his mistakes. But allowing him to come was out of the question. He wouldn't put his brother's life in danger.

Zeeran backed up a few steps, the incantation flowing from his lips. Blue light ignited around his hands, and Ladisias's eyes rounded with the realization of what was happening. The world contorted, but not before a hand reached out and gripped his coat.

* * *

His view became a smudge of color, but Zeeran could feel the hold on his arm, clutching him in a death grip. He wanted to shout to Ladisias, to instruct him not to let go, but the words wouldn't come.

The pressure on his arm vanished.

Ladisias was gone, and a heartbeat later, Zeeran's legs buckled beneath him. He blinked, the familiar clearing swirling around him. His heart hammered. Morzaun had never revealed what happened to those lost in transport during the spell. He could only hope no harm had befallen his brother.

He pushed himself from the ground and spun to face Morzaun's cottage. The man would answer for his actions, but first, he needed a few minutes to calm the emotions raging within him. His magic would respond in kind if he didn't get them under control, and facing his uncle without a firm hold on his power was unwise.

Zeeran marched to his cottage and threw open the door. So much anxious energy coursed through his veins. He needed an outlet. He needed to finish this and go home.

His thoughts settled on Sicarii, the woman who had stolen his heart and betrayed him. Could he forgive her for what she'd done?

Or tried to do.

He still didn't have all the details, but what Feya told him had been enough. The ache in his chest felt like a massive hole, one that may be impossible to mend. His uncle's plans no longer surprised him, but Sicarii had become his world. For her to do something so sinister tore him apart like a knife ripping fabric. Perhaps he could stitch it back together, but it would never be the same as before.

Would it?

Until he saw her—spoke to her—he couldn't say for sure, but at present, all the feelings were going to make him explode.

His gaze shifted to the table where a glass bottle caught the light coming through the window. The wine Sicarii had brought him might numb his emotions enough to keep them in line.

He crossed the room and lifted the bottle. Once he'd removed the cork, the sweet smell wafted to his nose. He knew better than to become completely imbued by alcohol, but something to douse the overbearing anger could only aid him.

Zeeran brought the bottle to his mouth and downed several swigs before placing the drink back on the table. He had one more thing to do before going to see Morzaun. He needed to see Sicarii and put her betrayal behind him in one way or another. Whether that meant forgiving her or leaving her forever, he wouldn't decide until she'd had the opportunity to explain.

He passed through the open cottage door and crossed the worn dirt path to Sicarii's home. Birds twittered as they flew from one side of the clearing to the other, joyously unaware of the impending storm Zeeran felt brewing. He rapped on the door three times, hard and slow.

Several minutes passed, and not a single sound stirred from within. He hadn't been gone for more than an hour. Would Sicarii have gone off into the woods?

He knocked again, this time louder, but only silence greeted him. Frustration swelled in his chest, and he moved away from the door and toward the window. He held up his hand to block the glare of sunlight and peered inside. Much of the room was shadowed, but the space was without movement. Perhaps she had gone out.

He turned, but his eye caught the glint of a dagger, halting his feet. He pressed his nose against the glass, and his heart leapt into his throat. Sicarii's body lay sprawled across the floor, unmoving. From his position, he couldn't see her face.

Concern replaced his anger, and without thinking, he darted back to the front door. He turned the knob, but the door caught on the latch above his head, preventing his entrance.

"Sicarii!"

The lack of response fueled his panic. He shoved his shoulder against the door, and each ram splintered the wood more until it gave way and he stumbled inside. He raced to Sicarii's side.

Her eyes were closed, her expression peaceful. Zeeran stroked his thumb over her cheek, and the coldness of her skin jolted his heart. "Sicarii!"

His hands fell to her chest. There was no gentle rise and fall, no soft thud beneath his palms.

"No." He studied her body, searching for an explanation, until his eyes landed on the green leaves and pink flowers clenched in her fists. He pried her hand open.

Foxglove. A flower that often grew in the meadows in Virgamor. They were beautiful, but sometimes the most beautiful of things could be deadly. If she'd ingested it...

His breath caught, Sicarii's sad expression before he left coming to the forefront of his mind. Surely she wouldn't have eaten them intentionally? A woman of her intelligence would know how they would affect her.

But perhaps that had been the point. She'd been so certain she couldn't escape Morzaun's grasp. What if she'd decided to put an end to her allegiance in the only way possible?

He placed his hands on her chest. "You're not leaving me. Not like this."

Tears swelled in his eyes, and the words to the healing spell fell from his lips. He couldn't lose her. She'd betrayed him, but not of her own free will, and he needed her in his life. Blue light erupted from his palms, but it flickered like a candle flame in the wind. He concentrated, willing his magic to resurface without success.

No! He couldn't lose access to his power now.

He drew a deep breath and allowed the words to flow through his mind, muttering them in a soft whisper.

"It will do no good."

Zeeran turned toward the open doorway where his uncle stood, and the man's lips lifted into a wicked grin. "You can't save her or yourself."

CHAPTER TWENTY SIX

Revenge and Magic

The air had been warm when he arrived back in Selvenor, but somehow Morzaun's presence made the room feel cold. A dark energy pulsed from the man and reflected in his eyes and smug expression. The way his uncle looked at him, without compassion or care, pinned him like a hunter who'd spotted his prey.

Zeeran slowly stood, his gaze fixed on Morzaun. "What do you mean?"

"I mean you can't save her. Her heart has stopped, and soon, yours will as well."

Zeeran's lungs constricted, but he swallowed his fear. "And do you intend to ensure that? Like you tried to stop Feya's heart."

Morzaun chuckled. "Ah, so that's why she's in this state. Though I cannot understand how she managed to skirt around our agreement. I forbade her from telling you anything." He gestured to Sicarii's still form. "Warned her death would be the result should she do so."

"She never told me anything! She took her own life to escape you."

His uncle cocked his head, amusement lining his features. "Then her soft spot for you ran deeper than I thought. But tell me, how did you find out about Feya if not from Sicarii?"

"I went to Verascene. Sicarii told me I should visit my family."

Irritation swept over his uncle's face. "I should have known she'd find a way to warn you, but it's no matter. She has fulfilled her role."

Morzaun entered the cottage, and Zeeran mirrored him with a step backwards. "And what role is that?"

His uncle shrugged. "After months of experimenting, I found myself ready for the final phase of my plan. Making the attempt on Feya certainly would have sped things up, but why rush when I have the perfect test subject here? One who so willingly joined my cause."

The confirmation that Morzaun had allowed him to stay simply to use him twisted his stomach. "I protected you, and you repay me by what? Planning my demise? It doesn't make sense."

Not that he expected anything logical from the man. Morzaun had lost more than his morals to his thirst for revenge.

His uncle closed the door, cutting off much of the light illuminating the space, and reached inside his cloak. A purple glow filled the room, but it didn't come from a relic. The flower pinched between Morzaun's fingers possessed the same lavender-colored aura as his mother. He'd never seen anything like it.

"The Puniceas," said Morzaun. "I can't give you much detail since I know little myself, but before I lost my power, a voice revealed its unique effects to me."

"A voice?"

"Indeed. The same guiding power that has taught me many spells, most of which are recorded in the book your parents stole from me." His brows tightened. "A book I will retrieve. They will not keep me from bringing peace to Virgamor. They will not prevent my return."

Return from what, or where? His uncle made little sense. "I don't understand."

"I am not whole without my magic, but someday, I will have it back." His dark eyes flickered over Zeeran. "And you mark the first step."

A wave of dread swept over Zeeran. Instinct told him to run, but without his magic, he would never come out victorious in a fight against Morzaun. The man had been second in command of Izarden's army. Fighting was second nature to him.

Perhaps if he kept Morzaun talking, he could formulate a plan or distract him long enough to gain control of his magic. "How am I a step toward regaining your power? My parents drained your magic. It doesn't just rest dormant within you."

Morzaun took a step forward, twirling the Puniceas between his fingers. "No, it doesn't. Think of it as more of a replacement. Your power will become mine, though I suspect the spell will require more than what you can provide."

Virgamor. Morzaun intended to take his magic? No. Not *just* his from the sound of it. "If you think I'm going to hand over my magic without a fight, you're sorely mistaken. How can you perform such a spell anyway?"

His uncle reached into his cloak again, this time removing his jagged dagger from within. Zeeran's stomach plummeted to his feet. The relics. Of course they were involved. There had been a reason Morzaun never revealed all of their abilities.

Morzaun tapped the blue gem on the hilt as he removed more distance between them. Zeeran pressed against the wall, and with all the energy he possessed, reached for his magic. He could sense it buried deep in his soul, out of reach or perhaps blocked. But how? Morzaun had certainly had a hand in it. Relics and glowing flowers—

He inhaled sharply. "The wine. You've poisoned me with that, haven't you?"

Morzaun tossed the glowing flower at Zeeran and it landed at his feet. His uncle's grin widened. "The extract of the Puniceas is harmless to most humans, but for those of us who possess magic, I'm afraid it renders our powers useless."

Zeeran's heart stammered. For months he'd struggled with his abilities. The condition seemed to come and go as it pleased, but there had been a reason, and he now knew the cause. "The tea. All this time?"

"With your arrival, I was given an opportunity to study the effects of the flower directly. Why would I throw it away? It was rather interesting to note how the dosage suppressed your power. Such observation gave me a clear understanding of how much would be required to render your power completely obsolete."

The sting of betrayal burrowed into Zeeran's chest. He'd believed Morzaun had used him, but this...this was far more than he ever could have fathomed. His uncle had but one objective—to steal his power and...

Morzaun chuckled, seeming to sense his realization. "Yes. I was always going to kill you. For a moment, I had reconsidered, but your decision to disobey orders, to hang on to morals that would inhibit my plans, only reaffirmed my original intentions were the best choice."

Shadows threatened the edges of Zeeran's vision, and his head felt airy, almost as if he were dreaming. His body flooded with heat, and a fresh wave of dizziness prodded at his balance. Zeeran braced himself against the wall, his breathing heavy.

"Interesting," said Morzaun, his tone genuinely curious. "It seems the extract effects more than your magic."

The man was right. At this rate, Zeeran would soon have no energy left to attempt an escape. He pressed off the wall abruptly, launching himself forward, his fist raised. His knuckles made contact with Morzaun's jaw, and an echoing crack resounded through the cottage as the man stumbled sideways.

Zeeran's feet fumbled in a desperate scramble for the door. Darkness pressed on his vision, blurring what remained until the smear of color captured his balance. He toppled, but a hard yank on the back of his coat collar ripped him backwards. He flew into the wall, the collision knocking the air from his lungs and leaving a throb at the back of his head.

Morzaun wiped the blood from his lower lip, his expression tightened with a scowl. "You thought you could win in a fight against me? And in this pitiful state, no less? I take great offense to the idea. Me, a warrior who fought at the forefront of Izarden's army. Who destroyed an army with the flick of my hands!" The man's chest heaved with rage. "You could never outmatch me, in wit or strength, despite the magic you possess. But soon, that will be unavailable to your defense, too."

Zeeran slid down the wall until he met the floor, gravity zapping the last of his strength. The room spun, making him nauseous. "Why bother with all of this? If you wanted my magic, what was the point in suppressing it?"

"You think me so foolish? How was I to take your powers without first severing your tie with them?" Morzaun crouched in front of him. "You would have resisted, and I have no intention of risking my life. This way, I can take what I need without much of a fight."

Zeeran's chin quivered, his gaze following the dagger in Morzaun's hand. "We're family. How can you be so cold? I was the only one who stood up for you, believed in your innocence."

"Gullible. Naïve. You became the perfect target when Sicarii failed to claim Feya's power. She was ideal, given her inability to use her magic, but fortunately the Puniceas provided me with another path forward." The blue gem on the dagger's hilt illuminated, and Morzaun passed him a look of false sympathy. "I imagine this will not be pleasant, but I promise to make quick work of it." He huffed. "On second thought, perhaps not."

Before Zeeran could say another word, pain erupted through his body. He screamed, agony pulsing through each of his organs with the faint sound of his uncle's incantation. The spell burned his skin, stabbed at his insides with a blade sharper than any dagger could be. His magic rose to his defense, or attempted to do so, but the foreign extract doused its efforts. Morzaun's spell ripped his power from his soul like flesh peeling from bone.

The blue light of the gem faded, and Zeeran sucked in a hard breath. His body thrummed with the lingering pain, and tears streaked over his cheeks. He could feel the absence of his power as if it were an appendage lost to war. It left him hollow in a way he couldn't explain.

Morzaun hovered over him, his expression hard as stone and the jagged dagger raised. "It's a shame it came to this. You were never as skilled as your brother, yet I could have trained you. But you have served your purpose, Nephew, and as much as this pains me, I cannot have you warning the others of my plan or the dagger's capabilities."

Pained him. Zeeran would never believe the false sentiments. Not that it mattered.

A plea died on his lips, exhaustion blanketing more of his vision in shadows. Morzaun plunged the dagger into Zeeran's abdomen, and a new surge of pain wracked his body. His uncle ripped the blade from him, and a warm liquid rolled across Zeeran's stomach. His lungs struggled for air, the lack thereof doing little to help in his fight to remain awake.

Alive.

Morzaun wiped the blade against his cloak, removing the crimson stain. “So long, Zeeran. Rest easy knowing I will use your gift to bring peace to this land.”

After grabbing the glowing flower from the floor, his uncle stood and walked away without looking back, his form blurring into a muddled mass basked in the soft glow of the Puniceas.

He’d been wrong. His uncle cared about more than removing Delran from the throne. Morzaun’s plan was founded on vengeance, yes, but it had been a scheme of both revenge *and* magic.

Zeeran closed his eyes, and then the shadows took him.

CHAPTER TWENTY SEVEN

Vanishing Memories

Everything ached, and Ladisias dared not move until the clouds above him ceased spinning. Once they had a fixed position in the sky, he sat up slowly and took in his surroundings. He'd landed in a small clearing, trees encompassing him on all sides. Nothing about the place seemed familiar, not even the smell. The taste of salt on the breeze was absent, and he suspected he was a long way from home.

Whatever spell Zeeran performed had completely stunned him. He'd clung to his brother's coat as long as he could, but the nausea that washed over him had loosened his grip, and he'd landed on the hard ground a moment later, dazed and his muscles throbbing.

And then he'd lost his lunch on the grass.

He caught a whiff of the regurgitated food, and the scent encouraged him to put some distance between his nose and the ground. Standing, he brushed the dirt from his trousers and listened intently for anything that might suggest the right direction.

Right direction? He scoffed. For all he knew, Zeeran had continued on for miles. He might never find him.

Still, he needed to try. The thought of his brother facing Morzaun on his own knotted his stomach. Their uncle lived on the verge of eccentricity and would not hesitate to cross lines. Family meant nothing to the man.

He'd fought his way through the brush for not more than a few minutes when he reached another clearing. This one was large and contained several cottages. He may not have found Zeeran, but at least he'd found civilization. Perhaps someone here knew of his brother or had seen him. If nothing else, they could tell him where exactly *here* was.

He started to step out of the shadowed forest but halted when his eyes caught movement near one of the cottages. A lone figure, cloaked in black, left the small home, and Ladisias sucked in a sharp breath. He hadn't seen his uncle since Zeeran left them, and the urge to throw a few punches at the man nearly had him giving away his position. Morzaun had betrayed them all, and while it had been Zeeran's choice to leave, it was only by deceit and trickery that his brother remained at the man's side for so long.

Morzaun pulled something from his cloak, and Ladisias's eyes caught the glint of sunlight off the item. Blue light emerged from it and surrounded Morzaun in a faint glow. His body deteriorated until nothing remained and the clearing grew quiet.

How? Morzaun's magic had been taken away. He couldn't understand it, but right now, the answers didn't matter. If Morzaun was here, then it was likely that Zeeran was also. He needed to find his brother.

Leaving the safety of the shadows, Ladisias crossed the clearing with hastened steps, keeping a wary eye on his surroundings. Morzaun could return at any moment, and there was no telling how his uncle would respond to his presence.

The cottage door remained ajar, cracked near the hinges, allowing the afternoon sun to brighten the room, and beams of light fell on a woman's motionless form on the floor. Her skin had paled, but her chest rose and fell with short, quick breaths. Dark hair framed her face, and several old scars adorned her face.

He recognized her at once as the assassin who'd attempted to kill Feya, and fury swelled within him. Had it not been for the trail of crimson beyond her and his brother's lifeless body, perhaps his anger would have conjured his magic on its own.

Ladisias rushed to Zeeran's side. Blood coated his clothes and the floorboards, still wet from a recent altercation, which could have only come from Morzaun judging by the state of the assassin. Ladisias placed his hands on Zeeran's chest and felt the faint heartbeat beneath his palms.

He opened his mouth to begin the healing spell, but movement drew his attention. The woman moaned, her dark lashes fluttering. She sat up and glanced around the room as though dazed. When her gaze landed on him, her hand darted to the sheath at her side, gripping the hilt of a dagger. He drew his sword, but before he could even point it at her, she'd dropped her weapon. Her eyes rounded as she stared down at his brother, and tears spilled over her cheeks.

"No," she whispered.

The assassin crawled toward them, and Ladisias pointed the tip of his blade at her. "Stay back!"

"You...you're his brother and have magic. Save him!" The plea in her tone was too genuine to deny. This woman may have tried to kill Feya, but she cared for Zeeran, though how deeply remained to be seen.

Ladisias pinned her with a glare. "I'll try, but stay back. I don't want you anywhere near him."

She swallowed but nodded. He lowered his weapon and set it on the floor to free his hands and place them on his brother's blood-drenched shirt. Green light filled the room as he muttered the incantation of the healing spell. He could sense the severity of the wounds and silently begged his magic to repair the damage.

His aura dissipated, and he waited, the last of his hope fading until Zeeran gasped. His brother's eyes flew open, but only briefly before his head lolled and they closed again.

"Is he alright?" the assassin asked. "Will he..." Emotion cut off her voice, and she seemed to contemplate something before launching forward. Ladisias reached for his sword, but she was at their side in an instant, brushing Zeeran's dark locks away from his face. "Tell me he will live. Please tell me you've saved him."

Ladisias had several questions to ask this woman and resented the idea of granting any of her requests, but it seemed they both wanted the same thing at the moment. He placed one hand over Zeeran's heart. It beat much stronger now, but still weaker than it should be. "I think he will make it, but he needs rest."

The assassin wiped her face with the back of her hand and sniffled before leaning down to press her lips to Zeeran's forehead. "Thank you."

"For saving my own brother? I would do anything for my family. That includes protecting them from people who have attempted to kill them."

She glanced up at him, a tear clinging to her lashes. "You must hate me for what I did—for what I tried to do—and I don't blame you. I have regretted my actions for months." Her attention shifted to Zeeran. "I have so many regrets, and it's the person I care about most who has suffered for my decisions."

Some of the anger filling Ladisias's chest eased. He didn't trust this woman, but he *did* believe her. Regret lined her expression, and every soft touch revealed her affection. This assassin was in love with his brother.

He could almost laugh. But he wouldn't.

Ladisias cleared his throat. "Zeeran's magic—I can't sense it at all anymore. I need to know what happened." He lifted the tip of his sword so that it hovered inches from her face. "And you're going to tell me everything."

She nodded, unperturbed by the blade. "I swore my allegiance to your uncle years ago. I needed help escaping...your uncle made it possible for me to leave my past behind, and in return, I agreed to work for him. A little more than a year ago, he sealed that agreement with magic using an amulet—one Zeeran had helped him retrieve from Verascene."

"The amulet?" Ladisias lowered his sword. The woman seemed cooperative enough, and sensing she was no longer a threat, he sheathed the weapon. "You're saying my uncle could access the magic within the gems?"

"Yes. He never fully divulged the details, at least not until recently, but he used the amulet to ensure my loyalty. If I were to willingly go against his orders, I would die."

Zeeran had been correct in his assumptions, then. The assassin was acting under Morzaun's orders, but she'd had little choice in the matter. "My brother said you told him to visit his family. Why did you do that?"

Her eyes glazed, and her voice quaked. "Because I couldn't tell him myself about your sister—about Morzaun's plan. Your uncle ordered me to keep his secrets, but I knew if Zeeran went home, his family would reveal the truth to him."

She stroked her dainty fingers through Zeeran's black hair. "After Zeeran saw your parents, Morzaun believed he would leave. I think Zeeran *was* planning to go home, but your uncle needed him. He ordered me to give him a bottle of wine laced with some sort of poison."

"Poison?" Ladisias glanced down at his brother. He couldn't sense Zeeran's magic, but so far as he could tell, the healing spell had restored his health. Was this poison the reason the magic remained elusive?

"I don't know much about it," the assassin continued. "Only that Morzaun said it would render Zeeran's power useless. He needed his defenses subdued so he could steal his magic."

Ladisias looked up at her sharply. "Steal it? What do you mean?"

She shook her head. "I don't know his entire plan, but the dagger, the one with the blue gemstone, is capable of absorbing a person's magic. Morzaun intends to use it to restore his own, somehow."

Ladisias felt as though he'd fallen into a lake of ice. Morzaun couldn't be allowed to regain his power. The man was unhinged, and the destruction he would unleash with the return of his magic was troublesome, indeed.

"You're certain of this? I don't know of any spell that would allow him to accomplish it."

"He mentioned a book, one with spells. But it was my understanding that your parents had taken it."

His mother and father had removed a spell book from Morzaun's possession. Upon inspection, they'd found it contained dark magic and quickly attempted to destroy it. But the binding was impenetrable to both physical elements and magic, and they were forced to hide the book instead. Not even Ladisias knew where his parents had put it, but so long as Morzaun never got his hands on the corrupt spells within, he couldn't regain his power, and that offered Ladisias's soul a little relief.

Still, the thought that the man could use the magic contained within the dagger—a weapon Ladisias had forged for him—filled him with fear. If his uncle had such intentions, then none of them were safe.

"I saw Morzaun leave. I can only assume he was successful in his endeavors. He's taken Zeeran's power."

"Are you sure it isn't simply the poison?"

"I can't be entirely sure, but would my uncle have left, have tried to kill him if he hadn't found success?"

Her shoulders slumped, resignation playing over her features. "I suppose not."

Ladisias tapped his finger against the ground. "Why did he not kill you?"

He didn't bother to hide the accusation in his tone. Whether this assassin cared for his brother or not, she'd still tried to murder a member of his family. She'd spent months lying to Zeeran, albeit against her will, but who was to say she wasn't lying now? Morzaun's power over her would still require it, would it not?

She tilted her head, her lips curling into a frown. "I know what you're thinking. You don't trust me, and you want to know how I've been able to tell you the truth when I couldn't speak a word of it before now."

The woman was intuitive, he'd give her that. "Yes."

She held out her hand, revealing pieces of crumpled Foxglove. "Because I died, and death severed my tie to your uncle. I ate this to stop my heart. With Morzaun's frequent reminders of the consequences for my disobedience, I knew my only chance of escape was death." The assassin reached into a pouch hanging from the belt around her waist and pulled out another herb, one he didn't recognize. "This has been known to counteract the effects of Foxglove...or at least had the possibility. The apothecary in Rowenport said it was my best chance, anyway. All I had to do was eat some once the effects took hold.

"I didn't know if it would work, but I couldn't live with the lies any longer." She met his gaze, her own pleading. "I love your brother. I thought once he learned the truth from his family, he wouldn't return. He would be safe."

Ladisias heaved a sigh. She spoke the truth, of that he was certain, but could he trust her in perpetuity? Now that she was no longer under Morzaun's control, she had no reason to harm any of them, but he couldn't take that risk. Besides, his father had yet to forgive Strauth for his actions against Feya. This woman had little chance, especially after working so closely with Morzaun.

He ran a hand through his hair. "How much do you love him?"

"I'd give my life for him. In a way, I nearly did. I'd hoped he wouldn't come back after he spoke to his family, that he would forget me and stay away."

Ladisias scoffed. Based on the short conversation he'd had with Zeeran, he suspected his brother loved the woman. He would have never left her with Morzaun.

And Zeeran would likely never rest until he'd seen Morzaun brought to justice. The man was a threat to their family, and not only had he taken Zeeran's power, but he'd attempted to kill him. His brother, with his short temper and unyielding determination, would never let that go.

"When Zeeran wakes up, the first thing he's going to do is go after my uncle," Ladisias mumbled. "We can't let him do that. Without his magic, it wouldn't end well."

"Agreed, but how can we prevent it? If I've learned anything about your brother, it's that he's stubborn. And persistent to the point of annoyance."

Ladisias bit back a laugh. There was a story behind her words. "He is, and I can take care of the issue, but I'm going to need your help."

Her brows furrowed. "My help?"

Ladisias looked down at Zeeran, an ache forming in his chest. The only way Zeeran would abandon the notion of chasing Morzaun was if he forgot what happened, but to erase the desire for justice that would surely plague his brother, Ladisias would need to eliminate *all* memories of magic, and those included him. They included his entire family.

He turned to the assassin. It would be her responsibility to keep his brother safe, and while he hated the idea of leaving his family in her hands, a bit of his pain eased. Zeeran would not be alone.

He swallowed, his throat dry with emotion. "I'm going to erase his memories. As far as he'll know, you are his only family. Against my better judgment, I'm trusting you to keep him safe."

She nodded. It would have to be enough.

With the glow of his aura, he erased every memory of himself, his family, and magic from Zeeran's mind.

EPILOGUE

Zeeran closed his eyes and drew in a slow breath. Sometimes the scent of salt riding the breeze brought him close to remembering, but his memories remained ever elusive. They slumbered, buried beneath a veil he couldn't seem to penetrate, which often frustrated him, but he took solace in the few he had. They were, after all, the most important ones.

In the distance, waves thundered against Croseline's rocky shore. He listened to the melody they created, and while not the canorous song of birds, the rhythm of the water and the music it made calmed him, a familiar balm to his soul that he might never understand.

But he couldn't spend all day standing there on the hill. There was always work to be done, and if he didn't see to his chores, his wife would worry. And then she would take it upon herself to do them for him, all while demanding he rest.

A smile lifted his lips, and warmth seeped into his chest. Perhaps they both should take an afternoon to relax from their labors. Although he remembered little of his past, one thing he'd discovered over the last few months was just how easily he could persuade her. His charms must have been solely responsible for winning her heart.

He made his way over the grassy hill, pausing briefly at the top to give the shimmering sea one last look before continuing on. The chatter of chickens met his ears as he approached the thatched cottage, sunlight glistening off the smooth stones of the outer wall. The birds parted to clear his path, but not without complaint, and Zeeran stopped by the shed to grab a few handfuls of grain. He tossed it out to animals, and their mad flock to snatch up the tiny pieces made him chuckle.

"There you are." The sweet voice of his wife pulled his attention. She walked toward him, her black hair waving behind her in the breeze. Her smile lit a fire within him, and the sparkle in her green eyes did nothing to douse it.

Months ago, he'd awoken to a throbbing headache and pain in his abdomen. Sicarii had assured him that his tumble over the cliff had left him bedridden and unconscious but still in good health. He could remember nothing of the fall–nothing, in fact, of his life beyond a few scattered images, all of which revolved around her. He'd been immediately comforted by her gentle care, the genuine concern in her eyes. What a blessing that of all the things his mind clung to, it was her. His solid foundation.

He longed to remember more, but he didn't regret spending the last few months getting to know her. He'd fallen in love all over again, which she frequently teased him about.

Sicarii stopped in front of him, and he lifted his arms to pull her into them, the distance more than he wanted. "Here I am."

"What have you been doing?" She ran her fingers down his arm, making him shiver. "You're not overly sweaty, so clearly nothing too strenuous."

"That is only because my *wife* insists I not do anything too strenuous. Honestly, I'm in perfect health, and she should let me keep some of my pride."

She took a deep breath and pressed closer to him. "I worry too much, but I can't help it."

No, he imagined she couldn't. Just because he couldn't remember the accident didn't mean Sicarii had been given the same privilege. He couldn't fathom how much he'd scared her. If the roles were reversed, he might never let her leave his side.

He leaned closer and brushed his nose against hers. "I understand, but eventually winter will arrive, and I expect you to at least let me chop firewood."

"Very well, but only if I come with you." Her voice dipped into a quiet whisper. "You never know what dangers are hiding in the woods."

There was more to her words than a jest. He could sense it, but Sicarii was slow to reveal much of his past. It often made him wonder if there were horrors she wished he never remembered, and while part of him couldn't help but be frustrated by the secrets, he didn't allow the feeling to fester. The past was behind him—behind *them*—and somehow that offered him a deep sense of freedom.

He lifted a hand to her cheek and caressed the scars there. She'd recounted the events that created them, and he'd promised himself to remind her how beautiful she was as often as he could. Sicarii had left her past behind, and he would do the same. So long as she was at his side, he couldn't resent his lost memories, not when his future remained bright.

"There's that look again." Her lips lifted and her eyes glittered with amusement.

"And what look is that?"

"The one that says you think I'm the most beautiful thing in the world despite the marks on my face."

He shrugged. "I can't help it if my face reflects my thoughts. It's beyond my control."

"And I still say you are blind."

He held her tighter. "I'm not blind. My mind may not be fully functioning, but my eyes can see quite well, I thank you."

She chuckled, and Zeeran swept a strand of her wayward hair behind her ear. He could remember the first time he met her, though the details surrounding the event were unclear. She'd been hesitant to open up to him, that much he knew, but the small flashes that filled his thoughts and dreams had only rekindled what he'd lost. He knew Sicarii. Her soul. He needed her like he needed air.

He loved her.

"I wish I could remember more," he whispered. "Even our wedding would suffice."

She shifted in his arms. "Well, we could always get married again?"

He grinned. Even if he'd not been completely besotted with the idea, he could never deny the hope filling her eyes. "I'd like that."

His lips met hers, and she returned every ounce of his offered affections until neither of them could breathe. What were memories compared to the present? Nothing more than stepping stones to a brighter tomorrow, and while he could not recall the path that had brought him to this moment, he rejoiced in every step the journey had required, for each one had led him to her.

Thank you for reading! If you enjoyed this book, please consider leaving me a review!

Want more? Visit my website www.brookejlosee.com for character art, excerpts, and more! You can also sign up for my monthly newsletter to get *The Prisoner of Magic* for absolutely free! Just follow this link: https://BookHip.com/NZQJTRW

Please enjoy a preview of the final book of this series, *War & Magic*:

CHAPTER 1

Ladisias narrowed his eyes, careful not to blink. He would not lose this time, no matter how much the effort burned. Perhaps if he had gotten a decent night's rest, this would be easier, but sleep often eluded him, and his eyes weighed more than an iron anchor.

An adorable, toothy grin made his own lips lift, and a soft giggle ate at his focus. He'd give the one-year-old credit; she possessed knowledge in the art of distraction, babbling with such cuteness, her nose wrinkled in the most endearing way. Were all women born with the natural aptitude to lure men to their doom?

Because he was certainly taken with those soft blonde curls and blue eyes. She could not yet speak with any sort of cohesiveness, but he would do anything she asked of him.

Except concede in their staring contest.

The door behind him opened, and Dahlia's head snapped toward the sound of it closing. *Victory.*

"Ah hah! You've lost!" he shouted, pointing to his niece.

"Mama," Dahlia babbled, completely ignoring him as she reached for her mother.

Feya approached them and lifted the little girl off the rug, her chiding blue eyes on him. "Does your victory require so much celebration? She is only a child, Ladisias. How difficult could it be to beat her at anything?"

Ladisias shrugged and shifted on the woven rug before looking up at his sister. Her petite frame towered over him since he sat on the floor, but should he stand next to her, he would be nearly two heads taller. His brother's height fell somewhere between them.

An ache pressed in his chest, and he swept all thoughts of Zeeran away, coming to his feet. He reached for Dahlia, and the little girl reached back.

Feya heaved a sigh, passing the child to him as she rolled her eyes. "Sometimes I think she likes you better than me. It's hardly fair."

"She is quite fond of Uncle Ladisias." Strauth's deep voice came from the doorway, and they all turned to face him. Dahlia immediately reached for the man as he drew closer, mumbling *Papa* repeatedly until Strauth took her into his arms and tossed her in the air. She giggled, drawing a wide grin from her father's lips.

Like the rest of his family, Ladisias had not cared for Strauth when they first met him. Discovering the man's part in a scheme to murder Feya had not helped matters, but the fool had gone and fallen in love with his target rather than follow through. Ladisias could be grateful for that, of course, and he had never let either of them forget his hand in ensuring the two of them could be together. Papa certainly wouldn't have given Strauth the opportunity to marry his daughter had Ladisias not interfered.

"She likes me a great deal," said Ladisias, "but I do believe Strauth is her favorite. He spoils her enough to claim that position."

"I do no such thing." Strauth tickled her, eliciting another giggle. "Aldeth spoils her more than anyone."

Ladisias chuckled. "You may have me there."

"She is surrounded by love," said Feya, her voice wistful. "That's all that matters. Now" —she stole Dahlia from her husband's arms— "you must get washed up. Both of you. Mama and Papa are expecting us for dinner."

Strauth placed a soft kiss on his wife's forehead, and Ladisias spun around and rushed for the door. The two of them were completely enamored with one another, sickeningly so, and he had no need to witness their displays of affection.

"I'll meet you there," he called over his shoulder.

His sister's soft laugh and words followed him out the door. "You won't find it so disgusting one of these days, Ladisias!"

Hah! He had no intention of wife hunting anytime soon, and even if he did, he would certainly not surrender his pride to act the lovesick fool. Besides, the odds of finding anyone willing to marry a magic wielder was...well, he had a better chance of becoming king, especially given how few inhabitants made their home on the small island of Verascene. He could certainly travel to the shores of Izarden, but that alone was risky.

No, his sister had found her husband by an act of fate. Strauth didn't possess magic and, not long ago, had been opposed to its mere existence. People could change, but history left too haunting of scars for Ladisias to hope that the rest of Virgamor would ever see his power as anything but dangerous.

He took the worn dirt path leading between the two rows of stone cottages. Warm air filled his lungs with every inhale, a hint of the salty sea tickling his nose. At one time, the place had felt like home. He'd spent most of his life on the island, and yet...

His soul felt disjointed, out of place, and lost. Perhaps it was the secrets hiding below the surface and the guilt pressing on him whenever he spent time with his family that left him entirely uncomfortable. How long he could keep them in the dark about Zeeran, he didn't know. Truthfully, he struggled to believe he'd managed to bury the information for the past year, especially with his mother's ability to see the future. Eventually, she would discover the truth.

He dreaded facing her when she learned he had kept her away from her son. She might never forgive him, and he wouldn't blame her.

He couldn't even forgive himself.

Several pigs snorted when Ladisias passed by their pen, and he approached the fence. He leaned over the wooden structure and peered at his reflection in the water trough below. Wisps of his light brown hair fluttered in the shallow breeze, and brown eyes stared back at him in the rippling water.

When would he be able to look at his reflection and see more than his failures? He hadn't kept his family safe. Feya had almost been murdered, and Zeeran...

Well, he had saved his brother from death but not before their Uncle Morzaun stole Zeeran's power. A stab to the abdomen could be fixed, but Ladisias had no way of restoring his brother's magic. Instead, he'd used a spell to wipe Zeeran's memory of all knowledge of magic in an effort to keep him safe, and since that included his family, Zeeran no longer knew much about his past.

Ladisias sighed. His family deserved to know that Zeeran was alive and well, but they would demand to visit him, and one glimpse of them might overtax the spell. He couldn't tell his parents and Feya without also jogging Zeeran's memories.

And he knew his brother. Zeeran would want justice should he remember his past, and without his power, Morzaun would finish what he started. As of now, the only people aware of his brother's survival were him and Sicarii, the very assassin hired by Strauth's brother to kill Feya.

Ladisias pushed away from the pigpen and continued down the path with a scoff. His siblings were, by all accounts, insane—Feya marrying a man who had once wanted her dead and Zeeran marrying the assassin meant to carry out the death order. Was love always so ridiculous?

No one could blame him for wishing to avoid it when he had such examples in his life. What would be required of him to find love? All four limbs?

That hardly sounded appealing.

He returned home and made quick work of cleaning himself up for dinner. With the sky shifting from bright blue to deep violet, Ladisias increased his pace to his parent's cottage. Even after building his own, he still thought of his childhood home as his favorite place in the world. The ever-blooming purple flowers that grew in the window boxes reminded him of his mother, and the sturdy walls represented everything his father had sought to accomplish when they first left Izarden. Papa had wanted to keep his family safe from those who wished to destroy all traces of magic, and Verascene had provided them all with security.

Ladisias knocked on the door and was immediately met by his mother's smiling face. Her hair was pulled back into a braid and pinned to the top of her head, but a few strands—a mixture of golden sunshine intertwined with gray—hung loosely against her cheeks. She grabbed him by the elbow and tugged him into her arms, and he chuckled when she attempted to wrap them around his broad frame. She could barely do so.

"It's good to see you," she whispered.

"See me? Mama, I haven't left the island in months. You see me every day."

"Even so, a mother is always happy to set eyes upon her children." Her smile turned sad, and guilt struck him like a musician did an instrument. It seemed to echo within the walls of his chest, creating a dissonance that mottled his emotions.

He wanted to tell her Zeeran was alive, but he simply couldn't. His parents would wish to see him, and that would risk everything—the memory spell, his brother's safety. He loved Zeeran too much to put him in jeopardy.

No, he must carry this burden of knowledge, even if it killed him to do it.

His mother squealed, and recognizing that the joy for his presence would surely be trounced by the arrival of his sister—and more specifically, Dahlia—Ladisias stepped inside to make room for them.

With Mama distracted, he utilized the opportunity to take stock of the cottage. Everything remained precisely how he remembered it as a child, though it was tidier now that Mama didn't have three children scampering about.

It was a humble structure, large enough to house three bedrooms and a kitchen, but not decorated in extravagance as the homes on the mainland were. The turbulent waters surrounding the island didn't allow for much trade or even passage. His family had the ability to leave because of their magic, but the rest of the inhabitants didn't possess the same fortune.

Perhaps the villagers were luckier than they knew. Verascene was safe from the reaches of dark magic. It was safe from a power-hungry king.

Despite the more primitive nature of the house, the place had always been Ladisias's home. But now he felt more like a stranger standing within its walls. Secrets had a way of pushing people apart even before they were revealed. It was as if the tide were pulling him out to sea, and he couldn't shout for help for risk of his family drowning along with him.

He continued to sweep the room until his eyes met his near reflection, though the wrinkles on Papa's face and his graying hair were not features Ladisias could claim. Sometimes it felt as though he were looking at a future version of himself for how closely they resembled one another.

Already seated at the table, Papa nodded to the vacant seat next to him, and Ladisias obeyed the silent instruction. He sat down, and neither of them spoke straight away. Papa watched as Mama fussed over their grandchild. Strauth hovered behind Feya, his amusement unmistakable in the way he grinned.

"Are Eramus and Evree to join us tonight?" Ladisias asked.

Papa shook his head. "It will be some time before they are out and about, I should think. A new baby tends to tax one's stamina. Coupled with their loss, I imagine they won't join us for a few weeks."

Ladisias nodded. He could understand his cousin's need for solitude. Evree had given birth to twins two days ago. One baby had not survived.

He couldn't imagine the toll such a thing would take on a person's emotions. To have a deep mixture of joy and sadness all at once would be nothing short of difficult. He, himself, had accompanied Papa that morning to assist in the burial of the infant. The solemness weighed heavily on his heart, a feeling Eramus and his wife must feel to even greater extent.

The others joined them around the table, and they spent their meal in happy conversation. Ladisias maintained his facade, teasing Feya relentlessly and praising Strauth for his growing abilities as a blacksmith. The gathering almost felt normal.

Almost.

It comforted him to know that just outside of Croseline, Zeeran was likely having dinner with his wife. He was probably smiling like a lovesick fool as they discussed what crop to plant on their small farm or perhaps when they would need to make a trip into the city for supplies. Ladisias had checked in on them twice in the first few months of their marriage, and each visit left him more reassured that not only would his spell hold, but that Sicarii would take care of his brother. The way Zeeran looked at her spoke volumes to his affections, and although Ladisias had been slow to trust Sicarii with his family, she seemed just as infatuated and determined to keep Zeeran safe.

"Is that not so, Ladisias?"

He glanced up from his plate to find Feya grinning from ear to ear. What was she talking about? "I'm sorry. Is what not so?"

Feya speared a chunk of potato with her fork and lifted it toward her mouth but didn't take a bite. "You see, he proves my point. His mind is off on some adventure and completely oblivious to the lot of us. Are you daydreaming about another trip inland or a new design for some weapon?"

Ladisias scowled. "I don't daydream about going inland, and no, I have no new weapon designs at present. My thoughts were occupied with other important matters, if you must know."

One of her golden brows lifted. "Such as?"

"I..." Bother. He couldn't tell them the truth. "Fine. It was a weapon."

It wasn't entirely absurd. His favorite pastime was creating swords or knives in the village forge. For a long time, he'd believed that smithing would be his occupation until the day he died, but something had shifted in him as of late. He loved Verascene, but for all its beauty and seclusion, it was also stifling. In a way, he envied Zeeran and his lost knowledge about magic. How freeing it would be to remove the constraints that kept them on the island, but where would he go?

Perhaps Feya was not far from the truth; he might enjoy a bit of adventure.

Securing another potato to her utensil, Feya pinned him with a disbelieving look. "You were thinking of something else. You never have such a somber expression when conjuring ideas for your next creation."

"Perhaps he was thinking of a girl," said Mama with a hopefulness that stabbed him. Double bother, that was the worst suggestion yet.

He shifted in the chair. "I can assure you, that was not the case."

"You cannot speak of women or marriage or kissing in front of Ladisias," said Feya. "It makes him highly uncomfortable." She smirked. "For now."

Who exactly did she think he would form an attachment to on the island? There were no other people their age, and he would never consider marrying a young, flirtatious chit. He didn't spend enough time on the mainland to set eyes on a woman for the purpose of courting her. It was not as though they could conjure him a wife from thin air.

He narrowed his eyes. He would not put it past either his sister or mother to try.

Tapping on the nearby window drew all of their attention, and a flutter of black feathers danced beyond the glass. Papa stood and rushed to open the window, allowing the small bird to enter. It landed on the table and hopped several times before Papa could scoop it into his hands and remove the tiny roll of parchment attached to the creature's ankle.

Ladisias waited on bated breath as Papa's eyes roamed the letter, and his pulse quickened when the furrow of Papa's brow deepened.

"What is it?" Ladisias asked when Papa finally looked up.

"News from Croseline. And not the good kind."

Titles in this series:

Blood & Magic

Love & Magic

Revenge & Magic

War & Magic

Want more stories from this magical world? Check out my other books!

The Matchmaker Prince

The Prisoner of Magic

The Witch of Selvenor

The Warlock of Dunivear

Origins of Virgàm

The Seer of Verascene

Shadows of Aknar

Path to Irrilàm

The Sorcerer of Kantinar

ACKNOWLEDGMENTS

This book was a difficult one for me, and I've been so blessed to have support to keep going with this writing thing even when it's not easy.

To my critique partner and bestest friend, Justena White, for always being there and keeping me going. I would be so lost without you, my friend!

To my sweet husband who supports me so much and cheers me on. I love you and couldn't manage this journey or life without you in it.

To my beta reader, Mindy Porter, for taking the time to read through and find my mistakes at the last minute so I don't have a full on panic attack. You're the best!

To my wonderful readers who put up with my crazy schedule and patiently wait for me to finish.

And finally to my Heavenly Father who gifted me the little bit of talent I possess and the chaotic imagination to create stories and worlds.

ABOUT THE AUTHOR

Brooke Losee lives with her husband and three children in central Utah where she enjoys fishing, exploring, and gathering as many rocks as her pockets can hold. Brooke obtained a BS in Geology at Southern Utah University but has always had a passion for all things books.

Brooke began her journey to authorhood in 2020 with the notion of publishing one novel. That book turned into a series of seven, and the Pandora's box of ideas was unleashed. Her works range from fantasy to historical, all featuring a sweet and clean romance.

To follow her writing journey and keep informed about upcoming stories visit http://www.brookejlosee.com.

Made in the USA
Middletown, DE
25 October 2023

Driven by an unyielding sense of justice and loyalty, Zeeran finds himself at a crossroad after his father agrees to aid in the capture of his traitorous uncle in exchange for a royal pardon. When Uncle Morzaun emerges from hiding, seemingly to surrender, Zeeran's dilemma comes to a head: let the man face trial and death or save him from the executioner's blade.

Choice made, Zeeran escapes the clutches of the army with Morzaun. They seek refuge in a secluded forest, far from the vengeful king's grasp, and Zeeran is introduced to the feisty assassin Morzaun has hired to achieve his schemes of revenge.

As Zeeran grapples with his own identity, he must navigate a treacherous path where his loyalty and heart are tested and everything he believes is called into question. Safety is an illusion, and Zeeran soon discovers that the true enemy is closer than he ever imagined.

ISBN 9781954136304
9000
9 781954 136304